# Blood Justice

# Blood Justice

## David Burton

By Light Unseen Media
Pepperell, Massachusetts

# Blood Justice



Original cover art, cover design and interior design by Vyrdolak, By Light Unseen Media.



Perfect Paperback Edition

ISBN-10: 1-935303-11-2
ISBN-13: 978-1-935303-11-4
LCCN: 2010928369

Published by
By Light Unseen Media
PO Box 1233
Pepperell, Massachusetts 01463-3233

Our Mission:
By Light Unseen Media presents the best of quality fiction and non-fiction on the theme of vampires and vampirism. We offer fictional works with original imagination and style, as well as non-fiction of academic calibre.

For additional information, visit:
http://bylightunseenmedia.com/

Printed in the United States of America

0 9 8 7 6 5 4 3 2 1

# Chapter One

Justine Kroft died for the first time at 11:26 p.m. on a Tuesday night. There was no physical reason for her to die at that time. She didn't fall down the stairs or off a ladder. The radio didn't tumble into the bathtub with her. She didn't eat anything poisonous, walk through a plate glass window or get hit by a stray bullet. Yet she felt death settle over her as surely as if the Reaper wrapped her in his dark cloak.

She had the first uneasy sense of death at about 8:30 p.m. that evening. Her heart raced for a moment. Nothing in an article about picking colors for a bedroom would cause her heart to race. Two gallons of periwinkle blue had already been ordered. Just a brief thump*thump*thump*thump* and back to normal. Only a faint feeling of unease remained.

At 9:00 p.m. she began to wonder why her daughter Brittany wasn't home from the library. Probably talking to Nick Cressman. Those two sixteen-year-olds could talk for hours about nothing. Brittany was a good kid, though punctuality was not a strong point. Justine decided to give Brittany fifteen more minutes before calling.

At 9:10 p.m., Justine's toothbrush slipped from her hand and clattered into the sink. Dread gripped her gut and twisted. She ran to the bedroom and dialed her daughter's cell phone. The ringing stopped after five rings, but there was no voice mail announcement. She pressed the phone hard to her ear, desperate to hear Brittany say, "Hi Mom." All she heard was an empty silence—no laughing, no voices, no breathing.

"Brittany? Where are you? Are you all right?"

She heard a scream, then nothing. Connection broken.

"Oh, God. Brit, what's happening? Brit?"

She dialed again. Voice mail. Again. Voice mail.

She called Nick's parents, Patty's parents, Claire's, Robin's, Jeff's. Brittany had left the library at about 8:30. Nobody had seen her since.

911.

"Something's happened to my daughter. She left the library at eight-thirty. It's less than ten minutes away. She's not home yet. I called her cell. Somebody answered but didn't say anything. I heard a scream in the background then nothing. It was Brittany screaming. I know it."

Justine paced the length of her bedroom as her face tightened. "Yes, I know it's only nine-thirty…I know kids will be kids…I know, four hours…I heard her scream. A real scream."

Stopped in the middle of the floor, Justine's body vibrated with frustration. "And you expect me to wait until you get around to sending somebody? I'm going to look for her, whether you do or not."

Within a minute of slamming down the phone she was in her Lexus SUV speeding to the library. The building was dark, save for a single light illuminating the entrance. At the far end of the parking lot, Brittany's ten year old Ranger pickup waited like a lonely white smudge. They'd bought the truck from a friend for five hundred dollars the weekend after Brittany received her driver's license. Faded white, scratched and battered, stick shift, Brittany had fallen for it, love at first sight. "It has character," she said.

Justine wasn't interested in its character when she screeched to a stop beside it. She only wanted to look inside and see her daughter asleep, exhausted from end-of-school-year studying and activities.

"Brit! Brit!" Justine stared through the window. The seat was in shadow. Was that Brittany lying down? She pounded on the roof. "Brittany! Wake up!"

Nothing moved. Justine fumbled with her key ring for the spare truck key and yanked the door open. "Brit?"

Nothing. No pretty young woman excited for the end of tenth grade, excited to go surfing with her friends, excited to start a poorly paid summer job helping a school friend's brother make a documentary on San Diego shoreline wildlife. Nothing but a crumpled jacket and a gym bag.

"God damn it!"

Justine's knees gave way and she dropped onto the seat's edge. The jacket she gripped held Brittany's scent. They had shopped for it together only a few weeks ago. The memory did nothing to soothe the desolation growing in her chest. Several minutes passed as she sat frozen. This was a crisis. Justine was good in a crisis, able to think and act fast when unexpected problems arose. That's why she was so successful. Yet, her mind was blank. There had to be a hundred actions she could take. She couldn't think of one.

The thunk of a nearby car door broke through her despair. A San Diego County Sheriff's Deputy approached.

"Are you all right, Ma'am?" His hand rested casually on the butt of his firearm as he peered into the truck cab from a wary distance.

"I am, but my daughter isn't."

"You must be the woman who called about her missing daughter."

"Yes. Yes. Something has happened to her. I know it." Her fist pounded her chest. "I know it, in here."

She explained the situation. Deputy David Axel rubbed his close cropped head for some long seconds. "I have a fifteen year old daughter," he finally said. "My wife swears she gets the same type of feelings with her. She knew the instant Toni broke her arm falling off her bike.

So I don't dismiss your instincts."

"But?"

"No buts. When a young woman goes missing these days, we take it seriously. But there are procedures, things we have to do first."

"But my daughter needs help now."

"Ma'am, I can imagine how you feel. I'd be tearing up the town if it was Toni who was missing. But really, the best thing you can do is go home and wait for her to come home or call. We need a photograph, a description, a list of friends. Is there a husband or boyfriend who might have—"

"No. I want to look for her."

"Where?"

"I don't know, damn it."

Deputy Axel took firm hold of her shoulders.

"I promise we'll do whatever it takes to find her. I'll do whatever I can. I hate to say it, but it could easily be my daughter missing."

Justine relished her self reliance, yet was thankful for Deputy Axel's grip. It kept her from totally losing control. Bad for her image, but when it came to Brittany, she didn't give a damn. His grip on her shoulders lightened as she relaxed. She had no doubt of his sincerity. Through his hands, she felt his understanding and support. The passion in his voice spoke of his love for his daughter.

"Thank you."

"You're welcome. I'll follow you home and get the information we need. She may be home already, wondering where you are."

Brittany wasn't home. There was no message. Justine made more phone calls to no effect. Her sense of dread grew like a cancer in her chest. At 11:20, pain ripped through her body from crotch to chin. Terror squeezed her lungs. She fought for every breath.

At 11:22 breathing did not seem important anymore. The pain vanished. Emptiness replaced dread. Grief replaced hope. Justine gasped once and dropped to her knees. There, with the patience of the dead, she waited for confirmation of what she already knew.

⧼—⧽

Justine had been a struggling, self-reliant single mom for six years since her husband left her for a more pliable woman. He and the woman died in a car crash the next day and Justine, taking that as justified karmic payback, had not told Brittany that her father abandoned her. For the past three years Justine had been financially independent as a successful Southern California commercial real estate agent, and to the world at large, content. As long as Brittany was a happy, successful student, that was all that mattered to her.

# David Burton

But Justine Kroft was a fraud. Her reputation as a "tough lady in a tough business," was based on her need to provide the childhood for her daughter that she hadn't had. It was all a façade. She'd known it all along, since her husband died and she had to support Brittany. Desperate and scared every step of the way, she gave up her life to provide for her child. From office manager in a commercial real estate firm she did what she had to do to become their top earner through sheer tenacity and fear of failure. Some nights while Brittany slept, Justine continued to read or study, though tears blurred the words. This wasn't her, what she wanted to be. Her husband's betrayal had sucked the substance and purpose from her. After his death, Brittany had given her emptiness meaning, a reason to struggle, a reason to succeed.

That all changed the day of the funeral. Until then she had maintained her stoic "tough lady" exterior. When the Sheriff's Deputies had come to inform her of her daughter's death, her face, as well as her heart, turned to stone. When she had to identify Brittany and only her daughter's face was revealed, she didn't shed a tear. Justine had known in her gut that her beloved child was dead. To have it confirmed hardened her all the more, because otherwise her shell would crack and never be whole again.

In the days before the funeral, Teresa Diaz, her office manager and friend, checked on Justine in the morning, stayed with her in the evenings, forced her to eat and helped with arrangements.

The unconscious effort to hold herself together sometimes left Justine disoriented and confused. As they left the funeral parlor, Teresa said, "It will be a lovely service."

"It will?" Justine said.

"Yes, it will."

At the car Justine asked, "Who died?"

Speechless, Teresa opened her mouth to answer, but couldn't bring herself to say the words.

Riding home in silence, Justine rested her forehead against the window and stared out, something Brittany often did.

The morning of the funeral her stoic veneer held intact. None of the emotions roiling inside her showed through. She did what she needed to do—shower, dress, eat, breathe—to prepare herself for an experience she never dreamed she would have to endure.

Teresa wasn't fooled. Not so long ago she had suffered a similar ordeal. She knew what was coming.

The non-denominational service was well attended by Brittany's friends and Justine's co-workers and acquaintances. No relatives attended. Justine and Brittany were a family of two. Many attended the actual burial, and though her legs wanted to buckle, Justine refused to let them. She even managed to acknowledge the tearful condolences.

The sad affair over, the attendees departed to their lives, sure that happiness would soon erase the sadness that for most of them, was temporary. After all, they had loved ones to console them and remind them that their lives had a future purpose.

Leaving the graveside, Teresa put her arm around Justine's shoulders as they walked toward the car. As she had so many times before to give or take strength and comfort, Justine reached out for Brittany. But instead of her child's solid warmth she felt the chill of empty air. Brittany wasn't there. Her strength wasn't there to hold Justine's shell together, and it cracked wide open. She dropped to her knees and tears brought out all the feelings of sadness, anger, frustration, emptiness, uselessness, despair, loneliness and fear that had boiled within her since death had taken both of their lives.

Justine lay in her bed and cried for almost three days. She only cried half the time for two more. Teresa finally made her eat, drink and clean herself, then went home to her family. That night Justine sipped coffee in her back yard. The cool air refreshed her face flushed from days of weeping. A crescent moon accompanied by its companion, Venus, shone bright enough that she could see the rest of the moon's dark circle.

*That's me,* she thought. A slim bright sliver of light on the edge, the rest an empty shadow of what she might have been. She had faked her way through a job that months before Brittany's death had come to feel like a slightly obscene and unfulfilling way to make a lucrative living. She had no family, no real friends, save Teresa, no cause she championed. She did have looks and money, enough for most people, but she was used to having a purpose. Brittany had been taken away, raped and murdered. What else did she have to live for?

She uttered a single cry of anguish, "Oh, my girl," and sobbed, once. She wanted to cry, to sink back into grief and misery and just…vanish. She was dead, after all, part of a double homicide ten days ago. She just hadn't lain down for good yet.

But she had no more tears. She had used up her grief, as well as any other associated misery. Except anger.

When Teresa returned in the morning, she found Justine in the backyard, dressed in martial arts clothes, running through a Kung Fu sword form.

"You look like you know what you're doing," Teresa said, uncertain.

Justine wiped sweat from her face. "I had a black belt in Kung Fu when I was twenty. I thought it was time to return to it." She absently spun the sword. "You never know when weapons training will come in handy."

# David Burton

❧ — ❧

Three weeks later Justine thought about that time of mourning as she waited in the Vista station of the San Diego County Sheriff's Department to see Detective Harry Frazer. She knew who she was now. Though she was dead inside, her living body was filled with purpose. She had worked with a new Sifu to regain her black belt skills and weapons proficiency. This was part of fulfilling her new purpose in life: to find and kill those responsible for her daughter's death.

# *Chapter Two*

Homicide Detective Harry Frazer of the San Diego County Sheriff's Department stood hands in pockets and stared out the window of a borrowed office, wishing for a natural disaster of some kind. Not a big one where people got killed, maybe a minor earthquake, or a small tsunami. Anything so he didn't have to talk to the woman sitting in front of the cluttered desk.

Working a case, Harry had no problem talking to whomever he needed to. But confronting a woman whose daughter had been brutally murdered left him tongue-tied. He had a nephew about the same age as Brittany Kroft. The boy's father had died of cancer several years ago. Though he'd never had any kids, and had never wanted any, Harry had grown to love the boy like a son. What could anyone say to him if the kid had been killed like the girl? Nothing that mattered.

Madson Trees, one of three detectives on his team, usually talked to the families. He was a people person. But his wife had won ten million dollars in the Colorado lottery and he had walked out and wasn't coming back. While on vacation in Mexico Tom Volovitch, the other detective on the team, had been hit by a bus. He wasn't coming back any time soon. Other detectives were helping out, but it was still Harry's case.

Harry closed the blinds he'd been fiddling with unnecessarily. *Keep it professional.* He was usually good at that.

Still, what to say to Justine Kroft? He'd been wondering about that for ten years. She'd been the wife of a friend, but barely noticed him. When the husband died, she looked him in the eye and seemed to listen to his lame condolences. Lame, because he knew about the husband's affair and had become attracted to Justine while he himself was still, he thought, happily married.

After her daughter was killed, Justine had let him drive her home. She hadn't cried, but had let him hold her in his arms while she gathered her strength to hold back the tears for as long as she could. She did, after all, have a reputation of toughness to maintain. He felt guilty for enjoying the contact with her, but not enough to let her go before she pulled away.

He sighed and turned to her.

She regarded him with a cool, unflinching gaze from the darkest green eyes he'd ever seen, eyes not looking for sympathy or sorry-for-your-losses. Christ, he felt like a high school freshman trying desperately not to look stupid when the prettiest senior smiled at him. He focused on her loosely braided blonde hair that flowed from under a dark cap. Not light blonde, maybe strawberry blonde, but natural, he thought, as she didn't strike him as vain enough to spend the time to color it so perfectly. The hair was still damp, from a shower, he guessed. He remembered she had a black belt in Kung Fu. Maybe she had just come from a workout and that's why she seemed so relaxed, except for her eyes, when her reason for being there was the grim subject of murder. For sure, a hot and sweaty workout then a shower with…where was that damn earthquake when he needed it?

"Hello, Harry," she said.

"Mrs. Kroft." Damn it, what was the matter with him? "Justine, what can I do for you?" His job depended on reading people, but he had no idea what went on behind her placid façade.

"I want to know exactly what happened to my daughter."

"I don't think that's a good idea. The case is still under investigation."

"Surely by now you've developed a timeline of events, know how many men participated, their movements."

"Justine, it's not our policy to discuss a case in progress."

"Screw policy, Harry. I don't want an overview designed to protect a grieving mother's sensibilities. I have no sensibilities anymore. It's been three months since I buried Brittany, plenty of time to collect and analyze forensic data and form a timeline. They're horrible, I know, but I want the details. I need to know what really happened to my daughter. I'm not going away."

That much Harry could read. And he was sure she'd catch him if he fudged the facts. He slumped into his chair and gathered his thoughts.

"This is for your ears only. If the perpetrator gets off on a technicality because you told someone who told someone, nobody except the bad guy is going to be happy. Understand?"

"I get it, Harry. I don't want you to get in trouble."

"This is supposition, but it's based on solid forensic evidence and experience." He looked right at her. "No sensibilities protected."

She nodded. Her body tensed, lips pressed tight. She silently pressed her thumbnails together, one over the other.

"Brittany left the library at eight twenty-eight. She walked toward her truck at the far end of the lot. Around that time several people reported seeing a van in the area. The occupants, two men, maybe three, were shouting and laughing, the radio turned way up. The van passed by as she reached her truck. They stop, jump out, grab her. It's over in a few seconds."

Her frown deepened. Otherwise Harry detected no change. How did it change her thoughts on the crime, knowing it was a random wrong place/wrong time act? Harry became aware that he really wanted to know.

"She fought. They punched her once to subdue her. Sometime after nine oh five they entered a house being refurbished. She was raped." Harry couldn't bring himself to say how many times and ways she'd been raped.

"She fought back. We believe there was a fourth man. She ran to him, possibly thinking he would help her. He did not. Two of the other men dragged her to a wall and tied her with wire, suspended by her wrists, legs spread."

Justine had stopped clicking her thumbnails and her knuckles had whitened, otherwise she hadn't moved. Harry had spent time at the scene. He could barely continue. Maybe the woman really didn't have any feelings left.

"We found no evidence of torture, which frankly is unusual. She was cut open in one continuous motion from vagina to breast bone. That is what killed her. The cut was deep and fast. She was unconscious in seconds. Her heart was removed and drained of blood, then discarded. There was very little blood at the scene, considering the wound."

Harry watched Justine. Had he gone too far? She stared into a corner, both fists clenched tight. "Go on," she said.

He inhaled deeply. "She was found by the construction crew at six-thirty the next morning, her clothes neatly folded beside her. Except for her panties, which have not been recovered."

Perhaps Justine did not need a moment to compose herself, but Harry did. "Is that what you came for?"

The woman took a deep breath. "Yes. Thank you. Do you have any DNA samples? There must have been some."

Harry wished *no* would suffice, but knew that it wouldn't. "No, we do not have any at this time. Any semen samples were washed away when she was...cut."

She blinked once. "The van. Have you found it? Do you have any suspects?"

"We have found nine vans that fit the description. We've questioned all involved with those vans. No arrests."

He didn't like the way she studied him, as if she could read his mind. Surely he wasn't that transparent.

"So none of those men are suspects?"

He should have known she wouldn't leave it alone. He sighed. Honesty could be a real pain in the ass.

"One of them is a possibility."

"Who is he?"

# David Burton

"I can't tell you that."

"Afraid I'll pay him a visit?"

"He has an alibi for that night."

She almost smiled. "Three other men who swear they were playing gin rummy together until eleven-thirty?"

Harry rose up and leaned his fists on the desk.

She stood up with him.

"Justine, we're working this case hard. When we make an arrest, you will be one of the first to be informed."

"You promise?"

"I promise. I'll call."

"I hope so."

After Justine left his office, Harry slumped in his chair and frowned. His instincts told him that the guy, Robert Westly, had some involvement in the murder. But with no probable cause, there was nothing he could do. By the book, as usual.

He thought of his sister and his nephew. Brittany was Justine's life. She was not going to let the investigation go. He wouldn't either. Harry could tell already that Justine Kroft was going to be a problem, if not professionally, then personally. Probably both.

# Chapter Three

Justine found a chair in a waiting room. Face hidden in her hands, she thought she might cry. But no, dead people didn't weep. Dead people delivered justice. *My girl. My life.*

Detective Frazer, Harry, believed one of the men questioned was involved. She liked the sound of that name, Harry. A good, solid, trustworthy name. She saw something in him she could connect with, though she had no idea what it might be. Not that it mattered. Her job was vengeance, to find and execute the men responsible for her daughter's murder, not to connect with a handsome detective, or give a damn about consequences. As a child, justice had been denied her and her parents. That was not going to happen this time.

ॐ — ॐ

*Ten year old Justine broke her arm while racing two boys on bikes. She hit a patch of wet leaves, skidded out, and tumbled up against a tree. She had some scrapes and bruises and a broken arm. No big deal. After all, she was winning at the time.*

*She wanted to go to school the next day, but her mom made her stay home. Justine had to admit, not out loud, of course, that the scrapes and bruises hurt a lot more the next day than she thought they would. So she only protested half-heartedly when her mom made her take some pills with lunch then go to bed.*

*A short scream interrupted her nap. Drowsy and confused, hearing voices downstairs, Justine slid out of bed and crept down the first few steps like she sometimes did when her parents had company. Peeking through the banister posts she saw her mother, naked, on the living room floor with a man on top of her. He had no pants on and his thin rear end rose and fell.*

*Justine's heart raced. She didn't understand what was happening, but was pretty sure it was bad. What to do, call out to her mom, go back to bed, run away? The man emitted several sharp grunts and stopped moving. He raised his body and that's when Justine saw the knife the man held against her mom's neck.*

*"I've waited a long time for that," he said. "You shouldn't have rejected me all those years, Judy. It could have been much more pleasant for both of us."*

*"Well now you've had me, Bill. Now get off." Mom tried to push him off.*

*With a hand on her forehead, he pressed her head to the floor. "It's not that easy, Judy. I don't think I can trust you not to tell somebody about our short affair."*

*"Do you think I'd want to admit to anybody I'd been with you?"*

*"I know you, Judy. You wouldn't want to, but you would. A pity, you were the best I've had." He leaned on the knife as he drew the long blade across her neck. Judy's body shuddered for a few seconds as blood spurted, then slowly relaxed into death. She didn't even have time to scream.*

*Justine was smart enough to stay silent. She pressed hands to her mouth to keep from crying out. Frozen in place, barely breathing, Justine watched the man, Mr. Service from down the block, touch her mom's private places before he washed himself in the kitchen, dressed and left.*

*Bill Service pled Not Guilty. Justine, eleven by then, was the star witness at the trial and she did well . Too well. Service's lawyer presented refutable, but believable, proof the prosecutor had coached her on what to say. He told the jury she had been on pain pills that day. How reliable a witness could she be? Mr. Service had been in the house only two days before, invited in by Mr. Kroft, so of course there were fingerprints and hairs. They proved nothing.*

*Service was acquitted.*

*As Justine grew up she didn't think of it so often, and even less after her father's slow decline into depression and a quiet death by sleeping pill. She was too busy surviving. But she never forgot the guilt of not saving her mother, and never forgot that justice was not always served.*

❧ — ❧

Justice would be served this time, Justine swore it. There had been no consequences for her mother's murderer. This time would be different. Whatever she had to do, whatever she had to give, Brittany's killers would get the justice they deserved.

If Harry thought a particular man was involved, she wanted to speak to him. The information had to be in a computer somewhere. She knew a guy who would take it as a personal challenge to find that information. If Harry's suspect was involved, he would tell Justine all he knew. She hated the idea of torture, knew nothing about it. But if the government could do it, so could, so would, she.

With a plan in mind, Justine stood up quickly, right in front of Deputy Axel. They both apologized, then recognized each other.

"Deputy Axel, I remember. You were very helpful that night. I appreciate it."

"I'm so sorry we didn't find her in time."

"You did your best." *Now it's my turn.* She laid a hand gently on his arm. "You were at the funeral with your wife and daughter. They're both beautiful."

His fingers nervously intertwined. "I had to go. I kept thinking about how I'd feel if something like that happened to my Toni. I doubt I'd be as strong as you."

"I didn't feel very strong at the time."

Axel had the appearance of a hard ass cop, but at that moment he looked like he was about to cry. "I'd do anything to keep her safe. Anything. There's been so many girls gone missing the last few years, you just want to lock them in their rooms. But even that doesn't always work. Several have vanished right from their bedrooms."

Justine had another idea. "I'm sure she'll be safe with you looking after her. Unfortunately, I can't look after Brittany any more. But I will do whatever's necessary to catch the people who did it. And that would make your Toni much safer."

"You should let the Sheriff's Department do it. We'll catch the sons-of-bitches."

"I have to do something. If not for Brittany, then for the safety of Toni, and other girls."

Axel nodded. "I understand. It's what I'd do."

Justine's smile dazzled. "Maybe you could help me?"

∾ — ∾

At 6:15 in the morning, Justine sat in Brittany's truck across the street from 568 Equine Lane in Vista, the next town inland from Oceanside. An older, semi-rural neighborhood, several of the large lots contained horses. Number 568 contained trucks. A late model F-150 rested in front of the detached two-car garage. A Toyota with huge off-road tires sat to one side of the ranch style house, while behind the house a pickup with no hood waited beside a van with no wheels.

According to David Axel this was where Rob Westly lived.

Westly had two men swear they had shot pool together until after eleven o'clock the night of Brittany's murder. He had refused to give permission to search the van.

Waiting, she unconsciously flipped open a new folding knife, familiarizing herself with the action. Not just any mass produced knife, she'd had it custom made by a man she'd helped develop a small industrial park, and incidentally kept out of jail. Justine was an honest, if aggressive, agent. Like all agents, referrals were her lifeblood. It had been a calculated risk—not quite illegal, though possibly unethical—to help Gabe Wheat out with a small lie and some of her own money, but it paid off in two profitable projects with him and several very lucrative referrals.

Wheat made custom knives for a hobby. Collectors paid thousands for his creations. Justine did not want a collectible, she wanted a weapon. She wanted a utilitarian tool capable of delivering an eye for an eye, an evisceration for an evisceration. Not able to find a folding knife with a blade longer than four inches that she could carry in her pocket, she went to Gabe's hillside Carlsbad house overlooking the Pacific Ocean.

"It's illegal to carry a concealed knife with more than a four inch blade," he said when she told him what she wanted.

"I don't care."

"Ahh. I assume it would be best if the knife couldn't be traced back to me."

"I probably wouldn't sign it if I were you."

Wheat doodled a quick design. Without looking at her, he said, "I can't imagine how you feel after what happened, and I don't want to know what you plan to do with this knife. I do know I want you to be careful. This blade will cut both ways. Don't let it hurt you."

"Thanks. But nothing will hurt me again."

⊱ — ⊰

At 6:35 the left side garage door rolled up and a white van backed out. Justine followed the van to an off road truck shop in San Marcos where it parked behind the yellow brick building beside rusting four-wheel drive relics.

Justine parked in the Burger King parking lot next to the shop. When Rob Westly exited the van she was sitting ten feet away, separated by a chain link fence that enclosed the back of the shop.

Westly slammed the door and walked around to the back of the van. The only things not average about Westly were his massive arms and shoulders. Otherwise, he was five ten, one seventy, with short brown hair, a small mouth and pug nose, clean shaven—just another guy.

Passing around the van, he scanned the street and the Burger King parking lot with a practiced sweep. Justine pretended to search through her purse. She felt his gaze linger on her for a moment, then move on as he entered the shop.

Ten minutes later a guy about twenty years old with a ball of curly black hair and an untucked blue-striped mechanic's shirt came out of the side door of the shop and slipped through an opening in the fence across from Westly's van. Five minutes later he ducked back through with two Burger King bags.

As soon as he entered the shop Justine slid through the fence. The van's side door was unlocked. She climbed in and gently shut the door.

Sour smelling sheets and blankets covered a small mattress on a raised platform across the back. A small built-in cabinet had a tiny plastic sink in the top. A fold-up table hung on the cabinet's side. A beat up plywood box held jacks, tire tools and jumper cables.

It only took her a few minutes to find blood spatters on the thinly carpeted floor by the sink. She scraped them into one of several small envelopes she had in her pocket, just in case. Brittany's torn panties had dropped down between the platform and van side. Justine sat on the makeshift bed and studied them. They were common underwear, pale blue, high cut on the sides, bought in packs of three anywhere, except these had a crude flower drawn in blue marker on the right front. Justine had washed them a hundred times and the flower had faded, but there was no mistaking it.

Justine opened and closed her knife with one hand. She had wanted a six inch blade, but Wheat had insisted a knife that size would be too unwieldy, both open and closed. They settled on a five inch blade ground to razor sharpness the full length of one edge and the first three inches of the other. The blade swung into a no- frills aluminum handle with black serrated plastic sides molded to her grip. It was light weight and quick with a balanced feel.

She considered waiting until Westly got in the van, then slitting his throat immediately and being done with it. Three to go. But that wasn't enough. Too easy, too quick. Plus, she wanted names. And she wanted him to suffer.

A voice came from outside. "They're in the van. I'll get 'em. I'll get 'em."

In the van? Justine dropped to her hands and knees and peeked out the side window. Westly, twenty feet away. She froze for a second. She didn't care what happened to her—jail, her body killed—but she had to be free and alive to avenge her daughter's murder. Damn it, what did he want? Which door will he open? She looked out again. Where was he?

A squeal from the rear door latch galvanized her into action. The door creaked open. A blast of morning light blinded her as she rolled onto the floor against the platform, open knife gripped against her chest.

The second rear door opened. By the sound she knew he pulled open a drawer under the bed. A scrape and something heavy landed on the mattress.

"Ah shit."

The end of an open spring shock absorber rolled into sight above her head. It tilted over the edge. The van bounced. Westly's meaty hand grabbed the shock as it grazed her arm. When he yanked the shock back, part of the bunched sheet tumbled onto her face. The rank odor of unwashed sheets assailed her nose. For two minutes she lay still, not breathing. With the tip of the knife she lifted the sheet. She noticed several brown stains. Blood? Were these filthy sheets where Brittany had been beaten? Was it her blood? Or her murderers'? Harry Frazer said she fought back. Was this where it happened? Justine wanted to think so.

She carefully folded the sheet and slipped out of the van and back to her car. Back home, while continually chanting in her head *Dead women don't cry Dead women don't cry* she sealed and marked the sheet, panties and blood scrapings. Just in case. Then she went to her office. Just another day.

# Chapter Four

No matter what Justine felt inside, she had to appear "normal" to the world, until she completed her task. She had no thoughts beyond that.

So she endured her co-workers' questions about *was she ready to come back to work,* and offers of *anything I can do for you just ask.* Justine forced a smile and thanked them and said working was better than brooding at home, alone. They were good people. They meant well, but she felt nothing for them. They were extras in a movie, there to serve the heroine and then be forgotten. Her eyes blurred for a moment when she thought of what else she had lost besides her daughter.

Under her desk, she opened and closed the knife. The act reassured her. She felt Teresa studying her from the door. Teresa carried an extra ten pounds and didn't give a damn, because at forty-five she looked thirty-five and wasn't afraid to show it.

"What?"

"You're not ready to come back to work," Teresa said.

Justine shrugged. "It's better than crying, drinking, or eating myself into oblivion every day."

"Maybe, but your mind is not on your work. You've been staring at that same page for ten minutes. Talk to me, *amiga.* Tell me how you feel."

Justine didn't need to tell Teresa how she felt. Teresa knew. Four months earlier, her sixteen year old daughter, Antonia, had disappeared. A sweet, cute, Hispanic girl, Antonia embodied Southern California as well as any blonde haired, blue eyed surfer girl. A chance witness looking out her window saw what happened. Antonia was walking home in the evening with a slightly overweight, plain girl. A van stopped and two men jumped out. One grabbed Antonia, the second grabbed the other girl, seemed to look into her eyes, then dropped her. The girl remembered nothing. In five seconds, Teresa's world went from happy to Hell.

Teresa and Miguel had three children: Antonia, eleven year old Carlos, and eight year old Maria. Teresa was the strong one in the family, but the abduction devastated her. Without her strength, the others coped by quickly moving on, leaving Teresa with nobody but Justine for support. In the weeks after Brittany's death, Teresa had returned that kindness.

"Not now," Justine said. "I need to go over some of these files. I won't stay long."

"I am worried for you, my friend." Justine forced a smile and a nod of thanks. Teresa admonished Justine with her eyes and left her alone.

Justine continued to stare at the same page. Teresa was her best friend out of a group of friends that, she had to admit, was too small. After two unproductive hours Justine left without a word.

At her home on the eastern edge of Vista, she listened to a message on her answering machine. "Justine, we are doing something. By tomorrow we should have a search warrant. Call me tomorrow and I'll explain. Maybe over lunch?"

The lunch invitation barely registered. If the police got hold of Westly, Justine might never get to him. It had to happen that night.

∾ — ∾

Westly left work at five-fifteen. He finished off a beer between the shop door and his van and popped open a new one before climbing in. Justine followed him down the 78 freeway into Oceanside, where he parked behind a bar close to the beach that was already rowdy with happy hour drinkers.

She waited ten minutes then entered the bar. Her dark pants, T-shirt and light jacket fit right in between the business suits and surfers with knee-length shorts and tank tops. The knife rested snugly in her right pants pocket. A small throwaway purse held some money, tissues, a comb, breath mints, and a fully loaded, .22 caliber semi-automatic pistol. Just in case.

Westly sat in a booth with a wiry, nervous guy he called Freddy who constantly stroked a scraggly beard. They had a fresh pitcher, so, with a beer of her own, Justine settled onto a bar stool on the right-hand end of the U-shaped bar where she could keep an eye on them. Half a dozen would-be escorts for the night offered her drink, smoke, two parties and a quickie in an apartment two buildings down, no names necessary. A mention of her jealous cop husband and a steely stare repelled them easily enough.

After about fifteen minutes, a scruffy guy somewhere between fifty and seventy pushed through the crowd of drinkers, most of whom were less than half his age, and ensconced himself next to her.

"Darwin," the young female bartender greeted him as she set a mug of beer in front of him. "Don't you be hitting on this gorgeous lady. I don't think she's interested."

Darwin studied his beer for a long moment then said with what Justine thought was a slight Italian accent, "It does not matter if she is interested or not, there is only one woman for me, and she is gone." He drank deep from his mug and gently set it down with a weary shake of his broad, square head.

With a quick meeting of eyes, Justine and the bartender traded sympathy for the man. "I'm Bayley," the bartender said. "You want anything, give me a shout."

After another deep draught of beer, Darwin launched into a story about evil grey monks leaking false information about WMDs so some idiot would start a war that would eventually escalate and wipe out all humans. Then the little grey wimps could take over the planet without having to do any exterminating themselves. Much of the story had to do with betrayal and loss and unjust condemnation, so that she wondered which war he was actually talking about. Justine agreed that so far, the evil monks' plan seemed to be working. She bought him another beer.

The toilets were in a corridor opposite the booth that led to a back entrance. The first time Justine followed Westly down the corridor, there were too many people he seemed to know. The second time nobody paid attention.

"Hi." Justine pressed herself against Westly, gently nudging him toward the exit. "I've been watching you," she said with drunken enthusiasm.

Westly studied her face, then lowered his gaze to her tight T-shirt, now thrust toward him. "Why's that?"

"Because I'm horny and I don't want to be."

"Oh, yeah?"

"Yeah. Want to do something about it?" She let her hand run over his ass, then along his hip to his thigh.

"Maybe. Why me?"

"Who else in this place?" She brushed her hand across his crotch. "You have a place close by?" She stuck her fingers halfway down his pants.

"I have a van in back."

"Ooo. I like camping." She tugged his pants as she backed toward the door.

Grinning, he followed along. "Just a quickie, right?"

She managed a giggle. "Well, not too quick."

Out the door she yanked him to the side and pressed him against the wall with her body. She bit his earlobe while probing his crotch with her leg. He was ready.

Nobody was around. She was ready.

Thick fog had pushed in off the water. It tumbled over the building tops in intermittent whirls and swirls. The van showed as a fuzzy edged shadow in the small parking lot across the alley.

"Where's your campground, Smokey? I have a fire to put out."

In the back of the van, Westly slid the side door closed and turned to Justine.

"Where's that fire?"

"Here."

Justine swung a pipe from the box by the door against his head. She laid him out on the floor and straddled him. Her hand shook as she pressed the knife to his neck.

"Who helped you murder my daughter?"

Still dazed, he shook his head, then winced and didn't move. Blood left a slow trail down his cheek. "Who are you? You're fucking crazy. Get off me." He shifted under her. The blade bit through skin to his neck tendons.

"I'm Brittany's mother."

The look in his eyes showed that he knew who she meant. "I don't know any Brittany."

"I found her underwear in here. Who helped you?"

"Get real, lady."

The power of his punch to her ribs drove her against the van's side. Each gasp for breath sent a spike of pain through her. It happened so fast she hadn't had time to cut him.

Westly sat up, then moaned and had to support himself for a few seconds. This gave Justine time to catch her breath, and worry. His punch had been much more powerful and quick than she ever imagined. Her Kung Fu training and her will failed her in the confines of the van. How could she hope to gut him like the useless animal he was?

He grabbed her left arm and yanked her to him. She slashed his arm and chest. He threw her onto her stomach and pounded on her back. She gasped in pain.

*You're dead,* she reminded herself. *No pain.* In one fluid movement, she jerked her knees underneath herself. "Fucker!" she growled. Rising, twisting, she smashed his face with her elbow. Stooped, but on her feet, knife still in hand, she knew she had to finish it.

She never got the chance.

Westly's foot lashed out, kicking her against the front seat. As she fell, she spun to land on her right side. The knife clattered into the door well.

*Get the gun. Finish him now, or he'll finish you.* Westly grabbed her before she could turn and get the purse. His hand held her arm like a vise. The other hand closed around her throat and squeezed.

Desperate, she pounded his body with her knee. He grunted with each hit, but did not loosen his grasp. She had one last chance. She seized his crotch and yanked.

"Ahhh!" His grip loosened. She twisted away, scrabbling for the door handle. The door slid open. Justine snatched the knife as she slid head first out the door onto the damp asphalt.

Westly swore as he lurched out of the van, swinging a pipe. The pipe caught Justine's leg just above the ankle.

She stumbled. Pain brought tears, yet she hobbled quickly down the dim alley leading deeper into the block.

Westly had to take a moment to clear his head, then, carrying a two foot length of pipe, he ran after her.

Single story commercial buildings lined the alley on both sides. There were occasional indentations for access and parking for the businesses, but no passage through to a street. That was good. On the open street the police were sure to get involved. The way the legal system worked, Westly could walk and she'd be in jail.

He gained on her fast.

A glance into a narrow opening showed her dumpsters along the back and a pile of scrap two-by-fours close to the corner. She turned into the opening, and flattened against the brick wall, knife gripped tight, ready to strike.

Westly ran around the corner. She swung the blade for his body. His swift reaction with the pipe just managed to deflect the blow. Back to the wall, he whipped the pipe down and smacked the knife out of her hand, sending a jolt of pain up her arm.

Justine ignored the pain—she had to. In one movement, she grabbed a broken two-by-four, whirled around and slammed the wood against his back. He stumbled. She hit him again. He went down. She drew back for a solid strike to his head.

Once again, he proved too quick and too tough for her. The pipe caught the back of her legs and swept her feet out from under her. She landed on her ass with a jolt that took her breath away. The knife spun out of her hand.

"You're done." He swung the pipe over his head like an executioner lines up his axe.

But Justine wasn't quite done. Holding the two-by-four by the ends, she blocked his blow, and the next and the next as she pushed backward with her feet. The third blow cracked the wood. It wouldn't take another. She stopped moving backward. Westly stepped up. She brought her leg back then jammed her foot against his knee. Not a crippling injury, but it slowed him down enough for her to crawl away and regain her feet.

Limping, but implacable, he came after her. She tried to dart past him and escape to the center alley. The wild arc of the pipe kept her trapped.

The two-by-four splintered in half, leaving a long sharp point at one end. She could barely hold it with two hands to parry the swinging pipe.

"Come on, Mom. Don't give up now. Your slut daughter put up more of a fight than you."

"You're a diseased creature, Westly. Do you know how sick you and your friends are? How could you rape a child like that?"

"She weren't no child with her clothes off, Mom."

"You sick fuck."

Justine ducked under a strike and jabbed the long splinter of wood into his side. Westly cried out and jerked away.

"Why did you cut her like that? Wasn't beating her and raping her enough?"

Westly froze. The hard glint in his eyes vanished for a few seconds. In the shadow light of the alley, he looked like a wax museum criminal. Justine saw him shudder as a normal person who remembers something horrible would.

She jumped sideways to run around him. He was wounded, weakened, and not as steady on his feet. If she could get the knife, she'd have a chance. She failed to consider her own condition. Westly body-checked her.

She slammed against a dumpster. Pain took her breath and her legs away. There was not supposed to be any pain. Dead people feel nothing. Dead people are entitled to their vengeance. Scratching at the lid, she slipped toward the ground.

Westly caught her and dragged her up by the T-shirt. How could he still be so strong? Pipe in both hands, he stuck it under her chin and forced her head back. He leaned over, put his face close up to hers face.

"That was Sinakov who done that. Not us. Not that it matters to you anymore."

The pipe pressed down.

Justine attempted to lift the pipe, poke his eyes, hit him, knee him in the balls. Nothing worked. He was too strong, too quick. No air entered her lungs. She didn't even have enough to spit in his face. *I'm sorry, Baby*. Justine closed her eyes so the last image she saw would not be Westly's bloodlust grimace.

Then the pressure let up and she could breathe.

# *Chapter Five*

Justine slid to the ground. Each gasp of cool, sea air soothed her dry throat. *I'm hallucinating,* she thought as she focused on the scene ten feet away.

A woman stood over Westly. She was ten feet tall from Justine's viewpoint, with black leather pants and a short-waisted leather jacket topped by wild dark hair. Westly, on hands and knees, was picking up the pipe. He lunged at the woman. Too quick for Justine's freaked out mind to comprehend, the woman snatched the pipe from Westly and smacked his head. Stunned, he offered no resistance when she lifted him up and dropped him on top of a dumpster.

Near death experience forgotten, Justine marveled at the woman's strength and speed, where she herself had been so inadequate. What happened next convinced her she was experiencing a dark dream before she woke up in Hell.

The woman held Westly's right arm, wrist up, and raised it to her mouth. She bit down hard. Westly uttered a brief cry. He thrashed about for fifteen seconds, helpless against the woman's steady grip. Blood ran across his palm. He lay quiet then. Justine heard a faint sucking sound as the woman's jaws worked at his wrist.

At last the woman released him. Head tilted back to face the sky, she let out a long satisfied, "Ahhhhh." Then she turned to Justine.

The thought *Vampire!* ran through her head, but didn't really connect. There were no such things, and didn't they always bite the neck? Suddenly a hundred questions vied to be asked first.

The strange woman had questions of her own. She had a slight French accent, easily understandable.

"I do hope I saved the correct person. You were trying to kill him, *ne c'est pas?"*

"He abducted, raped and killed my daughter."

"You are sure of this?"

"I am."

"Ahh."

The woman bit Westly's arm again. Finished, she licked blood from her generous lips. "Interesting. The blood of the evil tastes the same as the blood of the good."

"Who are you?"

*"On m'appelle Simone.* And you?"

# Blood Justice

Justine struggled to stand up. Somehow, Simone appeared beside her, raising her up with no visible effort.

"How did you beat him?" Justine asked. "He's so strong."

Simone leaned close. "I am stronger."

Justine studied the strange woman's arms. They were only arms.

Simone noticed her look and said, "I am also quicker. I hear better, I see better." Her tongue licked blood from her lower lip. "I taste better." She rested a hand on Justine's heaving chest. "I am better in every way."

Justine attempted to step away. The hand, strong as steel, gently gripped her neck. "What is your name?"

Justine hesitated. With one finger, Simone turned Justine's face to her. "Do not be afraid of me. I am not of the *Gendarme*. And I am sated. I mean you no harm." She leaned close until their cheeks kissed. "Just the opposite, if you so wish?" Simone's hand slid down until the back of her hand caressed the top of Justine's breast.

Justine did not know what she wished. The nearness of a woman so powerful intoxicated her. Her scent washed away Justine's pains. Her touch...it had been so long since anyone touched her like that. What did it matter whether it was a man or woman? Years ago, by chance, she spent an intimate hour with a woman. It had not been unpleasant.

She let her head rest on Simone's shoulder. How could she ever avenge Brittany's death? Westly almost killed her. Somebody else had to rescue her. What made her think she could pull it off? She should tell Detective Frazer what she knew and move on.

Simone's lips brushed her cheek, whispered a kiss on the corner of her mouth. It would be so nice to surrender and let someone else take charge of her. The hand slid over her breast to her side. She sucked in a slow, deep breath. A sharp pain from her ribs cut through her like an electric jolt. She jerked back.

"No," she said, more to herself than Simone. "I can't. Not now. I can't...I won't let Brittany down."

"Ah, *ma cherie*, a disappointment."

Justine backed away. "Who are you? What are you?"

Amused, Simone said, "You do not really want to know, I'm sure."

Westly rolled off the dumpster. He slumped against the base.

"Is he still alive?"

Simone knelt next to Westly. She sniffed. "There is some life in him yet."

Justine stalked to him. She drew the knife from her pocket and flicked it open. Without hesitation, she leaned down, jammed the blade into his crotch, and in one smooth motion sliced him open from belly to breastbone.

Westly gasped, then settled as his entrails spilled out. He may have already been dead. Justine didn't care. She'd done what she set out to do.

*I'm dead*, she told herself. *Despicable man that he was, killing him means nothing to me. It was my job.* She wrinkled her nose at the stink of fresh blood and shit and stepped back. Her stomach wanted to vomit everything she had ever eaten. But she would not show her weakness to this woman.

"I'm Justine Kroft," she said to Simone. "Thank you for saving my life."

"Justine. A seeker of justice. Appropriate. I knew who you were when you cut him open. I am glad I saved the right one. I too have lost someone close to me."

Justine nodded acknowledgment. Now that her first goal had been achieved, the rage she'd been living off of for weeks cooled. Each breath sent a jolt of pain into her body. Her legs throbbed and stiffened with each step. Her head was going to explode. She had no strength to delve into this Simone and the impossibility of what she might be.

She turned to walk out of the alley, a slow, painful process. Simone put an arm around her waist and took most of the weight off her feet.

"I sympathize with your desire for revenge, Justine. And I understand your desire to gut them like a fish. But it was not a smart thing to do. The others will now know somebody is after them. They will be waiting for you. Perhaps, looking for you."

"I'll be ready."

Simone laughed. "Not if they are like *Monsieur* Westly."

"I have a gun. Shit! In his van."

By the time they reached the van, Simone held all Justine's weight. Justine crawled in, retrieved her purse, and wiped any surfaces she might have touched. The few people smoking by the bar's back door showed them no interest.

At the end of the alley Justine stood on unsteady legs. Simone stood a few feet away. "You can't possibly be what you seem to be," Justine said.

Despite the dim, diffuse light from a fog enshrouded streetlight, Justine saw a darkness pass over Simone's face.

"Three hundred and fifty-two years ago, in circumstances much less pleasant than this, I thought the same thing."

"The power you have—I believe I may need it to do what I have to do."

Simone reached out and cupped Justine's cheek. She drew her near. "A cliché, I know, but be careful what you wish for, *cherie*. Many before you have had much time to regret their choices."

The first scream sounded from down the alley.

Justine did not shy away from a gentle kiss. She savored the coppery taste of blood on her lips. For a moment, she again considered allowing herself to submit to control from outside of herself.

"Go home, Justine. Heal yourself."

The second scream turned her head to the alley. When she turned back, she was alone.

# Chapter Six

Harry Frazer settled on a stool at the end of the Sundowner's U-shaped bar. Bayley, the tanned, freckled, sun-bleached blonde bartender, set a beer down without his having to ask. She flashed a warm toothpaste ad smile.

"Hey, Harry. On or off?"

"As off as I can get."

She rested her arms on the bar and looked into his close set brown eyes. "If she's got any sense at all, she'll come around."

Harry opened his mouth to say one thing then said another. "You're the expert on women. Certainly not me. How is Susan these days?"

"Still surfing the monster wave of my heart. Have I thanked you this week?"

"Not for at least two."

Bayley lightly touched his hand. "Thanks, Harry."

She moved on along the bar, pouring drinks as if her wrist hadn't been smashed with a hammer three years ago. She had lived with her husband in the condo next to the one Harry and his wife owned on the beach, two blocks from the Sundowner. Charming in public, a raging, obsessive, green monster in private, Bayley's husband had her completely terrorized and under control. Harry recognized the signs. He offered Bayley help. Eventually he had to give the husband the word according to the Law. When that didn't work and the Green Monster went after her with a hammer, Harry gave him two bullets. There were some questions, but no charges filed. Only Harry and Bayley knew what really happened, and they weren't telling.

Harry had lived alone in the condo for almost two years—his payment for putting his wife through school so she could get a job making three times his income. She had put in the requisite time and effort until a headhunter recruited her for a job in New York at an obscene multiple of any salary Harry could ever imagine making. Because of their job schedules, the only reason he knew she was gone was that he found himself living in the small condo on the beach instead of a four bedroom starter mansion in a gated community. He liked the condo better.

Bayley came back with a second beer.

"Darwin been in?" He shouted to be heard over the band in the next room and the rising cacophony of voices and laughter.

"He was in earlier, talking with some babe. She left, then he left. Too rowdy for him on a Friday night."

Harry considered Justine a babe, with her blonde hair a sensible length, green eyes, and nose almost too small for her wide, strong chinned face. He wanted to see her again and had been disappointed she hadn't returned his calls. He knew that nursing a few beers at the end of the Sundowner bar while thinking of her, and observing the peculiar variety of local beach area personalities, was better than brooding at home which inevitably led to a killer hangover. Christ, he was pathetic. What was he, still in high school?

To everybody in the Sundowner, except Bayley, he was just another anonymous lonely, middle-aged guy pensive over a beer and checking out the surfer chicks. Yet, with eighteen years in the Sheriff's Department, Harry could never completely turn off his cop instincts.

The first indistinct scream floated in through the back corridor. It barely registered. There could be any number of reasons for screams on a Friday night, good or bad.

Five seconds later, at the second scream, he cocked his head and listened for related sounds. Ten seconds later hurried footsteps down the sandy corridor brought him to full attention.

A young couple burst through the door right beside him. The woman held one hand to her mouth and clutched the man's arm with the other. They rushed to the bar.

"Hey," the man yelled at Bayley. "Call nine one one."

Bayley sized them up for two seconds. "What's happened?"

"There's a dead body up the alley."

"It was horrible," the young woman said.

Bayley glanced at Harry, who nodded. He flashed his badge. "Show me."

It was horrible. The body slumped on the ground against the dumpster at the alley's end. Blood from two gashes in the wrist covered the right hand. Viscera spilled out of the abdomen, which was slashed open from belly to breastbone. The stench of intestine leakage gagged him. Sirens approached as, hand over mouth and nose, he knelt down to check the pulse as a formality. Dim light prevented a good look at the man's face, which seemed familiar.

By the time he turned the crime scene over to an Oceanside detective team Harry had had a good chance to examine the body. That survey gave him plenty to think about on the long walk back to the Sundowner and a cold beer. He didn't have to wonder who killed Westly, and why. He knew that. What he didn't know was what he was going to do about it.

# *Chapter Seven*

"Y ou did not fall down any stairs," Teresa told Justine. "You were beat up. Did they rape you, too?"

"No one raped me. I fell down—"

Teresa jerked the bandages around her patient a bit tighter than necessary.

"Ow, not so tight."

Justine sat in a maple kitchen chair which matched the table and cabinets. The three-year-old kitchen had seen barely six months of use. She and Brittany had been so busy the last few years they'd had little time together. But when they did spend more than a few minutes sharing their lives, they were usually in the kitchen. They'd cook and eat and talk. Always Italian food—Brittany had a sixth sense about cooking perfect pasta, though there was no Italian blood in the family. Brittany said Italian was, "slurpy, sloppy, talking food." Justine couldn't imagine ever eating Italian food again.

Teresa stood behind Justine and massaged her taut shoulders. "Don't tell your nurse how to treat you."

"You haven't been a nurse for eight years. You've forgotten everything."

"Good thing I have you to practice on."

She continued the massage in silence, then pressed her lips to her patient's hair. "Justine, I'm your closest friend of...one?"

"I have friends," Justine said with little conviction.

"You have business associates and people somehow related to raising Brittany. Since your husband died, I'm the only one who will put up with your slightly obsessive parenting. You can tell me anything. No doubt, you've had a bitch of it the last few weeks. You know that I know exactly what you've been going through. I don't know what really happened to you, maybe I don't want to know, but you have to share, or it'll eat you alive. I know how to keep a secret."

Teresa's hands moved underneath the cool, damp towel around Justine's neck. Justine relaxed for the first time since Brittany failed to return home. If she told anybody anything it would be Teresa. She had no doubt Teresa was serious about keeping a secret. But friendship can only go so far. How much to tell? All? Part? Which part?

What would she do if Teresa could not keep a secret?

A rolling wave of sadness forced a sob from her when she understood with firm conviction that she would do anything, sacrifice anything, or anybody, to achieve revenge. What other purpose did she have now?

Teresa pulled a chair up and took her hands. "What?"

On the other hand, Teresa wouldn't believe her. "What I tell you might get you in trouble, serious trouble, if they find out you knew and didn't report it."

"They who?"

"Police."

"I can lie with the best of them."

"You might not want to be my friend anymore."

Teresa studied her. "It's that bad?"

Justine kept her expression blank as she looked Teresa in the eye and raised her shoulders a fraction.

"So, tell me," Teresa said.

The doorbell rang.

"Miguel?" Justine asked.

"He's with the kids. Besides, he'd call first. Trouble?"

"Maybe."

Justine struggled to stand up. Thanks to a Tylenol/Ibuprofen mix, the pain was bearable. A couple of Vicodin when she went to bed would take care of the rest. Teresa pushed her back down.

"I'll get it."

Teresa pulled a long knife out of a drawer as she headed for the front door. It was Brittany's favorite knife. Justine's eyes followed it out of the room. Though the front door was out of Justine's sight, it was close enough that she could hear Teresa at a side window, checking out the late night visitor.

"A man, forty something, dark hair, needs a haircut. A hottie, though. Alas, no flowers. Looks sort of official."

The doorbell rang again.

"Go ahead and answer it," Justine said. She sucked in as deep a breath as she could stand, and waited.

# Chapter Eight

Harry stopped his three-year-old Mustang convertible across the street from Justine Kroft's house. The house was two stories with a two car garage. From his one previous visit on official business he knew it had a smooth, beige stucco exterior, vaguely Spanish in style. Bougainvillea tumbled over a brick wall.

Lights from the first floor showed through tropical plants that partially obscured the front of the house. Shadows on the curtains indicated movement inside. A small SUV was parked in the center of the U-shaped drive.

Harry had no reason to be there. The forensic team had barely unpacked their latex gloves. He had absolutely no evidence that Justine killed Westly—except he knew she had, and knew why, and sympathized with her. It wasn't even his case, yet he was here, probably blowing any case the real detectives might develop.

Christ, he was such a fool. He was breaking all the rules and jeopardizing his career for an attractive woman who thought he was doing nothing to solve her daughter's murder. As he turned into her driveway, he tried to imagine what she would look like in an orange jumpsuit.

A handsome Hispanic woman about his own age opened the door. She gave him a quizzical look and said nothing. He did not fail to notice the knife she made little attempt to hide.

"Is Justine Kroft home?" he asked, falling back on his official voice.

"Who's asking?"

"Harry Frazer."

Her eyebrows raised.

He nodded toward the knife and held up his ID. "Detective Harry Frazer, Sheriff's Department."

"It's all right, Teresa," Justine called.

Teresa stepped back with a tight smile and ushered him into the kitchen.

A glimpse of bandages and the bruises on her legs and face caught him by surprise. Christ, how could he ignore them?

"What happened to you?" *Westly put up a hell of a fight.*

For a long moment she looked up at him with an expression that an imaginative, or needy, person might interpret as meaning *It's nice to see you.*

"I fell down the stairs." She winced. "Damn near killed myself."

"Did you call nine one one? Go to the emergency room?"

"Better. I called Teresa. She was a nurse."

Harry studied the woman leaning with arms crossed by the kitchen door. She studied him right back, with the air of a woman used to being in charge and not intimidated by the likes of a small town cop.

"Senior Nurse, LA General ER, twenty years," she said.

"Right." He nodded to her then turned back to Justine.

"Have you been here all night, then?"

"Yes." Her body tensed for a moment when she said it.

"I called you three times. Left two messages."

"I was sleeping. Something I don't do very often these days. When I got up, the stairs took me down. What were you calling about?"

Harry watched her every move. "We were going to search Rob Westly's van and house. I wanted to tell you that we were doing something."

She met his gaze. "I appreciate that. Did you say 'were' going to search? Who is Rob Westly?"

"A suspect in your daughter's murder."

"Did he do it?"

"Someone thought so."

"There's that past tense again."

"He's dead."

An eyebrow rose. "Too bad if he didn't do it. Good if he did."

"Don't you want to know why I think someone thought he was involved?"

"Why do you think Rob Westly was involved, Harry?"

"Because he was eviscerated."

"Eviscerated? A nice way to put it."

"Not a nice way to die."

"If he was involved in Brittany's death it was a perfect way to die."

"And there seemed to be a lot of blood missing."

"Maybe you should be looking for a vampire?"

Harry sighed. He pulled up a chair and sat in front of her, then leaned forward and spoke in a low voice. "Justine, may I speak with you, alone?" He looked over his shoulder at Teresa. She returned his look with a neutral expression. "Are you sure you want your friend to know what you've done?"

"That's what friends are for."

"In this case friends are the same as accessories to a crime. They can go to jail, too. You would not be cellmates." He checked to see if Teresa got the point. She remained neutral except for a slight tightening of her lips.

"Friends are free to make their own decisions," Justine said.

Totally still, Teresa watched them.

# David Burton

Christ, if he had a shred of evidence, he'd arrest them both for their own protection. "Justine, don't you think we checked out Westly and his friends? He runs with a tough crowd. I don't know how you found Westly. Did someone in the Department tell you? That's dangerous, to you as well as the case. Who told you?"

Justine clicked her thumbnails and said nothing.

Harry reached out and pushed down the towel, revealing the bruises on her neck. "I'd bet you were damn lucky you didn't end up with a lot worse than that. His friends will eat you alive if you mess with them." He stood up.

Harry had met many mothers grieving the loss of a child, especially in the last few years. He wanted them all to be safe and had done all he could to ease their grief. So why was he bending rules and putting the case and his career in jeopardy for this woman? She was attractive, yes, but that was a small part of the reason for risk. She was headstrong, determined and overconfident, was going to do what she wanted to do, and wouldn't, couldn't, tell anybody. Not unlike him when he decided to become a master thief. And she had suffered a great loss. His loss had been minor compared to hers, yet it still hurt and had poisoned his few attempted relationships in the two years since his wife left.

"I don't want anything to happen to you." Christ, was he talking as a cop or as a man? He didn't know. Next thing, he'd ask her to go steady. He had to get out of there. "Stay away from those people, both of you."

He searched Justine's eyes for some life, some emotion. For a moment he was terrified there was nothing there, and never would be. Then she reached out a hand. Her gaze softened when he took it. "Thank you, Harry, for coming to see me. I certainly don't want to be eaten," she glanced at Teresa, "alive."

❧—☙

As Harry entered the 78 freeway West, he continued to castigate himself for acting like a besotted teenager. Before he left he had handed her his card and said, "Please, call me any time, for any reason." He might as well have dropped to his knees and begged her to call him. Pathetic.

Up to speed, he considered her last words. She had emphasized "alive" as if it was part of some in-joke he hadn't a clue about. He suspected that whatever it meant, it would be no joke.

# Chapter Nine

Justine and Teresa sat across the table from each other, a half empty wine bottle between them.

"You were hit too hard on the head. A vampire?" Teresa threw her hands up, slopping a few drops of wine from her almost empty glass.

Justine hugged her robe tight around her. Her bare feet rested on the chair beside Teresa. "I know. I know. But you didn't see or feel what I did."

"There are no vampires. But whatever she was, I thank her for saving your ass. Vampires aside, what are you going to do now?"

"Find the other murderers. Make sure they get the justice they deserve. Will you help me?" Teresa stared at the table top. "You didn't ask me if I really killed the guy."

"That's what friends are for." Teresa drained her glass and set it down carefully in front of her. "Nurses are trained to save lives, not take them. But after all the shit I've seen men like that do to women, I can't work up much sympathy when some man gets what he deserves. I'll help you find these men, I'll help you get them into jail, I'll fix you up if necessary. I will not participate in killing anyone. No matter how much they might deserve it."

"Fair enough."

"The ruggedly handsome Detective Harry will help. Anything to get close to you."

"Why would he want to get close to me?"

"Because you are a very attractive woman who has lost a loved one and he wants to help. And he likes you. Why, I don't know."

"He wants to arrest me."

"I don't think he wants to, but he will if you give him a reason to. That's why you just lied to him."

*Lies which he may or may not discover.* Justine's stomach and fists clenched as she controlled a spurt of anger at herself. She was dead, and not supposed to have feelings. She didn't want to care what he discovered, but the pain throughout her body made her feel, and reminded her that she was, indeed, alive. She did not want to feel. It made her job as judge, jury and executioner of Brittany's killers harder to perform.

Then why did she feel guilty about lying to Harry? She had glanced into his eyes, and was caught by them. They were a deeper brown than she'd ever seen. But it wasn't the color that held her. They glistened as if permanently ready to overflow with tears, as if hurt and sadness lurked behind them. *He, too, has suffered a loss,* she thought, and laughed silently. *Two losers attracted to each other, how long could that last?*

"He'd prefer I forget Brittany ever existed and go back to my so called life."

"He only wants you to not go after those guys."

"What else do I have? How can I let it go? Have you let Antonia go?"

Teresa's face tightened. She shook her head. "At least you know what happened."

Justine touched her friend's hand. "You still have hope. I don't. I know I'll never see Brit again."

"It's hard to keep hoping. Miguel and the kids have moved on, but I can't. Antonia is my first child, I won't abandon her. We were too close." She filled their glasses and slumped back in the seat. "I do agree with Detective Harry, though. You should move on."

"Too many bad guys get away with bad things, Teresa. It happened with my mother, it won't happen with my daughter. I can't move on until they're all dead. Or I am."

Teresa absently rubbed Justine's feet with one hand. "I wish you would not speak like that."

Justine stared through a window into the darkness on the other side. "I wish I didn't have any reason to talk like that."

# Chapter Ten

Rob Westly's funeral was held the next Friday in Escondido. From her car Justine photographed those gathered around the gravesite. They included Harry Frazer who stood off a bit, making no attempt to hide who he was.

Many of the burial attendees were men in their late twenties and early thirties looking uncomfortable in suits, including Freddy, Westly's friend from the Sundowner. Justine briefly felt sorry for the new widow and her two young sons. But he had been a scumbag rapist and murderer and she was better off without him, whether she thought so or not. Justine had lost her daughter and her life, and that woman's husband was responsible. Maybe he beat her and she was glad he was dead. Maybe Justine had done her a favor. Maybe her tears were just for show. Maybe.

Freddy walked away with two of the other men. One was about six feet tall, muscled, with a close military-style haircut. The other was taller and thinner with blond hair in a ponytail. Freddy was talking to them, they weren't talking to him.

"The blond one with the ponytail is Jay Dunham, thirty five." Deputy David Axel leaned in the passenger side window. "A freelance truck driver, got in some bar fights in his twenties, but clean for about four years now. Has a black belt in something, Kung Fu, Judo?"

By a new pickup, Muscles pushed Freddy hard against the cab. Dunham tightened Freddy's tie until the smaller man's mouth gaped open. From Justine's point of view it didn't look like Dunham was offering words of friendly commiseration. Muscles yanked Freddy away from the truck and they sped off.

"The other one is Latch Standard, thirty three. Yeah, I know. I didn't name him. Ex-marine sergeant, now a security consultant. Both tough guys, both were tight with Westly."

After they were out of sight, Freddy flipped them the finger, then drove away in a small Toyota pickup with a beat-up camper shell.

"You know about Freddy Champ. Westly's cousin, a wannabe bad boy, though he seems to have more sense than that. I'll follow the tough guys."

Justine followed Freddy to the back of a carpet warehouse store. At four o'clock that afternoon, she followed him to a two story apartment building in San Marcos. A new Lexus SUV was out of character for the neighborhood, so she drove home. She showered, dressed in jeans,

T-shirt and jacket, ate something, and checked that her gun had a full clip and one in the chamber.

The sun had set, the day heat replaced by a dying breeze, when Justine returned to Freddy's two-story, pink stucco apartment building, one of several running at a right angle to the street. Open parking in front of the units, steps at each end and in the middle and more shadowy apartments behind completed the ambiance of the area.

Freddy's truck remained in its space. Justine parked Brittany's truck on the street, and walked to number 29, upstairs, far end. Cooking sounds and Mexican food aromas came through some open doors. The only activity around the building were a stout Mexican couple with two kids unloading the spoils from a major supermarket visit.

Low TV voices came from inside number 29. Justine made sure the gun at the small of her back was loose. She knocked.

"Who is it?"

"I need to talk to you about Rob Westly."

"Rob is dead. Go away."

"I was a friend of Rob's. I need to talk with you."

After a long ten seconds the door opened on the chain. Beer bottle dangling from his hand, Freddy peered out suspiciously. His eyebrows raised in appreciation as he checked her out.

"Who the hell are you?"

"Someone looking for justice." She jumped up and kicked the door in at the chain. It slammed against Freddy, who staggered back. Justine pushed inside and shut the door behind her.

Inside, the furniture looked like it was left by the original tenant thirty years ago. A couch and armchair faced a large TV with electronics stacked beside it on plywood and cinderblock shelves. An open pizza box with one slice of pepperoni, and two empty beer bottles lay on a heavy wood coffee table.

Justine drew the gun out, cocked the hammer, and pointed it at Freddy. "Sit down."

His head jerked back when he saw the gun. "What the fuck?"

"Sit down."

He sat. "If you're looking for money, you're in the wrong place, bitch."

"I want to know who murdered my daughter."

"I don't know your kid. I don't know nothing."

"Westly was one of the men who kidnapped, raped, and butchered my girl. You know that."

"No." But he did. A twitch in his eyes told her.

"There were three others besides Westly. I think you were one of them."

"I didn't do anything to any girl."

"*I* think you did. That's all that matters." She stood over him, gun pointed at his crotch.

"You shoot and there'll be cops all over you."

"I don't care."

With a quick move, Justine flicked open her knife, leaned forward and pressed the blade against his neck. Simultaneously she jammed the barrel of the gun against his groin, the muzzle pressed to the cushion. "Don't flinch," she said. She pulled the trigger.

He flinched. "What the fuck? That hurt, God damn it." Blood trickled down his neck. He grabbed his groin with both hands.

Justine had his attention. Her eyes as much as the knife pinned him to the couch. She pressed the gun's muzzle to his crotch.

"I want to know who murdered my daughter. Westly, you—"

"I told you, I didn't have anything to do with that."

"But you know who did. Those two guys at the funeral who didn't seem too happy with you. Them?"

"They'll kill me if I say anything."

"I'll kill you if you don't."

"Shit, lady..."

"There were four men, Westly and your two funeral friends. Who's the fourth?"

Freddy's eyes widened. He squirmed on the couch, obviously more scared of the fourth man than of her.

"You...you don't know what sort of shit you're fucking with, lady."

Justine pressed the gun hard. "I don't hear any sirens yet, Freddy. Shall I try another shot? Give me names. I'll leave and I never heard of you."

He exhaled sharply through his nose. "Go ahead. Kill me. At least I'll really be dead."

"What the hell's that mean?"

Justine's body vibrated with her need to know. Here she was with a man who could tell her who murdered Brittany and he wouldn't tell her. Her mind raced. She wanted to shoot him. She wanted to cut him, beat him, make him talk. But she was not at all sure she could do what she needed to do.

From outside came the sound of two heavy car doors closing. Freddy's head jerked toward the door. His body went rigid, then completely limp. "Lady," he said after a few seconds. "If you want to live, go out the bathroom window and forget whatever you're trying to do."

She looked toward the door. The gun drifted that way, too. "Are they here?"

"Sorry lady, I got to save my own ass."

"What?"

Freddy's fist against her cheek sent a jolt down to her feet. Her ass hit the coffee table hard, jarring the gun from her hand. Her vision blurred. She flailed about with the knife. Freddy kicked her off the table. She tumbled to the floor and rolled to her knees. The gun. She lunged for it. A boot pinned her hand to the carpet. A jab with the knife drove it away.

Freddy knocked her over with a kick to her hip. Continuing to roll, she stretched for the gun. Freddy grabbed the back of her jacket and yanked her up, then slammed her face against the wall and held her there, feet off the floor.

Justine tasted blood. The rough wall ground into her skin. She couldn't get a good breath. She still gripped the knife, but with her face pressed against the wall, she could do nothing with it.

Freddy spoke in her ear. Beer breath almost made her gag. "Lady, you should use that knife on yourself. You won't like what they do to you with it."

Pressure on her face barely allowed her to say, "They who?"

"Them."

Standard and Dunham from the funeral stood just inside the door, hands in leather jacket pockets, quizzical frowns on their faces.

"Need some help with your new toy, Freddy? Want us to break her in for you?" Dunham asked.

"I can handle her, Jay," Freddy said.

Justine's knuckles scraped the wall as she twisted her knife arm down. Freed, she jabbed the blade into Freddy's thigh. He cried out and slid to the floor clutching his leg.

Stumbling over him as she pushed off from the wall, she snatched the gun up and whirled to point it at the two men. Their guns, big ones with silencers, were already out and trained on her.

"What's going on, Freddy?" Standard asked.

"She's looking for whoever killed her daughter. I think she killed Rob."

They stared hard at Justine. She had no idea what to do.

"What did you tell her?" Dunham asked Freddy.

"Nothin'. Shit, my leg hurts, man. I gotta see a doctor."

Standard said, "Later. He wants to see you now."

"Why's he want to see me. I ain't done nothing. I didn't tell her anything."

"Then you don't have anything to worry about, do you?" Dunham said.

"Come on, Freddy. You wanted in with the big boys, here's your chance," Standard said, grinning.

Justine saw the terror on Freddy's face.

"Latch, I can't go now. I...I gotta get to a doctor."

"You're going," Dunham said.

"What about her?" Standard asked.

Justine couldn't help herself. "Who wants to see him?"

"Shoot her. Blame it on Freddy," Dunham said.

"Let's fuck her first."

"Yeah. She's hot, just like that kid. We'll have to take her somewhere."

"He won't be there, I hope. That was nasty with that girl."

"I think it only works with virgins," Dunham said.

"I think that's bullshit. She wasn't a virgin anymore when he did that shit."

They considered options.

"Of course, if she killed Rob, he'll want to deal with her."

"What the hell, better take her to him first."

"Where? Where is he?" Justine shouted. Why weren't they scared of her? She had a gun pointed right at them. She could pull the trigger anytime. Yet they ignored her.

Frustration twisted her gut and made her breath come in short, sharp bursts. Those two men raped and killed Brittany. She wanted to shoot them. Wanted to empty her gun into them, take their guns and shoot them in the groin until nothing was left but shreds of bloody flesh. But who was the fourth man? How could she get them to tell her, when they ignored her?

Without thinking, she jerked the trigger. The bullet creased Latch's belt. He yelped and jumped sideways.

Freddy crawled toward the back of the apartment.

"Who's the other man, God damn it?"

Standard was having a hard time not shooting her.

Dunham smiled and said, "Relax. We'll take you to him."

"Just tell me where he is."

Dunham's smile faded. "We'll take you." To his partner he said, "Leg."

*Leg? What the hell does that mean?* Then it came to her. She jumped sideways.

Standard fired. The gun made a loud "chuff" sound. The bullet stung as it carved a shallow groove in her calf. She ducked around the corner leading to the bedroom and backed against the wall.

If the dead don't feel, why did her leg hurt so much? Forget the pain. Pain was nothing. Nothing could hurt her more than she'd already been hurt. Hurt made her brain speed. So what to do, shoot or run? Wait, then track them down individually and bring them the justice they deserve, or shoot now and be done with it? Shit, if they were vampires, bullets were useless, weren't they? It'd be over for her. But they stood in the sun for an hour that afternoon. Did the sun really turn them to dust? Do something. Do something.

A familiar voice interrupted her indecision.

"Sheriff's Department. Stop, and put those guns down."

Justine peeked around the corner and saw Deputy Axel standing just inside the door, gun in one hand, badge in the other, covering Dunham and Standard. Dunham had his back to Axel, Standard faced him.

"You don't want to get involved in this," Standard said. "It won't end well for you or your family."

"Don't threaten me. Put the gun down. You too, Dunham."

"Yes, sir, Officer." Dunham, arms in the classic hands up position, slowly lowered his gun, dropping it across his body and around his side.

Justine realized his plan. "Deputy Axel, look out!"

Four gunshots sounded, two loud, two subdued. Dunham shot Axel. Justine shot Dunham, her bullet leaving a long crease across the back of his leather jacket. Axel shot Standard in the leg. Standard shot at her. Stinging dry wall chunks forced her back.

"Run," Freddy said as he limped out of his bedroom, carrying a backpack. "Out the bathroom window."

Justine peeked around the corner. Axel lay still on the floor, blood trickling from his mouth. Dunham saw her, fired, and started toward her.

Justine ran, reaching the bathroom before Freddy. He slammed and locked the door while she stood on the toilet and yanked open the window.

"Hit the screen," Freddy said. She did and it flew off.

A fist drummed against the door. Dunham said, "Don't run, Freddy."

Freddy stepped up and cupped his hands. Before boosting her through the window, his voice a harsh whisper, Freddy said, "Sinakov is the one you want. Stephan Sinakov."

Sinakov. That was the second time she'd heard that name.

"Open up, Freddy." Dunham kicked the door.

"Where is he?"

Freddy launched her through the window, his reply stopped cold as bullets ripped through the door and slammed him against the wall.

Justine glanced down at Freddy's bloody body, heard another kick on the door, then rolled across the covered parking roof, dangled from the edge and dropped to the ground. Expecting to be shot in the back at any second, she ran for cover around the next building. A bullet splintered against a small flatbed truck, spraying her ass with tiny burning fragments.

A minute later her little white truck cruised slowly past the first screaming police cars arriving on the scene.

# Chapter Eleven

Justine and Teresa leaned on the rail overlooking the Oceanside beach across the street from the Sundowner. The sun had set hours before and the temperature had cooled nicely. A slight breeze brought the smell of salt water and the soothing sound of Pacific waves.

"Teresa, how are Miguel and the kids going to survive without you? You don't need to be here. It might be dangerous for you."

"Little Carlos is becoming quite a good cook. They won't starve. You are down here searching for a vampire, which is *mucho loco*. And friends don't let crazy friends walk around alone in the dark looking for vampires."

Teresa stared out at the dark water, pulling her jacket tight about her. "Truth is, since Antonia disappeared, it hasn't been so good between me and Miguel. He accepted it much too quickly. I still haven't. The less time we spend together right now, the better."

"Carlos and Maria?"

"They've always been closer to him than me. I love them, but Antonia was my perfect kid. They will get along without me while I help you look for what cannot exist."

Teresa returned to inspecting every female that walked past. They'd been there since eight, wandering in and out of bars and restaurants looking for Simone Gireaux.

Justine leaned elbows on the rail and stared out into the ocean darkness. "I don't know she's a vampire."

Teresa kept scanning. "But you think she is. Assuming she's for real, why would she help you?"

"She lost someone, too. I got the feeling she never had the opportunity to avenge that loss."

Teresa nudged her. "Hey. Isn't that your detective?"

Harry Frazer sauntered hand in pockets toward the Sundowner. He lifted his head, taking in the cool sea air. "We're looking for vampires," Teresa said. "Wonder what he's looking for all casual in shorts and that flashy shirt?"

Justine's focus never wavered until he entered the bar. She hadn't seen him since Westly's funeral, and hadn't spoken to him since he called her the day after Freddy's death.

"I'm fine," he had answered her polite inquiry on the phone. "The question is, how are you doing?"

Carefully, she said, "I'm doing fine." Though in fact, her leg hurt, her face hurt, her ass hurt and most of the rest of her body hurt and she'd been brooding on the couch all morning. "Why is that the question?"

"Deputy David Axel was killed last night."

"Oh. I'm so sorry. He was very kind to me. What happened?"

"Freddy Champ also died last night."

"Oh?"

"Do you have a gun, Justine?"

She did, duly registered. "You know I do."

"Do you still have it?"

"Far as I know. Why?"

"I'd like to test it."

"Why?"

"A blonde, white woman wearing a black jacket was seen running right after gun shots were heard."

"And I'm the only blonde, white woman with a black jacket in California? So you called me."

"She had a limp."

"I don't."

"Where were you two nights ago?"

"Here. With Teresa."

"Teresa is a good friend, isn't she? She'd do anything for you."

"As I would for her."

"I hope she remembers my warning about accessories to a crime."

"I'm sure she does. She's very smart."

Justine waited through a long pause from Harry. She heard phones ringing and people talking in the background. He was in his office. She pictured him in his chair, leaning back, thumbs twiddling, his too large shirt spreading out, adding thirty pounds. He must have lost weight recently. She wondered why.

"You haven't asked why I called you about Champ's death," Harry said. Justine hesitated. She shouldn't be talking to him. He wanted to prevent her from avenging Brittany. Yet, she liked the sound of his voice, low and sincere.

"I'm sure it has to do with Brittany's murder. Was this man one of the men responsible? If so, I'm glad he's dead. If not, I'm sorry."

"So you didn't know him?"

Voice unaccountably tinged with sadness, she said, "No, I really didn't know him."

Harry had asked her to meet him for lunch when he could tell her more, meaning ask her more. She could work through the pain in her leg that made her limp, but hiding the bruise on her face would be too obvious. He'd insist on asking questions she didn't want to answer. She'd love to, she said, but she had so much to catch up on at work.

Maybe another time.

They disconnected and Justine continued to brood about Harry. Both were unwillingly doing their duty as they saw it. She felt like they were circling each other, trying to figure out whether they were friend or foe, whether to hit or kiss. Like pain, he made her feel something besides empty inside, though that emptiness allowed her to do her job.

It was obvious to her now that despite her resolve, she was weak compared to Dunham and Standard and this Sinakov. Westly would have killed her without the intervention of Simone's strength. Dunham and Standard saw her as powerless, even with a gun in her hand. Simone did not have that problem. Justine needed that kind of power to succeed, no matter the cost.

Justine pushed off the rail and walked after Harry.

Teresa watched her walk away then followed, talking, for all the attention Justine was giving her, to herself. "Hey, why don't we follow Detective Harry and see where he's going. Maybe he's meeting Simone. Maybe he's meeting Sinakov. Maybe they're brothers. Maybe he is Sinakov. We could make a citizen's arrest and then I could go home and eat my son's cooking which is better than my own."

Teresa took her friend's arm and gently stopped her.

"So do we a have a plan, or are we just going to admire him from across the room?"

Justine glanced at her then sheepishly shook her head. "How about watch from across the room and see what happens? We are still looking for Simone."

"And if he sees you, or me, which he probably will?"

"Then we're just out for a drink or two at the beach."

Teresa rolled her eyes, opened the door and ushered Justine inside.

The Sundowner was in full swing, music rocking, tanned flesh, loud shirts and pitchers of beer. Justine and Teresa found a tall table and stools along the wall with a clear view of the smiling, shouting, drinking crowd, and the bar.

Though it was packed three deep at the bar, Harry had already ensconced himself on the last stool on the left by the back wall. Justine watched Bayley set a beer down in front of him then tenderly touch his hand. She rested her arms on the bar and they leaned forward to speak. Harry patted her hand and, smiling, Bayley went about her business. Harry lifted his beer mug to someone across the bar.

"See anything interesting?" Teresa asked, knowing full well what Justine saw.

"No." She sat back and sipped her beer. "Sorry, you're going above and beyond to help me and I'm ignoring you."

"That's what friends are for. Maybe she's his daughter."

"No kids."

"Justine, why don't you go talk to him. Oh, Harry, imagine meeting you here. Maybe you could get some helpful information from him."

"I don't need his information. Besides, he's a cop. He wants to put the men in jail and I want to kill them."

Teresa's lips pursed in frustration. "Wouldn't it be...? Never mind." For the hundredth time she checked her jacket pocket.

Justine attempted to put Harry out of her mind while scanning for Simone. The events in Freddy's apartment had shaken her. She had a gun on those men and they ignored her! How could she go up against them? Yet, how could she not? The argument had bounced around her head a thousand times. They had brutalized her only daughter, the one person she lived for, the one person she cared about, including herself.

All her life Justine had imagined that she'd grow up to be like her own mother, a happy homemaker with a loving husband and a smart, good kid. Then that son of a bitch husband betrayed her and her perfect universe shrank to two against the world. Now it was down to one against three men. No way in hell was she going to leave the job of justice to anybody else. Revenge was her universe now. Though Harry Frazer held some attraction, she couldn't allow him to become a distraction.

Suddenly she gripped Teresa's arm.

"You see her?" Teresa asked with some skepticism.

"There, to the left of the hallway. Dark hair, red jacket. Come on."

Justine led Teresa through the packed tables and into the standing crowd. They lost sight of the dark haired woman, but pushed quickly through the mob of drinkers. The crowd thinned out a few feet from Harry. Justine pressed through toward where Simone might be.

Two arguing guys blocked Teresa. When she reached the opening, Justine was gone, and Harry looked right at her. She looked after Justine, then moved toward Harry.

Harry said, "What are you doing here?"

"Hunting vampires," Teresa said. She searched the crowd for Justine. "What are you doing here?"

Harry held up his beer. Harry the detective noticed her searching the room. "I suppose she...Justine is here, too?"

"Smart, as well as cute. You'd be a catch for some woman, Harry."

"That's what I thought."

Teresa raised her eyebrows asking for more information. Harry stared into his beer and shook his head.

Staring into her own beer, Teresa asked, "Do you know who killed her daughter yet?"

"You know I can't talk about that."

"You'd talk to Justine."

Harry held up his hand. "She's a whole different case."

"I don't think so. You have any suspects?"

He finished off his beer. "There's always suspects."

Teresa sucked in a deep breath. Eyes on the crowd, she withdrew a folded photograph from her pocket. Laying it on the bar, one finger tapped the faces of Latch Standard and Jay Dunham at Westly's funeral. "But are you checking out the right suspects?"

Harry studied the photo. "Where'd you get this?"

"You know I can't talk about that." She leaned close and said, "Just arrest the bastards and get them safely locked up. That would save a lot of trouble for everybody."

Harry flipped the photo over. On the back was written the name *Sinakov.*

Before he could ask about the name, Justine approached out of the throng, lips twisted in a frustrated scowl.

Teresa surreptitiously folded the photo and stuck it in Harry's shirt pocket. *Sotto voce,* she said, "Best she doesn't know you have that." Then she offered Justine what was left of her beer. Justine downed it in one long gulp.

"Any luck?"

"No."

"No vampires?" Harry asked.

Justine raised an eyebrow at Teresa, who answered with a shrug and a crinkled corner of the lip.

"No vampires. I thought I saw someone I knew."

"Would you like a drink?" Harry asked.

"She'd love one," Teresa said. "Nothing for me. I'll be back." She pushed Justine into her little bar space close to Harry and moved off in the direction of the bathrooms.

⊱ — ⊰

He motioned to Bayley for two beers. He and Justine couldn't seem to find anything to say until he introduced her to Bayley.

"First name basis with the hot bartender," Justine said. "You must be a regular."

"She lives in the same building as I do. With her partner."

"Oh." That information cheered her more than she thought it should. Jeez, she felt like a freshman in high school with her first major crush on Steve Harding when she found out Janey what's-her-name had dumped him. She hadn't listened when everybody told her not to get involved with the guy—just like she wasn't listening to herself to not get involved with the handsome detective, sad brown eyes or not.

# David Burton

She was working up a smile for Harry when strong fingers gripped her arm.

"Come with me. Now," Simone spoke in her ear.

"It's you." Justine forced her thoughts to focus. "Why?"

Simone spun her around and made her look. Dunham and a clean cut man with stylishly rumpled brown hair stood at the entrance, scanning the bar.

Justine stiffened. What should she do? She had no confidence in her ability to deal with them, whether to attack, defend or flee.

A second before Simone spun her back around she noticed a man behind the two murderers. Attractive, with styled blond hair framing a broad face, his head was turned to speak to a striking woman with dark hair. In that one second she recognized his arrogance, an arrogance that came with great power.

"Come." Simone dragged Justine toward the rear exit.

Justine glanced back and caught Harry's quizzical look. He stepped off the stool to follow her. She shook her head to stop him. Then she was propelled down the corridor.

"My friend is back there."

"They do not know her. It is better they do not."

Outside, Simone guided her left, down the alley toward where they first met. When they were out of sight of the exit, she said, "You have been searching for me. Why?"

"Who is Sinakov?"

Simone jerked her to a stop. "Where did you hear that name?"

"A guy named Freddy, a friend of Westly's told me, just before Dunham killed him. Do you know him?"

"I know of him."

"Is he a. . .?"

"A vampire? Justine, do you believe there are vampires? Truly believe?"

She wanted to believe after what she saw Simone do that night. But, truly believe?

Simone grasped her arm in an unbreakable grip and raised it to her open mouth. Her lips curled back and her jaw opened unnaturally wide and in the streetlight's glow, Justine saw two teeth extend down a half inch. No trickery, no hallucination, no wishful thinking. The teeth touched her skin, two pin pricks she was helpless to prevent.

"Justine!" Teresa stood fifteen feet away.

Simone's eyes locked on Justine's. The teeth retreated to become part of the striking woman's perfect smile.

Justine inspected the two tiny drops of blood on her wrist. "I believe," she said. She had to.

Beside her, Teresa said, *"Cristo.* Justine, it is a trick."

"It is not safe here. We can talk elsewhere," Simone said.

"Yes. Yes." Justine straightened herself. "I want to talk with you."

The outlines of two men appeared in the light from the rear entrance.

"Come." Simone walked quickly away from the men. Justine followed. Teresa didn't. The men stalked toward them.

Justine grabbed her friend's arm and pulled her into the dark center of the alley. "Come on. Come on. You don't want those men to get you, or find out who you are."

"Justine," Teresa pleaded. "That woman cannot be what you think. God would not allow such a thing."

"Who knows what God allows? He allows monsters like those two. Why not a vampire?"

"She is dangerous. I feel it."

"Not as dangerous as them."

Ahead, Simone ducked into a side alley. Dunham and Clean Cut broke into a run.

*"Vite! Vite!"* Simone called. She stood on top of a dumpster at the end of the alley. "Give me your hand."

With no visible strain, she yanked them up with her. Then she jumped up seven or eight feet to the roof of a building. Lying over the edge she extended her hand. "Quickly."

Justine raised her hand and Simone hauled her up.

Teresa hesitated. "No, wait. Justine, please. It's all a fake, somehow, for some reason. God would not allow—"

Dunham and Clean Cut rounded the corner fast.

"Teresa, please." Justine cried. "God does not want you to die. Let Simone save you. Just reach up."

The men had drawn their silenced guns. A bullet smacked into the wall above Teresa.

"Come on!"

Pushed out of her confusion by the bullet, Teresa raised her hand. A bullet struck her forearm. She cried out and dropped to her knees.

"Teresa!" Justine prepared to jump down and help her friend.

Simone pushed her down. "Stay." She jumped, landing between Teresa and the men. Clean Cut fired from twenty feet away. Simone grunted when hit, but stayed crouched by Teresa. Her body jerked with two more hits. Dunham watched from the side. He'd stopped when Simone barely reacted to the first shot.

"Stay away from her," Clean Cut yelled. "She's ours."

Simone snapped her head around, eyes blazing. "Stay down," she told Teresa. Like a blur of shadow she jumped to another dumpster, a car, a low roofed shed, and landed behind Clean Cut.

"She is not yours. You are mine."

Clean Cut, two jumps behind, spun around. "What the fuck?" He swung the gun. Simone snatched it from his hand and flipped it away. He stared at his empty hand. "How the hell...?" Then he got it. "Shit. You're a...."

"*Oui, je suis.*" So quick it was almost magic, she reached behind her head and drew out a thin sword with a foot long blade. It flashed. Clean Cut's empty hand fell to the ground with a flat smack. Simone grabbed the arm and directed the spurting blood away from her.

Clean Cut cried out, trying to pull his arm back. Simone held it in an unbreakable grip. Eyes locked on his, she took the bloody wrist and stuck it in her mouth. She sucked greedily.

"Jay, help me, man." He struck at her, but he was already growing weak.

Dunham, gun gripped two handed, took a few tentative steps forward. Simone stopped feeding. Clean Cut flopped about like a rag doll when she twisted around to glare a warning at Dunham. Clean Cut attempted to stand, then passed out.

Simone released him. She spit blood at Dunham. "Ptew. He has rotten blood. Maybe you have better?"

Dunham backed up, keeping a wary eye on Simone. "Who are you? What Family are you from? Who is your Master?"

"I come from no Family. I have no Master," she said with pride. "What do you know of such things, mortal?"

"I serve the Sinakov Family."

"The Master of your Family is here? Where?"

Dunham tensed. In the dim pool of light from a dirty bulb over a many-times-painted door, Justine saw him tremble with an inner effort. The gun clattered to the worn asphalt.

"*Where?*"

Suddenly, Simone jerked back and Dunham sagged. Justine followed Simone's stare. In the entrance to the alley stood the silhouette of a man. A woman stood behind him.

Even from the rooftop Justine recognized the man as the one behind Dunham in the Sundowner. Was that Stephan Sinakov? The one she hunted, the one she needed to kill? He was a vampire. She felt the power of him in the twitch of her muscles, and the whirlwind in her head. The chaos of her thoughts coalesced into a question: *Who are you?* Along with the question came a deep compulsion to answer. Justine fought that compulsion. He was forcing her to answer, and she could not let him force her. She was powerless to resist him, to resist everybody, to resist all that Life threw at her. On this one small challenge she could not give in. Deeper than the compulsion, she felt that if she failed now she would fail to keep her promise to Brittany, and that was unthinkable. Alive, Brittany had been her reason for living—dead, she still was.

Pain flashed through her head. She dropped to her knees, hands attempting to prevent her skull from exploding. The only way to stop the burning was to answer. *Who are you?* Unable to scream, Justine leaned forward, touched her head to the roof. *No. No. No.* "Ahh, no," the word came out as a mangled groan. "No," a wheeze as the last air was forced from her lungs. "I...I am...."

Suddenly the pain stopped, as if a thousand volt electric wire had been jerked away. She raised her head and delicious, cool, ocean air rushed into her lungs with each gasping breath. Her muscles had no strength and her bones burned.

As her vision cleared through tears, she focused on Simone and the man. Like gunfighters, they faced each other the length of the alley. Tension filled the space between them as they battled with their minds.

Off to the side, Dunham raised his gun.

Justine tried to shout a warning to Simone, but her dry throat allowed only a strangled croak to escape.

The cry, "Look out!" came from below her. An empty bottle spun through the air and shattered at Dunham's feet. Startled, he jumped back. His shot clanged against an empty trash can.

Justine managed to peer over the edge. Below, Teresa knelt on top of a half open dumpster. She launched another bottle at Dunham.

Sirens sounded, closing fast.

The tension broke. Simone sagged a moment, then turned to Dunham. Faster than a mortal eye could follow, she slammed him with a side kick that sent him hard against a brick wall. Then she leaped to Teresa, picked her up and jumped to the rooftop.

"Come, Justine. We must go." Carrying Teresa in both arms, she strode toward the building's front.

Justine, mouth open in awe, eyes bright with craving, struggled to stand. She followed a couple of steps before looking back. The silhouetted man had not moved. She knew with no doubt that she would not survive another encounter with him. Nevertheless, her inner voice urged her to attack and kill him.

Simone spun her around. "Come. Now."

"He's Sinakov, isn't he? The one I'm looking for."

"Now is not the time for this."

Justine, her mind fired up though her body was weak, tried unsuccessfully to escape Simone's grip. "When is the time if not now?"

"When we can both survive the attack." She easily dragged Justine across the roof.

Desire for the power Simone had demonstrated burned white hot in

# David Burton

Justine. Images flickered across her mind's eye: Simone shot, and barely noticing, Simone handling Clean Cut and Dunham with ease, Simone standing up against the silhouetted man. Once again she felt the mental and physical power that filled the alley. That's what she wanted and needed. The humiliation of being ignored by Dunham and Standard still rankled. To own the power she believed necessary to avenge Brittany's death, she would give anything. Even her life.

# Chapter Twelve

Harry and Bayley watched Justine melt into the Friday night Sundowner crowd.

"You know that woman?" Bayley asked.

"Which one?"

"Suddenly you have so many women in your life you have to ask that? The blonde."

Harry took a long pull on his beer. "Yeah. Her daughter was murdered a few weeks ago. Why?"

"Oh, shit. That sucks. I'm glad Susan doesn't want any kids. I'm bummed for a week if a goldfish dies. If my kid died I couldn't handle it."

Harry covered her hand with his. "Yeah you could. You're stronger than you think. Why did you ask about the blonde?"

"She was sitting with Darwin that night the guy was killed out back."

A customer along the bar called to her for a refill.

Harry grabbed her arm before she could turn away. He glanced in the direction Justine had gone. All he saw was the back of a tall guy with a ponytail entering the back corridor. He leaned close to Bayley so he wouldn't have to shout. "Are you saying that was the 'babe' sitting with Darwin that night? Are you sure?"

"I never forget a babe, Harry. What's going on?"

"She lied to me. Has Darwin been in tonight?"

"No. It's Friday night, he's usually not here until eleven, midnight."

"If you see him, tell him I want to talk to him, ASAP." He slid off his stool. "Bayley, not a word to anyone. Anyone."

Harry pushed his way out of the back exit. He scanned up and down the alley. It was empty, except for two men and a woman turning on to the street at the far end. One of the men was tall, with a ponytail.

"Shit." He remembered the photograph and yanked it out of his pocket. Was that the same guy he just saw? He ran to the street. There was, of course, no sign of them. Winded from the short run, he walked back toward the bar. He needed to speak with Darwin, who lived in a highly illegal lodging situation, a tiny room built onto the back of a car repair shop. But code violations were not Harry's job.

Something caught his eye in a side alley. Warily he checked it out.

The man was dead. Even in the dim light he could discern the paleness. Bled to death, it looked like. But where was all the blood? This was the third crime scene without the proper amount of blood. He had thought Teresa was joking when she said they were looking for vampires. What if she had been serious? Christ, if the media got hold of that idea it'd be chaos. He could see the headlines. *Police Search for North County Vampire Killer, Southern Cal Vamp on the Loose, Oceanside Vampire Starved for Blood.*

An hour and a half later, Harry needed a beer. He sat on his stool in the Sundowner. He now knew Jay Dunham had been the ponytail guy he'd seen earlier and who Latch Standard was. The search was on for them. The forensic team, the Oceanside detectives, and his new junior detective, Gurvitz, were doing their thing.

After grilling him on why another body had been found so close to the bar, questions for which he had no answer, Bayley told him Darwin had not been in. Harry finished his beer, then went to visit the old man.

Most people saw Darwin as a scruffy homeless guy shuffling around with nothing to do and no inclination to find something to do. Harry knew better. The ten by fifteen foot cinderblock room had originally been built as storage space for old oil and automotive chemicals, back when you could do that sort of thing, and old car parts that might be just what was needed in five or ten or twenty years. After a series of burglaries, the owner of the garage let Darwin live there temporarily, in exchange for bookkeeping services. That had been ten years and no burglaries ago.

Light flickered through the incongruous stained glass window set in a heavy oak door salvaged from a vintage mansion. Harry knocked.

"Nobody home," came from inside.

"Darwin. It's Harry Frazer."

A shadow interrupted the flickering. He heard the smooth thunk of two heavy locks, then the shadow went away. Harry entered. The near right corner looked like ten computers had exploded. The opposite corner looked like a bookstore had exploded. Darwin sat cross-legged on a couch, his attention on an ancient 36 inch TV showing a B monster movie on the SyFy channel. He patted the couch cushion next to him. Harry sat down and watched a dragon from the future disembowel the hero's girlfriend. She lived long enough for the hero to promise that nobody would stop him from avenging her death.

Justine had made the same promise. Westly was dead. He understood the photograph from Teresa to mean Dunham and Standard were guilty, and next. She wanted him to arrest them so her friend would not be able to kill them. Not that they didn't deserve it. What he really should do was arrest Justine. But he had no real evidence. All he had were his growing feelings for her. When he did get enough evidence, he'd have a hard decision to make.

# Blood Justice

Commercial.

"So, Harry, I didn't know you were a monster movie fan."

"I'm not. How can you watch that stuff?"

"It pays to be prepared."

"You think a dragon from the future is going to threaten humanity's survival?"

"It also pays to keep an open mind. You should know that."

"What about vampires?" The older man gave him a skeptical look from under his brows. "I know, that's crazy. Forget it. I need to ask about something else. Bayley told me that a few weeks ago on the night the guy was killed behind the Sundowner you sat next to a blonde woman at the bar. Do you remember her?"

Darwin's face went blank like it always did when he wanted to dredge up some fact from his diverse memory. "I remember."

Harry showed him a photograph of Justine. "Is this her?"

Darwin studied it in the TV's light. "It is."

Harry took back the photo. Did he have enough to arrest her? No. He had opportunity. He had motive. He did not have a weapon, or fingerprints or a witness. He could ask her to come in and answer questions. That was assuming he could bring himself to arrest her no matter what evidence he had.

Darwin watched him looking at the photograph. "Is she a vampire?"

"No. What did you talk about? What did she say?"

"She agreed with my theory on how we got into this war."

"So you did all the talking."

"Then she asked me if I believed in Hell. Naturally, I thought she meant, would those idiots who started and perpetuated the "Liberation" go to Hell. But that's not what she meant. What she meant was, does a person go to Hell if they kill to serve justice. If the person they killed is himself a brutal murderer."

"What'd you say?"

"I told her I'm skeptical about Hell after death, but I do believe in Hell on earth. She said she knew about that. As long as justice is served and a soul is sent down, she thought Hell wouldn't give a damn."

"Of course she thinks that." Harry sighed and pushed to his feet. He was tired. "Thanks. Go back to your monster. I'm going to bed." At the door, knowing he shouldn't ask, he said, "Does the name Sinakov mean anything to you?"

Darwin only spent two seconds accessing his internal data bank before saying, "You're back to vampires, right?"

"I didn't mean to be."

"Sinakov is one of the oldest vampire Families. First heard of in the Black Sea area. Odessa had a rash of killings blamed on a Stephan

Sinakov. He and his Family vanished after draining the blood of the chief prosecutor. They moved west into what's now Romania. Was an advisor to Vlad the Impaler around 1475. Said to be one of the most vicious Families. They gave vampires a bad name."

"How the hell do you know all that?"

"I read." Without taking his eyes off the TV, Darwin pointed to the book corner. "Second case, third shelf down, fifth from the right."

Harry stepped over piles of books on the floor in order to give a wide berth around an ancient card table with several precarious stacks of books propping each other up. Right where Darwin said, he found a thick, clothbound volume with *Blood Relations: A History of the Great Vampire Families* embossed on the spine.

"You can borrow it," Darwin said. "Make sure you bring it back. I don't want to call the book police on you."

Snug in his bed, Harry opened the book to the Sinakov section. He figured he'd fall asleep within ten minutes. After five minutes he came upon an engraving that depicted a woman tied to a cross, her body slit open, and a man catching her blood in a bowl.

Harry slept neither long nor well.

# Chapter Thirteen

Do you know the...man in the alley, Sinakov?" Justine lounged on one end of a couch in her home. Teresa slept with her head on Justine's lap, unconsciously protecting her wounded arm with a free hand.

"I do not think so." Simone reclined deep in a thickly upholstered armchair, legs stretched out, ankles crossed on the coffee table, arms folded tight across her body. "However, there was some familiarity to him. We may have met before." A thoughtful frown marred her broad face.

Breaking a long silence Justine asked, "Why my daughter?"

"No reason."

"I want to kill him."

"I believe he now wants to kill you, also. You are mortal. He will succeed."

Justine gazed down at Teresa, stroking her friend's hair. "Unless I'm already dead."

"Ahh, Justine, you do not know what you ask. What you must give up."

"What about what I gain? I've seen what you can do."

"Do not mistake what I am for being alive. You will die before you become...one of us. It is not an easy transition."

Justine's face hardened as she punched out her words. "I'm already dead. I require only the thought of revenge to sustain me. I will sacrifice my body, my soul, my existence to achieve justice for my daughter. After that, I don't care."

"You say you are already dead. You are not. You are warm and very much alive, and very angry. Neither death nor revenge will bring back your daughter. Do not make the decision to die lightly."

In a quiet, but hard-edged voice, Justine said, "I've lost everyone I have ever loved to Death. Why shouldn't I join them?"

"What of your family? Are there others? Friends?"

"I have no family or friends, now. Except for Teresa." She squeezed Teresa's arm as if reluctant to let go.

"That is very sad."

"What they did to Brittany is very sad. She was my life, I won't, can't, let it go. You said you lost someone once. Do you know who killed him, or her?"

Simone's eyes, dark even in bright light, went darker and deeper.

# David Burton

"Yes, I know who took him."

"Didn't you want to just get even? Do to them what they did to you?"

Simone grinned without humor. "Not exactly, but I understand what you mean. If I turn you, I must kill you. It is usually a most unpleasant experience, beyond the pain. There will be much to learn. There are dangers, even for vampires."

"When can we do it?" Tears dripped from her cheeks onto Teresa's face. Justine gently wiped them away. Her voice caught when she said, "The ache in my chest is unbearable. Help me, please."

In one fluid motion Simone left her chair and knelt in front of Justine. She placed her hand flat on Justine's chest. "Even when the heart stops beating, the pain does not go away." She sat back on her heels. "I will do as you request, but you have to consider for one day what you are going to do. What of your job? Money? What will you do if you survive your revenge?"

Simone rose up, went to a small built in bar and poured scotch in a glass. Eyes closed, she swirled it under her nose, then savored a sip.

"It is true that your senses become more acute." She took another sip of scotch. "Taste, smell, hearing, sight..." She let her hand trail down her body. "...touch. It will be very strange to you."

"I have thought about it."

"But that was before you knew it would really be possible. It is different now. Think about it. If you wish to continue, say goodbye to those you will miss. Say goodbye to your life."

"Simone, my life is already—"

"No, it is not," Simone dropped onto the edge of her chair. "You are about to die and be reborn immortal. A gift as well as a curse. You may exist for a thousand years, Justine. Take advantage of this most rare opportunity to say your farewells and prepare." The passion drained from her, replaced by melancholy. "I still dearly wish I had had that chance."

❧ — ❧

Teresa had reluctantly allowed Simone to tend her wound while Justine was upstairs preparing the guest bedroom. "You've done this before."

Simone smiled ruefully. "In three and a half centuries one learns many useful things."

"I still don't believe you are what you say you are."

Simone shrugged and held out two pills. "It took me quite a while to believe, also."

Teresa downed the pills and lay back on Justine's soft leather couch. "Justine wants to be like you."

"I know." Simone gathered up the leftovers of her medical

ministrations from the glass coffee table. Their eyes met over bloody towels. Simone smiled, a bit self-consciously, Teresa thought, and dropped all the towels in a trash bag.

"I wish you wouldn't change her. She is stubborn and strong. She doesn't need to be a...vampire to...see that those men get justice."

"She does if she has hopes to defeat Sinakov."

"But she will die if you change her?"

"True, but do you not believe in life after death?"

"Are you mocking me?"

"No. I do not make fun of people's beliefs. They are all wrong, or all right. Whatever it takes to get them through their lives."

"What do you believe in? Is there a vampire God?"

"For some, yes."

"But not for you?"

"There has been much suffering because of Gods and none has ever helped me. Has God helped you?"

Teresa stared at the ceiling. "I believe in God. But lately, no, He hasn't done a damn thing for me."

Simone set the trash bag beside her on the table. "Sinakov knows of her now. He knows about Westly. He will come for her."

"Can't you kill him?"

"Possibly, but I would not cheat Justine of her revenge."

Tears spilled from Teresa's eyes. "Brittany was a wonderful girl. She used to baby sit my two kids. They loved her. We all did. She called me Aunt Terry."

***

Simone carried Teresa upstairs to the guest bedroom. She left Teresa and Justine alone.

Justine draped a light blanket over her friend then sat down and watched her. Justine told herself they would still be best friends afterward, but she knew that wasn't so. She missed her already.

"You're going to change tomorrow night, aren't you?" Teresa said, her voice thick with sleep and drugs.

"Yes."

"Then stay with me tonight."

Under the blanket, foreheads and knees touching, they slept.

# Chapter Fourteen

Simone turned out all the lights on the first floor. One by one she sent out her senses at each window. She detected no watchers, though she had no doubt they would be there.

The couch in the living room provided a view of the front and side of the house. A half hour rest on the couch gave Simone time to gather her thoughts, and assimilate the blood of the clean cut man she had fed on earlier. It was always best to sleep after feeding, but many times it was not possible as a matter of survival.

Her task for the next night was relatively simple. Bite, suck some blood, swirl it in her mouth and inject it back into Justine.

That blood would initiate the change. Then it was only necessary for Justine to die. That was the easy part—for both of them.

Justine would go through with the change. As Teresa said, she was stubborn and determined. Guiding her through the transition might be difficult. She would want to charge right in after Dunham, Standard and Sinakov. Patience must be learned. Time took on a different meaning when you were virtually immortal.

Simone felt the sound more than heard it. She rose to her feet in an instant. Head cocked, she listened: a whispered command, the click of a heavy vehicle door gently closed.

They were coming.

Simone slipped out the back door and began her hunt.

She tracked him first by his smell. He was young, less than a year since changed. He had not yet developed the sweet, musty odor vampires acquired over centuries.

The watching vampire perched above the ground in a large orange tree by the neighbor's six foot privacy fence. It was a good observation post with a view of the first and second floor main rooms. He was just a dark blob in a dark tree, easily missed.

A slight breeze blew from inland as the land cooled. She approached from downwind on the other side of the fence. As if she had practiced the moves a hundred times, Simone silently leaped the fence, made two crouching steps, reached up, grabbed an arm, and yanked.

Taken by surprise, the young vampire landed on his back. Before he could recover, Simone grasped his leather jacket, flipped him and dropped him on his face, arms outstretched. She planted a knee between his shoulder blades, then jammed her short sword through a

# Blood Justice

hand, pinning it to the ground. He grunted as he struggled. She grabbed his long hair, bending his head back to quiet him.

"What Family do you serve, Young One?"

"Sinakov." His answer came in a wheeze. She let his head down.

Simone tensed, her body like sprung steel. "The Master's name?"

"Stephan."

∾ — ∾

*It was the year 1642 in Suben, a hamlet in eastern France close to the Swiss and German borders. The band of vampires came out of the Jura mountains as full night fell. They rampaged through the outlying areas first, then the village, raping, torturing, feeding, fighting amongst themselves for blood. They spared none.*

*Simone and her eight-year-old son, Henri, lived with her sister and her husband, their three children and his parents on a farm at the far side of the village. When the alarm reached them it was too late to run or hide. The leader, Stephan Sinakov, and six of his servants caught them in the barn where they had an underground storage pit.*

*The father, husband, and Simone's nephew fought valiantly, but were quickly cut down. The Blood Lust was in the attackers and they did not even bother to feed on them. Simone's sister tried to protect the younger girl, but it was a futile gesture. One attacker ripped the girl from her arms, another stuck a pitchfork through the sister's throat and into a post. She drowned in her own blood, listening to the girl cry out for her. Mercifully the child's death was quick, the six vampires fighting for her delicate young blood.*

*Sinakov held Simone and Henri with an iron grip on the back of their necks. He made them watch the carnage. When it was done he said to his servants, "There is one more for you."*

*He held up Henri.*

*"Please, let him live," Simone pleaded.*

*Sinakov nodded toward the storage pit. One of the blood spattered vampires jumped in and came out with Camille, the elder daughter. At fourteen, she was a sweet innocent girl, the favorite of the family and the whole village. Huddled on the floor, surrounded by monsters, the girl whimpered with fear. "Aunt Simone, don't let them hurt me."*

*Sinakov said, "Choose."*

*"What?"*

*"Choose. One lives, one dies. Choose, or they both die."*

*"No. No. I cannot choose." Her heart pounded with new fear. The stench of fresh blood made her gag. How could she choose Henri over Camille? Tears burned on her cheeks. She fell to her knees. "Please, don't make me do this."*

*"Decide, woman. Or watch them both die. Is this one not your son? Surely you will choose him."*

# David Burton

*She reached for Henri.*

*Sinakov held him away. "You choose to save your son?"*

*Simone covered her ears so as not to hear Camille pleading for her aunt to save her. She could not look at the girl.*

*"Say it, 'My son, save my son.' Say it!" Stephan jerked her to her feet. "Say it!"*

*Heart breaking, barely able to speak through her sobs, Simone said, "My son. Save my son." She clutched Henri to her breast and collapsed.*

*The vampires cheered. In a few seconds the clothes were ripped from Camille's young body.*

*"Aunt Simone," Camille cried. "Save me!"*

*"Stop! Stop! Do not harm her," Simone cried. "Take me."*

*Sinakov ripped Henri from his mother's arms.*

*"You want your son to die?"*

*"Take me instead."*

*"No. The boy or the girl. Choose."*

*"You will kill us all."*

*"One will die for good and all. One will survive. You have Stephan Sinakov's word."*

*Simone had no hope of saving her own life. She would rather die than become one of those beasts. The children would, too.*

*"One will live and one will die. That is the choice?"*

*"Yes."*

*"Then I will pick." Heart racing, not thinking lest she not act, she reached out to her cowering niece. "Camille, dear one, come to me."*

*The girl, grasping at a glimmer of hope through her terror, crawled to her. Henri still dangled from Sinakov's hand an arm's length away.*

*"Forgive me, dear ones."*

*Simone yanked a knife from Sinakov's belt and lunged at Henri. The blade sliced the boy's throat. Blood flowed from his neck before she swung the blade at Camille.*

*The master vampire was too quick. He snatched the knife from her hand and smashed her to the ground.*

*The rest was a swirl of blood and pain and horror. Sinakov cut off her clothes with the knife, leaving stinging cuts the length of her back. He then raped her over an old barrel while she endured the screams of Camille's ravishment.*

*"Bring me the girl's sweet blood," Sinakov called to his fiends. "I must regain my strength."*

*They tied the ravaged girl to the barn wall, arms stretched out. They slit her open and gathered the blood in an old cup, which they brought to their Master.*

*He wrapped his hand in Simone's hair and pulled it back. "You could have saved her, stupid woman." Then, laughing, he poured some of the blood into her open mouth. She choked as it overflowed her face and neck.*

# Blood Justice

*Sinakov drained the cup. "More!" he called to his minions.*

*Simone wanted to die. All whom she loved were dead, Henri by her own hand. The guilt would drive her mad, death was preferable.*

*Sinakov's teeth sank into her neck.*

*Then the soldiers attacked.*

*Abandoned, she slipped to the dirt floor. As in a dream she heard cries and curses, gunshots and swords, followed by silence, except for the crackle of flames. Then blackness.*

*She awoke, covered in ash stuck to dried blood, in a tiny space formed by the barrel she had been raped over and an unburned section of roof. Thinking she was in Hell, she climbed out into devastation.*

*All the village had been burned. Bodies lay everywhere, their stench suffocating even in the cool of sunset. She scavenged for clothing. Trousers from the baker's son, a tunic from an old man, a jacket from the mayor's wife. A search for Henri found only some small burnt and scattered bones.*

*She wondered that her wounds had healed, though she had slept only a day, maybe two. She had been taught to expect Hell to be different, with flames and fearsome demons. Not so...quiet.*

*In the morning, when the barely risen sun burned her skin, she understood what she had become. Over the nights, years, decades, the constant fight to survive had pushed the flame of revenge to a quiet corner of her mind.*

❧ — ❦

Hearing the name Stephan Sinakov again woke old emotions in Simone. The flame gathered heat. The figure in the alley had been too strong for her to get any real sense of him. Yet, he had a vague familiarity. Was this the same Stephan Sinakov that murdered her family and left her for dead to survive and thrive alone? He would be seven or eight hundred years old by now.

"Young or old?"

"Young."

"Does he know who I am?"

"Only that you are one of us."

Simone expelled a deep sigh she had been holding in since the encounter in the alley. The shadowed man was not the Stephan Sinakov she knew, the last face she saw before she died.

"Where is he?"

"I don't know. I am not allowed to his refuge."

"Where is your dormitory?"

"Carlsbad. Let me up. If you damage me he will destroy you."

"Don't give yourself so much credit, Young One. He already tried to destroy me."

The Young One surged up, determined to throw her off.

# David Burton

Simone had too much experience to be taken by surprise. She jerked her sword free of his hand and rose to her feet behind him. Suddenly released, the Young One raised his head. With a quick, powerful backhand strike, Simone sliced through his neck.

The head thumped to the ground. The body shook, then collapsed. Simone had heard that the head could reattach to the body. She didn't believe it, but she kicked the head away, just in case.

"Your Stephan didn't care about you, anyway, Young One."

She dragged the body to the back of the yard by a garden storage shed, out of sight of the house and neighbors, but exposed to the sun. A couple of hours of sunlight and it would decompose to ash and dust.

Then she went hunting the mortal vampire followers sure to be waiting somewhere close.

# Chapter Fifteen

"Two dead, Sir," Gurvitz, the new junior detective, said to Harry. "Throats cut, no other obvious wounds. Lots of blood."

"That's refreshing."

"They still had their wallets. Bill Picotto and Pierce Calder."

"I know Picotto. A minor thug dreaming of the big time but not enough brains to make it."

"Same with Calder. Has a long sheet, but nothing major."

"Who's the vehicle registered to?"

"Picotto."

"Shit. That's a Lincoln Navigator. How the hell does a loser like him afford wheels like that?"

"Maybe he found some brains?" Gurvitz said, scribbling in his notebook.

"Well, they weren't in his head. Let's find out where."

They stood at the apex of a sharp corner looking down at the big SUV standing on its nose seventy five feet below. The Medical Examiner backed out of the passenger side and looked up. He waved at Harry.

"I guess I have to go down there, don't I?"

"Yes, Sir."

Harry stared down at the rocks and thick brush with some trepidation. "There's probably snakes down there."

Gurvitz suppressed a smile. "It's still cool yet for snakes, Sir. Give it a couple hours to warm up."

"Great." Harry took the notebook from Gurvitz and wrote some names on it, then handed it back. "See if Picotto or Calder knew any of these guys." He thought a moment and added another name.

Harry descended the slope with the help of ropes set up by the Rescue Team, thereby keeping his dignity intact. He liked the outdoors and nature, but he preferred to walk on the beach or level, shaded paths—with no snakes.

What the ME showed him drove out all thoughts of snakes. "They're both like that?"

The ME nodded. "Probably done after death. Autopsy will tell more. But the skin is barely broken, just the clothes sliced open up the front. Why? I couldn't tell you."

Harry stepped back and looked up and down the ravine, calculating distances. "It's a message," he said, and scrambled up the slope.

Fifteen minutes later he peered into the windows of Justine's house. He walked all the way around, checking doors. All locked up, no car in the garage. Beside the garden shed he found a small mound of what looked like ashes and fine dust. He took a sample, just in case.

When he called Justine's office and learned that neither Justine nor Teresa had been in he drove to Teresa's house, parking across the street in the shade of a Eucalyptus tree. He rang the doorbell several times before the door opened on the chain.

"Where's Justine?" he asked Teresa.

"I don't know."

"We should talk."

The house was larger on the inside than it looked from the outside. The interior was colorful and cluttered with serapes draped over clean, well-used furniture, and walls painted in bold hues of blue, rust and yellow. Pictures of Teresa and her handsome, sturdy husband, and two kids, a boy and a girl, took up much of the wall space. There were none of her missing daughter, Antonia.

Teresa, wearing brown pajamas adorned with ducks and her hair loose, settled on a couch facing a big screen TV and pulled a red blanket up to her chin. Harry thought she had been crying. He sat across from her in a matching loveseat.

They studied each other for a minute before Harry said, "When you said you were searching for vampires, you weren't kidding, were you?"

She licked her lips. "No."

"You know there's no such thing as vampires."

"No."

"Have you seen one?"

"I've seen some things which I cannot explain otherwise."

"Like what?"

She shrugged and said nothing.

"This Sinakov, is he a vampire?"

"If there are such things, probably."

Harry sat on the edge of his chair, elbows on knees.

"Teresa, what the hell's going on? Who was that woman with Justine last night? You gave me a photo of two men. One was at the bar last night. He's disappeared. The man with him was found dead close to where Westly was found. A hand had been cut off, and he was light on blood. Two men were found dead this morning, less than a mile from Justine's house. Aspects of their death link them to the death of Westly and Justine's daughter. Then there's the death of Freddy Champ. All these things can be linked to Justine. And indirectly to you, by the way."

Harry covered his face with his hands, rubbing his eyes, then his temples. "Justine is obsessed with punishing the men who murdered her daughter. I understand that. I am assuming that you think Rob Westly, Jay Dunham, Latch Standard and this Sinakov are the perpetrators. Is that correct?"

Teresa nodded.

"Okay. Do you have any evidence, any proof? We have Standard in custody, but we can't hold him just on your say so."

"No, sorry."

"Do you know where Jay Dunham is? Are we going to find him with his guts spilling out?"

"I don't know."

"Where's Justine?"

"I don't know, really."

Harry hung his head. "At the very least, she has to come in for questioning about her connection with all this. I don't want to arrest her, though I should. I want her to be free of her grief, to be able to move on and have a life."

"With you?"

"Christ, am I that transparent?"

Teresa sat up cross-legged on the couch. She couldn't quite meet his gaze. "Don't get too obsessed with her, Harry. I hope I'm wrong." She spoke slowly, not believing what she was saying. "But, she may not be what you think the next time you see her."

"What the hell does that mean?"

She shrugged and shook her head. Then she lay down, drawing the blanket tight to her face, wet eyes staring at emptiness.

Harry knew he wasn't getting anything else out of her. He moved toward the door. Teresa's words stopped him.

"Be careful, Harry. And keep an open mind, no matter what you see."

Harry sat in his unmarked sedan and tried to make himself believe in vampires. *No way.* Although Teresa, who, despite being misguided, seemed level-headed and practical, had obviously half convinced herself they were real. It gave her last words some weight.

He had his hand on the ignition key when a dark SUV parked directly in front of the house. Harry's cop antennae began to quiver. His hand moved closer to the gun holstered on his right hip.

The left side doors opened. Two tough, confident men got out, wearing jackets that no doubt concealed guns. Harry could make out the silhouette of one person in the passenger seat. The men wasted no time moving to Teresa's front door and knocking.

Harry waited, gun on his lap, one hand on the door handle. With his cell phone he called for backup. He told them he had a possible situation, but to approach slowly and quietly. He could be wrong.

The door opened on the chain. One man spoke. The door slammed shut. The talker stepped back and nodded to the slightly bigger guy. The big man landed a kick just above the doorknob. The chain stopped the door. A second kick, and the door flew open. The men charged through.

Harry was already out of his car, running across the street, gun against his leg, one eye on the door, one on the SUV. He made it half-way across the lawn when the men emerged. They had Teresa between them, hands held behind her back.

"Sheriff's Department," Harry yelled. "Stop there."

They didn't stop.

"Police. Stop right there. Let her go. I will shoot."

The man closest to Harry said, "You think we're afraid to die?" He reached into his jacket with his free hand, drew out a .45 semi-automatic pistol and fired.

The kidnapper's bullet just grazed the top of his left shoulder. Harry was a much better shot when he didn't have time to think about it. He fired twice.

Both shots hit the man's head. He fell forward, dead before he sprawled on the grass.

The larger man drew his gun out and dragged Teresa in front of him.

Harry yelled, "Teresa, down!"

All she could do was drop her head. The man fired. His shot put a hole in the neighbor's front window.

Harry's shot put a hole in his forehead. Teresa managed to stay on her feet as the man fell away.

Harry steadied her. "Are you okay? Who are these guys?"

"Behind you!" Teresa cried out.

Harry spun and dropped. He caught a quick image of a pale face glaring at him from under a jacket hood before a fist bounced off the top of his head. "Run!" Harry shouted, then shot the guy in the gut. That slowed him a fraction, allowing Harry an instant to grab the pale man's legs and take him down.

Teresa ran for the house.

In his younger, wilder days Harry had been in more than his share of fights, but he'd never tangled with anyone with the strength and speed of this guy. Pale Face easily flipped over, leaned forward and punched Harry's head. It felt like a horse kick. He grabbed Harry's gun and flung it into the neighbor's bushes, then ran into the house.

Harry jumped up, took a moment to let his head stop spinning, and followed. On the way he yelled into his radio, "Back up. Now!"

Inside, at the end of a long hall, Pale Face dragged Teresa from a room. Harry knew he couldn't take him head on, so he moved out of sight and waited. As Pale Face exited the hallway, carrying Teresa under one arm like she was a five pound doll instead of a hundred and forty pounds of terrified woman, Harry's right fist sunk deep into the stranger's belly. Anybody else would be on their knees gasping for breath. He just stopped. Harry cocked his left arm back and struck.

Instead of shattering the man's jaw, he smacked into his palm. The palm closed over Harry's fist and forced him to his knees. On the way down, Harry slammed his leg behind the other man's calves.

Pale Face went down, dropping Teresa. A second later the man was on Harry, one hand on his chest, the other on his chin, bending Harry's head back, exposing his neck. Behind the man, Teresa gaped with horror, then tightened her face and ran out of sight.

At least she would be safe.

"Who are you?" Harry croaked.

"I am your death. And your Maker, if I choose."

And that's when Harry had no choice but to believe.

He watched his attacker's mouth open wider than it should have been able to. Harry's vision narrowed to focus on the two canines lengthening as he watched, broad and sharp. Harry may have been dying, but he knew what he saw, knew the strength and speed of the...whatever he was. *Holy shit, they're real!*

The mouth closed on his throat.

*"No!"* Teresa yanked the hood back. She stood over them, a machete held high with both hands. The vampire raised his head. Teresa swung the big blade down with everything she had.

Teresa had to strike three times before the head thumped on the floor next to Harry. The body shook, then pushed up as if preparing to stand. Then it collapsed on Harry. Barely keeping it together, Harry shoved the quivering body off him.

Crouched by the sofa while still fighting panic, the detached trained observer in him wondered at the sudden lightness of the body. Where had the muscle that provided the strength gone? And where was the blood? The man/thing had been decapitated right above him. He should be covered with blood. *The guy was a vampire. The guy was a vampire.* Harry kept repeating it in his mind to convince himself the last few minutes actually happened.

Teresa stood next to him, staring down at the body.

*"Cristo. Cristo.* I believed it, but I didn't believe it. That was a vampire, wasn't it?"

"I...I think so."

Sirens approached quickly.

She shook herself and said, "Do you want the other cops to see this?"

That question brought Harry back to the now. "God, no. How could I explain it?"

# David Burton

"Help me take it outside."

Harry got it immediately. Not allowing himself any hesitation he picked up the body, which weighed about half what he would have expected. Teresa picked up the head by the hair. The hair pulled out with a small patch of sickly, white skin. Wincing, she picked up the whole thing and led the way out the back.

A small covered patio extended ten feet out from the house. She pointed to the flat, solid cover. "I think it takes a couple hours in the sun."

Sirens died and doors thunked out front.

Harry grabbed the headless end, Teresa the feet end and one, two, three they slung the body up, out of sight.

"Go," she told Harry as she reached for the head. On his way through the house he instinctively hunched his shoulders when he heard a thump from the backyard.

# Chapter Sixteen

At four-thirty in the morning Simone had awakened Justine and told her now would be a good time to take Teresa home. Nobody was watching. Simone carried Teresa out to the Volvo and sat with her while Justine closed the house.

Justine locked locks that hadn't been used in years, and filled a briefcase with papers she might never need. She turned off the gas and unplugged things. She tried to move about the house with dispassionate efficiency. It used to be a home, now it was just a house. Still, memories came and with them a tightening of the throat, a wetness of eye.

The excitement of moving day, making love with her husband in the middle of the living room surrounded by boxes. Brittany's first steps in the same place. The yellow lab puppy. A swirl of birthdays and holidays when they were all happy together. The last time she saw her husband, wishing he was dead. Holding Brittany while she cried for her father, and pretending she too was sad. More tears when the much loved dog was put to sleep. Holding each other tight while watching late night scary movies. Laughing at the idea of vampires. The loneliness and rage of the last few weeks.

Justine locked the door and drove away without looking back.

Justine thought her friend was asleep until Teresa said softly, "Simone says it will be hard to control your hunger, at first. You might attack me if you see me in the first days."

Justine stared grimly ahead. "I would never attack you. You're my only friend."

"I told you I will not help you kill anyone. But if you need blood, you can have mine."

Holding hands, they drove on through the darkness.

At her door, Teresa said, "It's all a trick, a scam of some kind. And even if it is real, I'd rather have a live best friend than a dead one."

Justine hugged Teresa, letting only one tear loose. "Too late for that." They separated, but Justine held on to Teresa's hands. "I know you don't agree with what I'm doing, but you understand, don't you? If it had been Antonia…?"

Neither let go to wipe away tears.

"I do understand," Teresa said. "If I knew where she was or where to look I would do anything to bring her home. Anything."

Justine watched day break from a bench by the Oceanside pier. She ate a huge breakfast at a local cafe, savoring crisp bacon and syrup soaked pancakes. Then she walked on the beach and planned her day. By noon she had rearranged her finances, surprised to learn she was worth over a million dollars. As long as she made the deal and had enough to give Brittany what she needed, and a little more, she hadn't thought about how much more she had. It was the getting that mattered, not the total amount. A quick stop at her office took care of what little business she cared about. She left without a word to the others. She had her will amended to leave everything to Teresa's kids. Just in case.

She thought little about the coming change. Half a day to settle her affairs, nobody else to say goodbye to. Work that was no longer challenging or interesting. What did she have to work for now, anyway? Giving up her life didn't seem like much of a loss.

After a cheeseburger and fries at Angelo's she walked the beach, soaking in sunlight for the last time. Justine liked the water, liked to swim. She'd been on the varsity team in school. Seemed like a long time since she'd been in the water just for fun. She looked up and down the beach. Nobody close. A quick strip to her underwear, a quick dash into the water. God, it was cold. Would she feel the cold as a vampire? It would be a definite plus to be able turn down that sensitivity.

Her rhythm quickly came back and she powered out through the breakers. A couple hundred yards out, she floated, facing west. The sun in the clear sky warmed her face. Would she ever gaze at it again without fear and pain? Probably not, but the moon was beautiful, too.

Back on the beach, Justine ignored the looks, discreet or open, of passing walkers, strollers, and joggers. Two kids sporting long, sun-bleached hair, peeled down wetsuits and surfboards made a detour up the beach to check out the almost naked woman. Justine waved them close.

"May I borrow your towel?"

Eyes and mouth wide open, the tall one unwrapped a bright-striped towel from his neck and handed it to her. They observed with frank interest as the big-boned lady dried herself. Big-boned. A long past boyfriend had called her that in the most admiring context. She couldn't remember his name, but he'd been a good guy and she wondered where he was now. Dry, she dressed, smiled her thanks to the boys, and continued her last walk in the sunshine.

From the Oceanside harbor jetty she watched a sailboat slip from the calm harbor to the open ocean. She and Brittany had sailed a few times on client's boats. Brittany had loved it and had hoped to one day sail across an ocean. Now that was something neither of them would ever have memories of, along with graduations and first days of college, birthdays and anniversaries, road trips and mother-daughter chats about raising children. The boat continued out to sea, slowly vanishing into the sunset. Justine felt like that boat, disappearing into darkness with no compass to guide her on her journey to the end of the world.

She ended her walking at the Sundowner, where she took the second seat from the right end, the same one she'd watched Westly from. The same bartender she'd been jealous of—was it only last night?—served her a beer.

"You're early if you're looking for Darwin."

"Darwin? Oh, the old guy. I wasn't looking for him, but I wouldn't mind his company again. You have a good memory."

"Beauty and the Beast, hard to forget."

"I wonder which one of us is which. Actually it was you I came to see."

Bayley raised a wary eyebrow.

"About Harry Frazer."

"What about him?" Bayley continued to wipe the bar top while she challenged Justine with her eyes.

"I think I like him. You know him much better than I do. How long have you known him?" Justine asked, concentrating on wiping the condensation on her mug with a fingertip.

"You mean, am I now or have I ever slept with him?"

"Yeah, I guess that's what I mean."

"No and no. But I love the guy. I don't want him to get hurt."

"I don't want to hurt him."

"What do you want to do to him?"

"I want to trust him."

"I trust him with my life."

Justine smiled to herself. It wasn't her life she wanted to trust him with. But she wasn't about to get into that with a woman she didn't know. "Why?"

Bayley went away for a few seconds, leaving a small, sad smile. When she came back she started talking. Justine knew Bayley wouldn't reveal any secrets, but that was okay. She had her own secrets.

The sun had set a half hour later, and they were still talking when Darwin sat next to Justine. The after-work people were demanding their alcohol infusions. Bayley left Justine and Darwin alone to administer to her patients.

They drank in silence for a few minutes until Justine asked, "Do you know anything about vampires? Real vampires?"

"You know Harry Frazer," Darwin said. It wasn't a question.

"Yes. Why?"

"He asked about vampires, real vampires, just the other day."

"He did?" Justine wasn't sure what to think about that. Surprise, shock, fear? Why would he ask that? It couldn't be a coincidence. "What did he want to know?"

"He asked about Sinakov."

Justine didn't even think to hide her shock. "Sinakov. How did he know...? What did you tell him?"

He told her the basic history that he had told Harry.

For a minute she considered abandoning her plan—tell Harry what she knew and let the police deal with Sinakov, Dunham and Standard. No. The police would never get Sinakov. What would they do with him if they did? What if Harry was killed because she gave up? The guilt would crush her. Christ, why did she care about Harry? She barely knew him, he'd put her in jail if he could. Yet, he had asked Darwin, apparently seriously, about vampires. Why?

Besides Harry, quitting would mean betraying her daughter. Immortality would not provide enough time for her to forgive herself for that. It was all she had.

Only one of Sinakov's own kind had a prayer of getting close to him. It had to be her.

"What do you think it would be like, being a vampire?" Justine asked Darwin.

"Dark."

She chuckled at that. "I suppose. Though I hear sunlight is not as dangerous as in the movies."

"You'll have a long time to learn to live with it."

She lost her smile. "Just so I have long enough to do what I need to do."

"And what would that be?"

The intensity in his eyes unnerved her, but she matched his seriousness when she said, "Justice."

"After that?"

Justine shrugged and shook her head.

They nursed their drinks for a few minutes, ignoring the increasing press and commotion about them.

Darwin said, "You speak as if you will actually be a vampire in the near future."

"Do you believe that could really happen?"

"I have an open mind."

"But, would you really want to know that it's possible, with absolute certainty?"

He smiled into his beer. "Yes, I would. Come see me when you know, with absolute certainty."

# Blood Justice

❧ — ❧

Justine looked up from the street at Harry's front door. It had been painted recently to match the weathered blue-gray wood siding of the two story condo building. Wood steps rose up to number 7.

Justine walked quicker as she approached Harry's place. She'd wasted too much time. She didn't know why she needed to see Harry, just that she had to see him because tonight she would die and things could never be normal between them. Then she had to go to Simone and become a vampire.

She rang the door bell.

Harry answered, holding a shirt in his hands. The bloody bandage on his shoulder drew her eyes, then she noticed the bruise on the side of his head. She reached out to touch his injuries, then pulled back.

Their eyes locked. In his eyes she saw mirrored the desire that suddenly coursed through her own body, all else forgotten. She had wanted this man since he told her what happened to Brittany. The horror of it should have pushed her away, never wishing to see him again lest he remind her of her little girl's agony. But he had the courtesy and courage to tell her the truth. That meant something to her. It wiped away the fact of his friendship with her lying, cheating husband.

All the anger and fear and loneliness of the past six years swelled up in her chest. She jerked as the heat and power of it snatched her breath away.

He opened his mouth to speak. She stopped him with a hard kiss as she pushed inside. Her fingers gripped at his flesh, pressing her body tight against his. She wrapped her legs around him. He carried her into the bedroom and slammed her against the wall. Their mouths groped each other as a drowning person grasps for anything that will save their life.

*Not close enough!* Hands trembling, Justine yanked her blouse over her head. The bra followed. She pressed against him, kissing, rubbing, clutching, reveling in the feel of his skin against hers.

*Not close enough!* Justine moaned when he let her down. Harry backed away, their breathing frantic with lust. In an instant he was naked. He ripped the blanket and sheets off the bed. Naked also, she came into his arms. He threw her on the bed and fell on top of her, mouth on her belly, breasts, mouth, neck. In a frenzy, they fumbled his erection into her. Justine wrapped herself around him, her universe only concerned with each thrust into her. Finally, close enough.

Together, they came quickly. For Justine, it was a never-ending blissful oblivion for which she had yearned for what seemed like all her life. When they caught their breath, Justine aroused him with her mouth then mounted him and worked herself into two more orgasms and

# David Burton

Harry into one. They lay in each other's arms for a long while before Justine broke the silence.

"What happened to you?"

Justine knew from the slow rise and fall of his chest and long hesitation that whatever he said would be bad. Eyes wide open, post-coital euphoria gone, she waited.

"As far as I can tell, two wannabe vampires shot at me while attempting to kidnap Teresa. Then a real vampire tried to bite me, but instead, Teresa cut his head off."

Justine jumped up and knelt beside him on the bed. "You're serious, aren't you?"

"Nobody is more surprised by that than me."

"Teresa?"

"She's fine. She and her family are taking an open-ended vacation to an undisclosed location."

"You say 'vampire' like you're not kidding." Dread washed over her. He wasn't kidding. Was he going to arrest her? Did he know about Westly? Freddy? Sinakov? Was he one?

"I wish I was." Harry sat up and knelt facing her. "I know what you're planning to do to yourself."

"How did they find Teresa?"

"Yesterday I'd have said you were crazy to be thinking of doing something impossible."

"Why were you with her?"

"Now I know it's not impossible. God, I think it's not impossible." His eyes found hers. "Please don't do it. I know about Sinakov."

"How?"

"We can find him together. Finish him for what he did to Brittany."

"He's too strong and smart for a mortal to beat him."

"Becoming a vampire is suicide."

"It's power and speed."

"What about after you've gotten your revenge?"

"There is no after. Only him."

"What about me?"

Justine had no answer.

"What about Teresa? She doesn't want you to change, either."

"I've already said goodbye to her. And now I've said goodbye to you." She looked around for her clothes.

Harry grabbed her by the arms. Still naked, they confronted each other.

"Please, Justine, don't do this. For ten years I've cared about you. I don't want to lose you now. I'll become a vampire if that's what it takes."

"That's ridiculous. You have no reason to do that. You have a life.

# Blood Justice

You're a cop. You do good things. What do I do? I facilitate the paving of Southern California. Not exactly a higher calling. This is my fight, not yours."

She shrugged him off and got dressed. All the while she repeated to herself, *This is my fight. This is my fight.*

Harry sat on the bed and watched her dress. "I can arrest you."

"Do you think that will change anything?"

Harry pulled on his pants and waited awkwardly, obviously wanting to say something.

Dressed, she said, "I'm glad we had this time together. I'll have a long time to remember it. Keep doing good things." Tenderly, she touched his shoulder wound and bruised head. Then she kissed him—a gentle, but passionate kiss that conveyed all she felt, consciously and unconsciously, about him.

"See you, Harry."

*It's my fight, It's my fight, It's my fight,* kept the tears back until she was out the door.

# Chapter Seventeen

The girl lay curled in a tight ball at the foot of Sinakov's bed. She listened to the sounds of sex above her: a faint rhythmic creak, her master's grunt and sigh as he finished. The female made appropriate noises of pleasure, though the girl knew she was only in his bed because he was the Master, not because she cared for him.

The girl was slight, barely five feet tall. She had been changed on her eighteenth birthday, ninety-three years ago. Her father had been a proper butler in London. He served only the best families. She was born and bred for loyalty and service. After the initial shock of finding herself dead and a vampire, she felt she had died and gone to heaven. She was immortal, her Master was immortal—an eternity of service to the same Master, what could be better than that?

She could move from room to room like a mouse, which she somewhat resembled, furtive and inconspicuous. Other vampires could not detect her. So she knew most of what was said and done around her Master. She spooked most others and they avoided her if possible. A few, who had attempted to remove her, had been harshly punished.

Her Master threw off the bedcovers and stood up. His body appeared emaciated, skin, bone, and muscle forever the same as when he was changed. Still handsome, his once broad face reflected the privations of slavery and harsh treatment—skin tight over the bones, a story written in scars over his body, and haunted eyes that had nothing to do with being a vampire.

As always she was there with his favorite silk dressing gown. He shrugged it on with no acknowledgement, as it should be. She was his servant, there to serve, not to be noticed.

The female in his bed sat up, not even bothering to cover herself. Then she noticed the girl. "Eww. Was that here when we were doing it?"

"Of course," he said, unperturbed.

"Well she can't stay here. I'm not doing it with her creepy little eyes..." she fluttered long-nailed fingers "...peeking up at me."

The Master slowly turned his gaunt body to look down on the female in the bed. "That is where she sleeps." His voice was matter-of-fact. Only the girl knew how dangerous that was. She stood back, head bowed, a small grin on her thin lips.

"Well she can't sleep there when I'm here. I'm your number one woman now and I don't want her there," the female said, too self-absorbed to realize the dangerous position her mouth had put her in.

"I see," the Master said. He casually walked around the bed and sat next to her. He stoked her cheek, then grasped her face in a vise-like grip. Voice still outwardly calm, he said, "Then you have a choice, either you come here when I say and do what I say with not a complaint, or you never enter this room again. Choose." He rose and moved toward the adjoining bathroom.

The girl knew about the choices. He spoke of them often when she massaged lotion into the chain ring scar on his ankle. He usually sat naked on the edge of the bed. She would kneel before him, his sex in the shadow above her, used on thousands of women, mortal and Vampire, through the centuries, but not for her, never for her.

He spoke about mortal years of living in cages, and being chained like a pet, then as a slave, and choices, terrible choices. If she could have cried, she would have cried for him. Even a mortal should not have to live like that.

The female was not bright enough to make a choice. She must have thought the enhanced breasts she flaunted gave her some power. "I shouldn't have to choose. I worked hard to be your first companion and I should have a say about who's here when we...you know. She creeps me out. I forbid—"

In a blur of movement, he picked her up by the neck. "You forbid nothing. You are nothing." The crack of the female's neck sent a delicious chill up the girl's back. The Master threw the female into a corner. She would heal, of course, but would be paralyzed for a time.

"Call Dee," he said. "Tell her to feed the dogs." He went into the bathroom and shut the door.

Ignoring the wide-eyed female, the girl left to find Dee.

Later, the girl watched him drink coffee by the rail of his small private deck. He gazed down at the heavily fenced dog runs extending into the expansive backyard from the center of the house. Though it was night, her Master had a clear view.

A screen door slammed and Dee, a female about thirty-five when she was changed, carried the bedroom female down steps to a gate in the kennel fence. Four large and frenzied dogs howled and barked and lunged against the wire. Their cacophony did not drown out the screams of the female. At a sharp command from Dee the dogs reluctantly backed away from the gate, their rear ends bouncy with impatience. Dee swung open the gate and threw the screaming female twenty feet from the dogs. The first dog sunk its teeth in before she hit the ground. Her shrieks died a few seconds later.

Her Master watched the beasts for a minute then entered the bedroom. He noted with approval that the bed had been made with clean sheets. After handing the girl his coffee mug, he checked his hair in the mirror and left the room.

# Chapter Eighteen

Simone sat on the stone wall that separated the lawn from a steep drop to the road below. The four thousand square foot house on the hillside in Carlsbad stood dark and empty behind her. The elderly couple who lived there were off to New England to see the fall colors.

On a clear day the Pacific Ocean was visible about three miles away. Dark now, an ocean of lights spread out before her. She'd been there for almost two hours. She didn't mind. Time meant little when you measured a life span in centuries.

Most vampires preferred the company of others, whether vampire or mortal. Simone preferred a more solitary existence. She had learned in her early days after her change not to trust others, vampire or mortal.

A car stopped in a small pullout below her. From her perch she had a good view of the winding road in either direction. There were no other cars visible. A woman exited the car and stood by the safety rail looking out at the last indigo sliver of daylight fading into the far horizon. Simone easily identified Justine. Still, she waited, all senses tuned to the immediate area.

Several cars passed. None contained anyone but local mortals. Simone slipped off the stone wall into the thick brush that covered the steep fifty foot slope to the road. She descended halfway, then stopped and waited again. Nobody followed.

"Back when I was alive, that many lights meant an army was going to attack in the morning," Simone said.

"Oh. Simone. You startled me."

Simone rested a reassuring hand on Justine's shoulder. "You are nervous about what we are to do?"

"Apprehensive. Well, a bit nervous."

"That is as it should be. Most mortals would be terrified to be changed as you want."

"I will do what I need to."

"Then you still want to do this? Once it is done, it is done. You cannot go back."

"Yes."

Simone leaned close and sniffed. Her nose, then her lips brushed Justine's cheek. "Ah, the detective, yes? One last time as a mortal. How I envy you. To have had a last hour with my husband before his death would have made the years pass easier." She rested her cheek on

Justine's shoulder.

"Did your husband love you?"

"He did, and I him."

"Did the vampires take him?"

Simone, hands in pockets, leaned against the car. "No. Two deserters from the army stole two chickens. When Raphael found them in the forest, they killed him. That is what his life was worth then, two chickens."

"I'm sorry. It must have been hard losing him suddenly."

"I had his family and my family to take care of me."

"Now I envy you."

"Getting revenge will help, for a while."

"A while is better than never. Can we go?"

Simone guided them along rising roads to a single level house at the end of a short cul-de-sac perched on the crest of the hill two rows of million-dollar homes above where she had waited for Justine. She used a clicker to open and close the garage door. Without a word she led Justine into the house.

The kitchen was simple and modern with black appliances, deep burgundy solid surface countertops, and Euro style wood cabinets. It had the air of never having been used.

A wide opening with a swinging door stepped down into a sunken living room with a grouping of heavy comfortable furniture arranged to face the twenty foot wall of windows. Simone went to the center one and cranked it open. Immediately, a cool breeze with a hint of salt water pushed through.

A spectacular view spread out below with the demarcation between city lights and ocean darkness clear. Simone had turned on only the kitchen overhead and left the swinging door open. Justine stood a few feet away, arms crossed.

Simone asked, "Do you see the ship on the sea?"

Frowning, Justine looked. "No."

"You will. All your senses will be enhanced. You must learn to control the senses, or control your response to what your senses tell you. It can be *tres* overwhelming. The power you seek will take some time, a week, perhaps more, to grow within you. Then you must learn to control the power. And know the limits. All that strength will do you no good, if you cannot properly use it."

Simone took Justine's hands in her own. She enjoyed the warmth in the mortal hands, felt the heartbeat in them, faster now than before.

"You will be immortal. Be patient, Justine. It will go better for you. You also must remember, your wounds will heal and diseases will not affect you, but decapitation, fire, and more than a half hour of sunlight will terminate your existence. As your saying goes, 'There is no free ride.' Questions?"

Though her tone was flip, Justine kept a grip on Simone's hands. "Will I be able to fly?"

"No flying. No bats. Are you ready?"

Justine's voice caught in her throat on her first attempt to speak, but came through strong the second try. "Yes."

"Come then."

Simone led her by the hand down a hall to a small guest bedroom. The room was simply decorated in beige and blue. A large window looked out on a small swimming pool.

By the bed Simone leaned close and said, "You must disrobe."

Justine began to shrug off her jacket.

Simone stopped her. "Please, allow me."

She ran her hands over Justine's chest and shoulders, slipping the jacket off with one smooth motion. She laid it on a chair. From behind she caressed ribs while lifting the T-shirt. Justine raised her arms without hesitation. Simone slipped the bra straps off her shoulders and the garment slid to the floor.

Simone's hands moved to the soon to be dead woman's hips. She asked gently, "Have you ever had sex with a woman?" Hands still collecting the warmth of Justine's body, she moved to face Justine. She began to undo her pants.

Justine was a full bodied woman, smooth and sleek with curves where they ought to be. Simone was not as generously endowed, though in three hundred and fifty years nobody had ever complained. She was not really a lesbian, but in her time she'd had many men and found them repetitive and ultimately boring. Women were much more interesting at the moment, and Justine was the type of woman she was interested in.

Justine stepped out of her pants. "Yes, once, a long time ago."

Simone pulled down Justine's panties, feeling the muscles under smooth, tanned skin. "Did you enjoy it?"

They were eye to eye now. "I was a bit drunk, but it was not...unpleasant."

Simone unbuttoned her own blouse and let it fall. She pulled Justine close. Their breasts touched, sending a thrill through her body. Justine shivered, too, though knowing she was about to die dampened any intimate response.

Simone and Justine lay together on the bed. Simone caressed Justine's stomach. "The change you are about to go through can be, if you let it, very liberating. Promise me you will keep an open mind."

"I will."

Simone moved her hand between Justine's breasts and let it rest on her chest. She closed her eyes and concentrated on the quick throb of

# Blood Justice

the heart underneath. "I love the feel of a beating heart. There is nothing quite like it."

Justine put her hand on Simone's, pressed it tight. Simone smiled gently, and let her lips brush the mound of Justine's breast. She slowly moved her lips to Justine's. "It's time," Simone whispered.

Justine's heart seemed to stop beating for a long few seconds then resumed a bit quicker.

Simone moved to lean over Justine. She brushed the hair from her face, looked deep into her eyes, and kissed her, at first tentative, then harder, tongue darting. She thought Justine responded.

As they kissed, Simone raised Justine's head. For a moment she looked deep into eyes wide with conflicting emotion. Then, Justine let her head fall back, exposing her neck. Simone opened her mouth wider than should be possible, and sank two extended teeth into her willing victim.

# Chapter Nineteen

A splash from the pool outside her window woke Justine. Her eyes opened, and quickly closed to block the bright light. She lay still for several minutes, marshalling her memories, attempting to decipher where she was and how she got there.

At the same time she listened to the ripple and swish of water, the hum of distant vehicles, the scrape of sheets on skin when she moved. All those noises occurred in a strange vacuum of sound. Something was missing. Her chest felt strange. She pressed a palm there, attempting to discover what was different. This jogged her memory. She sat up as if jerked by a hangman's noose.

She had no heartbeat. She found no pulse. She put hands over her ears and heard no background rush of blood as she had her whole life. She was dead.

Justine rolled off the bed and stood, inadvertently jumping two feet straight up. Taken by surprise she landed on the bed, then slipped off, rear end bumping hard on the floor.

"What the hell?"

She stood slowly, then took careful steps to the window. The mini-blinds leaked dim light. She grasped the cord and pulled. The blinds leaped up and banged against the window frame. Startled, she dropped the cord. The blinds dropped down on the sill. Justine jumped back, hit the bed, and sat down with a bounce.

Out of sheer habit, hand to chest, she waited a minute for her heartbeat to settle. "Okay, slow, slow." But there was still no heartbeat. What had she done? Yet, though the silence in her body was peculiar, she felt good; no aches, no pains, wide awake, strong. She couldn't really be dead and feel this good. Simone wouldn't...

Then Justine remembered the details—naked in bed with Simone, her hands on her, a kiss, a brief, sharp pain on her neck. "Oh shit." Justine felt her neck. They were there, two small scabs. "Oh shit."

The sun had set. A strip of blue sky on the horizon faded quickly. Below, naked in the lighted pool, Simone looked up. She waved for Justine to join her.

Wearing a thick bathrobe, Justine gingerly made her way to the pool.

Simone, in a dark green bathrobe, met Justine at the door and escorted her across the flagstone patio to the umbrella covered table. "Welcome," she said. Justine winced. Simone smiled and lowered her voice.

"You will adapt soon enough. Have some wine. One of death's great pleasures."

Justine would have knocked the glass over had Simone not been ready to yank it out of the way.

"For a little while, before you move, you must think first."

Justine slowly picked up the glass and held it gently with both hands. "How long since...?"

"Two days."

"I'm a...?"

"Vampire? Yes."

Justine was both elated and terrified. What had she done? What would she do? How would she cope? Finally she had the power to punish the ones who hurt her daughter and destroyed her reason to live. Now that she was dead, she felt more alive than ever.

"Drink the wine," Simone said. "But prepare yourself."

The bottle was on the other side of the table, the label in shadow, yet she could easily read it. A Chablis, one she'd had before, a favorite. She sipped. Her body quivered as the flavor burst in her mouth and swirled in her head. Wonderful, and too much. The intensity overpowered the subtleties of flavor that made wine enjoyable.

Simone told her, "Try again. This time consciously subdue the taste. Try to turn down the sensitivity of your mouth."

❧ — ☙

And so it went for the next week. Simone coached her on how to see, hear, smell, taste and feel again. It took two days before she could move about the house without bumping into furniture or walls. Simone began to teach her Tai Chi. The slow, controlled motion helped her focus on smooth movement, and awareness of where her body was in relation to itself and its surroundings. The similarity of movement to Kung Fu helped her take control.

Simone preached patience. At the beginning of her new "life," Justine had none. After three days, when Simone wasn't looking, Justine jumped right in and went through her Kung Fu forms. The beginning forms were no problem. She hit each move sharp and strong as if once again testing for the next color belt. As her confidence grew—what did Simone know, anyway?—her performance quickly deteriorated. Her body could move faster than she was used to thinking. Out of control, her limbs tried to kick, spin, crouch and punch at the same time. She ended up on her face, twitching as if she held a high-voltage wire.

When Justine could move normally, she pushed to her knees to face Simone who sat patiently at a poolside table. "Why am I not surprised?" Simone said.

# David Burton

*Oh shut up,* Justine thought. Then, as she tried to stand, the minor cramps she had been ignoring hit hard. Fire coursed through her veins, every movement agony. She moaned and doubled over, the pain of her head smacking the stone a relief from the twisting pain in her gut. A minute, an hour, a day of pain later, Simone knelt beside her. She held Justine's head and tipped a blood-filled glass to her lips. Justine gagged at her first sip of blood.

Her mind rebelled at the idea. Warm, the coppery flavor flowed heavy across her tongue. The pungent aroma nauseated her, even as her body, knowing what it needed, drank heartily. The thick liquid flowed into her stomach like a soft bomb. Warmth spread quickly, easing the cramp, nausea and fire.

"Patience, *ma cherie,*" Simone said as she gently smoothed the hair from Justine's face.

Justine nodded and did not think any more bad thoughts of her friend. As Simone had warned, the euphoria of discovering new strength and sensitivity had faded. Her body now had to adapt to a new way of functioning.

"Come with me," Simone said. She led Justine to a small bathroom by the pool.

"What are we doing here?" Justine asked.

"I do not wish to clean the stones."

"What...?" Her stomach spasmed and she barely had time to reach the bowl before she retched out the rejected blood. After a few minutes Justine sat on the floor, arms draped over pulled up knees.

Simone leaned a shoulder against the door. "The transition can be tough," she said.

"No shit."

"It will pass in two or three days. If you try to force the change, it will be worse."

"Patience, I get it." Justine looked up at Simone. Even completely still, the woman emanated power and grace. Justine had imagined those qualities for herself, referencing many of the vampire movies she and Brit had watched together late on a Saturday night. Now here she was, sitting on a bathroom floor after puking her guts out. Reluctantly, she accepted that she had a lot to learn. "Was it this hard for you?"

Simone's lips formed a faraway smile, then she reached out to help Justine up. "I had no friend to help me."

❧ — ❧

*As Simone huddled in the forest after the burning sun drove her into the shadow, she asked God why He allowed this horror to happen to her and her family. She wanted to die, not be one of those damned creatures. The village*

# Blood Justice

*priest was dead, hacked to pieces, so he could not answer her question directly. But God had not seen fit to save the priest, despite his faith, so maybe that was enough of an answer. Faith in an uncaring God would not save you. Faith in one's self might.*

*Not all in the village were killed. Simone saw the survivors from the trees, but could not approach, for the sun began to burn her within a few minutes. After dusk, she tried to contact them. They would not open the doors of the remaining buildings where they huddled in fear. They prayed to God to protect them, but would not help one of their own.*

*One man opened his door to her, Monsieur Tremain, the butcher. The odor of blood permeated the man. Before, it had nauseated her, but as she ducked through Tremain's door out of the dark, the scent drew her in like a warm fire on a bitter and lonely night. She knelt by the fireplace, soaking the warmth into her cold body.*

*"Please help me," Simone said. "Something is happening to me. The others are scared and will not let me in."*

*Tremain, a mustachioed man made strong by years of hefting carcasses, came right to the point. "I will help you, Simon Gireaux, and protect you from the others if you help me."*

*"What help can I provide you, then?"*

*"The beasts killed my wife. You will replace her."*

*Simon had seen how Tremain treated his wife. The suggestion revolted her. Better to risk the dark of the forest and the violence of frightened and ignorant people than endure the man's abuse. "If you will not aid me as one villager aids another, I will not accept your proposal, Monsieur Tremain. You would treat me little better than Stephan Sinakov and his band of brutal creatures. Open your door and I will trust my survival to the kindness of the wolves and bears."*

*She was loathe to leave the warm fire, and the smell of the place, that formerly repulsed her, now stimulated her senses and invigorated her body. Yet, she stood and moved unsteadily toward the door. Her late husband had been a good man who treated her with kindness and respect. As she felt then, there was no reason to settle for a cushone like Tremain.*

*The butcher grabbed her, dragged her into the bedroom and threw her onto the sour smelling bed. He began to undress.*

*"Did you not see for yourself, woman? The priest is dead. The prefect is dead. The mayor is dead. The soldiers are gone. You will be my wife and I will protect you only as long as you do not disobey me. Disrobe, I would look at you."*

*Images of the unspeakable brutalization of sweet Camille still flashed in her mind. No, no, no. Simone would not let that happen to her. The idea infuriated her. The residual smell of blood intoxicated her. A quick search for an escape route revealed none.*

*"Disrobe, woman," Tremain ordered. He yanked the belt from his breeches*

# David Burton

*with a snap. The knife he always wore fell free. He grabbed it and held it as he struck her leg with the belt. "I care not what injury you bring to yourself."*

*With no plan but to obtain the knife, Simone launched herself at the man. They tumbled through the door into the main room. She rolled over him and landed on her back, astonished at her strength and speed. But she had the knife.*

*Tremain wrapped the end of his belt around a fat-fingered fist and struck her with it. "Damn bitch! I'll throw what's left of you outside to feed the beasts."*

*The sharp pain on her face galvanized her. She was on her feet without realizing it. Tremain swung again. Simone caught the heavy buckle and yanked him to her. A swipe with the razor-sharp blade flayed his arm. A backward swipe cut deep into his neck. Simon watched him stagger, drop to his knees, and sag to the wooden floor. He was no longer a danger.*

*That's when the first cramp struck.*

*Pain made her curl up tight on the floor and cry out for God's mercy when she could inhale enough air. When she did breathe in, the scent of fresh blood broke through the pain and drew her attention to Tremain's quivering body. Mortal mind and vampire body working against each other, she crawled to him.*

*Blood seeped from his neck with small pulses, pooling around his head. Simone's body knew what it needed. Though her mind cringed at the act, she at first tentatively licked the warm liquid, then sucked greedily. The pain in her gut eased. The bloodfire dimmed to a soft warmth. She uncurled like a new flower in the sun. She hardly noticed when the mortal shuddered and exhaled his last breath.*

*Pain gone, strength restored, Simone paced the small room. She knew what she was, now. Dead, a beast, a horror, a creature of the night, hated and feared by all. Immortal, it was said. Yet, she wanted to die, almost as much as she wanted to "live." Stephan Sinakov was the name of the fiend that slaughtered her family. Revenge burned hot in her. Simone vowed to stay alive long enough to seek vengeance for their deaths.*

*Soon after, she set the foul bed aflame and slipped into the night. Terrified, exhilarated, completely alone and beholden to neither God nor the Devil, she headed into the mountain forest, where even the wolf and the bear avoided her.*

❧ — ❧

Simone informed Justine of the ins and outs of being a vampire. At first, Justine ate small amounts of regular food. The food was not necessary for nutrition, only to satisfy her life-long habit of eating.

"Feeding approximately once a week will keep you healthy," Simone told her. "One liter is enough. In little bits or all at once. More is better. You will not get fat."

"And less?"

"Have you ever had, how do you say, low blood sugar? Much like that. The cramps, also. You will not die, but maybe you will wish to.

Very unpleasant."

"Where do you...find the blood?" Justine asked.

Simone swept her hand in a circle, indicating the world. "There are three billion mortals on this planet."

"I wish to kill only three."

"It is not necessary to kill in order to feed. You can make them forget."

"How?"

Over the next week the pain, nausea, and weakness diminished with each episode. Drinking blood became a natural act. She didn't question where it came from. She continued to work out, slowly at first, building in intensity as the sickness diminished.

Decapitation followed by burning, Simone told her, was the most effective way to destroy a vampire. A stake in the heart worked, until it was removed. Bullets, especially a shotgun blast, would cause pain, and slow them down, but would heal. Most vampires fought with swords—they were quiet, effective, and not so regulated as guns.

Simone gave Justine a sword with a thin curved blade about two feet long to practice with. She used her own sword that had a very thin, foot long, double-edged blade that she wore strapped to her back.

"You are very good with the sword," Simone said after a particularly severe sparring session around the pool. Both had numerous cuts on their bodies. "You have experience with the blade." She shrugged off a tattered T-shirt.

Justine wrapped a flap of skin in place. "When I was sixteen I had a foster dad who owned a martial arts studio. Weapons were his specialty. He made me learn them all."

"You did not want to learn them?"

Justine stared unseeing into the water. "Not at first. But I was good at it, and he was a good teacher."

"You liked this man."

"The first two foster homes after my father died didn't work out. Mr. Harrow was the first one to really care for me. He and his wife were good people."

"Are they still alive?" Justine frowned. Simone had stripped, ready to enter the pool. She gently touched Justine's arm.

"No. They died in a small plane crash almost ten years ago." Her face bunched and she turned away.

"You were alone then."

"I had my husband and Brittany. But he...died soon after."

Simone wiped away imaginary tears. "And then Brittany was taken from you."

Justine sighed. "So I am alone."

# David Burton

"*Non, cherie.* Your friend Teresa cares for you. As does Harry, I think. And me."

"You have done so much for me, but I wonder why. What do you get out of helping me?"

"You are a woman who has lost her child. I understand that. So I help you. Now I think there is greatness in you, Justine—if you survive. I would like to see what you do with it."

"I don't feel like there's any greatness in me."

"All the more reason to suspect it is there."

Often, after sunset, they swam in the pool. Following Simone's lead, Justine became comfortable swimming nude. Justine was in awe of the power of her new vision as often they sat in the hot tub and watched the night sky while they talked. Justine asked Simone about the tattoo on the back of her neck—a Gothic V with an arrow through both legs.

"It means I am aligned with no Family."

"Is that good or bad?"

Simone hunched her shoulders. "Both. A Family member is a known quantity, an independent is not. A member has the protection, the knowledge of sure retribution, of the Family behind her. Nobody wants blood feuds again. Being independent has no such protection."

"Could you join a Family?"

"I could."

"But you haven't."

"Since I was changed I have survived on my own."

"And it's hard to give up that independence."

"Yes. And I have friends."

Justine followed a long shooting star a mortal would not have seen. "What about me? Am I in your Family?"

"You are a Young Blood, or Young One. If you survive your task, we'll talk."

The sensitivity of her other senses increased as she gained control of them. The touch of Simone's skin, or her scent as they practiced with the swords or passed close through a doorway, caused warm tingles in Justine of an intensity she had never known. Justine tried not to think of Harry at those times. After all, she might never see him again, and what would he think of her if she did?

Being with a beautiful, naked woman made it easier to distract her thoughts. Simone's body was leaner than Justine's—a good, strong peasant's body before it was broken down by a short lifetime of hard work and starvation, Simone said—but was attractive and desirable nonetheless. Simone also explained that pregnancy or STDs were no longer worries. Immortality meant freedom to experience the feelings and desires that came with her new life. Those heightened senses meant heightened pleasure if she chose to explore them.

Simone touched Justine as she talked, first with hands caressing, then thigh against thigh, then mouth and tongue. At first Justine resisted, this was not right for her. But, again, her body knew what it needed and opened to new desire. And as the novel sensations spread, her mind let go and accepted bliss.

On the tenth night they went out.

"I take it we're not going to a fine dining establishment," Justine said. They both wore sneakers, jeans, T-shirts and jackets. It was a cool, overcast night, and smelled like rain.

"I admit it is not a family restaurant." Simone wouldn't say more.

On the outskirts of Escondido she parked in a dusty parking lot in front of a bar. The neon light on the roof proclaimed that they were at the La Hacienda. Lighted beer signs graced the windows of the weathered exterior. She kept her distance from a long row of motorcycles.

"You're kidding," Justine said.

Simone turned to her. "You have been saying you want to go after your men. If you can't handle this place you are not ready to go after Standard and Dunham. Certainly not Sinakov."

Justine stared at the bar, not really seeing it. "I hate that they're still free. I gave up my life to go after them. I feel like I'm wasting time."

"You have much time left. And much to learn. Remember, your existence can be ended, and the ones you want will do just that if they can. Come. Let's see if anybody has some good blood tonight."

"In here?"

"Blood is blood," Simone said.

Two striking women did not go unnoticed. They had plenty of offers, most good natured, some crude, by the time they reached the bar at the back. Justine was tense going in. She wasn't quite as confident in her abilities as she acted. When drunk, drug-crazed bikers didn't attack her, she relaxed a bit. Beers in hand, Simone led her to the pool tables where she put a quarter down with two others, signaling she challenged the winner of the third game.

"I had never played this game until I came to America," she told Justine as they leaned against the wall and watched a good player humiliate a so-so opponent. "I have come to enjoy it. It helps if you're good. Do you play?"

Justine shook her head. "Nothing serious." Leaning close, she asked, "If I drink the blood from a drunk guy will I get drunk?"

"A little, but no hangover."

The good player was a lanky guy in his twenties with tattooed snakes spiraling down his arms, their jaws his thumbs and index fingers. He quickly put away his next two opponents.

# David Burton

When Simone racked the balls he said, "Are you sure you want to humiliate yourself, lady? If I win you have to blow me."

Simone didn't miss a beat. "If I win you have to blow yourself."

That brought some lewdly creative comments from some spectators. The player glared at them and they shut up.

A scraggily bearded guy put a quarter on the rail. Simone picked it up, kissed it, and inserted it between his lips. "Save your money, *mon ami.*" To the player she said, "I break the balls, do I not?"

She did, and ran the table.

Barely concealing his humiliation before the growing crowd, the player racked the balls for the next game.

During the third round a drunk biker staggered up to Justine and draped an arm around her shoulders. He had about a hundred pounds and six inches on her. "Hello, Darlin'," he said with drunken exaggeration. "Those fools are watching them rack the balls, but I been watchin' your rack. Those the ones I'd like to roll around the table with my cue." He groped her chest and said in her ear, loud enough for all to hear, "Come on, le's give 'em a real show on that table."

Justine winced at his fetid breath. "I don't think so." She grabbed the hand on her chest, spun out underneath, and with one hand bent his wrist, forcing him to his knees. "My rack is not for show...Darlin'."

All action around them ceased. It took him a few seconds to realize what had happened. "Let me up, God damned bitch slut."

Justine applied a little more pressure until his head touched the floor. Simone leaned on her cue, bright eyes intent on Justine. She gave the slightest of nods.

"You should learn how to treat a lady," Justine said. "Or someday you'll get into trouble you can't handle." She let him go. To the onlookers she said. "Somebody take him away. I don't want to put him down again."

He did go for her, but a couple of guys bigger than him dragged him away. Simone nodded her approval. Justine ignored the buzz from the surrounding group about how that woman took down that drunk ass motherfucker.

Half way through the next game Justine saw a familiar face: Jay Dunham. He leaned on the bar across the room, surrounded by three men. Physically, the four fit right in with the bar crowd, yet were apart from them. The other drinkers gave them space.

He had not yet seen her. A lust for violence exploded in her. She had to grab the cue rack to prevent herself from rushing to the bar with her knife and slitting Dunham open where he stood. Despite Simone's opinion of bad guy blood, Justine could taste Dunham's blood, sweet with revenge. Her practical side reminded her that killing somebody in front of a hundred witnesses was not a good idea, vampire or not. Nevertheless she moved through the crowd toward him, uncertain what she was going to do.

Dunham saw her. He started toward her. His buddies steered him out the door. Justine followed.

Outside, around the corner, two women joined him. Justine did not need to be trained, guided, mentored, or have hundreds of years experience to know that the two were vampires.

Dunham had the numbers, he could afford to be gracious.

"I hear you've been looking for me. It would be better for you if you didn't find me."

"You mean better for you. I will kill you for what you did."

"There's no chance you will ever be able to kill me. I'm tougher than you, and too well protected."

"So what do you do for Sinakov that he protects you so well?"

The mention of Sinakov brought them all to attention.

One of the women, about thirty when she died, big boned and attractive, rushed Justine at speed and grabbed her neck. "What do you know of Sinakov?"

Justine knocked the woman's hand away, spun her around and shoved her with a foot on her ass toward Dunham. The woman sprawled at his feet. The stunned expression on Dunham's face clearly conveyed the realization that he wasn't as safe as he thought he was a minute before. A few seconds later he collected himself.

"So, you have been changed since we last met. That makes a difference. Who did it?"

"None of your business."

"You want to kill me. It is my business. Who changed you?"

An arm wrapped around her neck. Her own arm was bent up behind her back. She struggled against her captor, but the other vampire was bigger, stronger, faster and more experienced.

Justine forced herself to calm down. She'd been thinking of herself as a badass, able to kick any butt, vampire or mortal. Now she knew she couldn't. She was as powerless as she was before.

That pissed her off. Her anger took control. She flailed and twisted, kicked and hit, tried to bite and scratch. All to no avail. She cursed her frustration. Finally she went limp, seething, but impotent.

Dunham came within ten feet of her. "Who dared change you? If you don't want your new immortality to be short-lived, you'll tell me."

Justine sneered. "It was Sinakov himself. He wanted me to kill you."

"Bullshit," Dunham said. Though she saw he thought about it. "Why would he do that? He needs mortals to take care of things during daylight."

"You know what he did to my daughter. He didn't last this long by leaving witnesses."

The tall mortal considered her answer for ten long seconds then smiled. "Nice try. Bring her," he said to the large vampire that held her. "We'll let Sinakov figure you out. Maybe he'll let me kill you." He turned to a nearby SUV.

"No. I think she will kill you one day."

The vampire holding Justine grunted and dropped to his knees, dragging her down with him. His grip relaxed. She spun away and came up next to Simone. Simone rammed a knee into the big man's spine, then stepped back as he fell over.

All the others stared in disbelief as he struggled to his knees and crawled toward them. Then they tensed to full alert.

Dunham asked the obvious question, "Who the hell are you?"

"A friend," Simone said.

Dunham glanced at the big man rising to his feet with the help of one of the women vampires. "Not his friend," Simone said.

"What do you want?"

Justine stepped forward ready to tell him what she wanted. Simone stepped in front, holding her back.

"We only wish to go home and have a good night's sleep."

"I'll put you to sleep." With enhanced speed, the big vampire rushed Simone.

Just as quick, she drew the big blade from her back. She spun sideways and chopped down. His hand raised a tiny dust cloud when it plopped to the ground.

"Ahh. You foreign bitch. I can take you with one hand."

He might have really thought it was true, but it wasn't. He went for her. Simone dropped, sweeping his legs out from under. The man jolted hard to his knees. She jumped up and pushed his head down. Two chops of her short sword severed his thick neck.

The woman vampire screamed and rushed Simone.

Simone pointed the blade at her. The woman stopped just out of reach. Simone held the head out. "Sorry, self-defense." Glaring hate, the woman took the head then signaled to the other woman to help her with the body.

Dunham said, "We should talk. I know somebody who could use someone like you."

"I have no interest in being used by Sinakov," Simone said.

"What do you know about Sinakov?"

"More than you. Otherwise you would not be with him. *Bon nuit,* Jay Dunham." She firmly grasped Justine's arm and steered her toward the front of the building.

Justine attempted to resist. "Wait. Let me take him—"

Simone kept walking. *"Tete toi,* Justine," she said low. "This is not the time for what you want. Come."

Simone drove several blocks to the first stoplight, turned left, made a U-turn, then parked in a 7-11 parking lot where they had a view of the La Hacienda.

Justin couldn't contain herself any longer. "Why didn't you let me at Dunham? He was right there. I'd have made him tell me where Sinakov is. Then I'd have slit the sick bastard open and watched him suffer and die on his way to Hell."

"And what would the other women, and the mortals, be doing ?"

"I could have handled those women."

"You were lucky. They would not let that happen again. Those mortals were armed and experienced."

"We could have controlled them."

"What if a mortal from the bar called the police? Would you fight them, also? Become a fugitive? Justine, we are immortal, we are strong, but we are not invincible."

Justine sat erect in her seat, fists tight with barely controlled tension. She wanted to rip into Dunham, tear into him, shred his body to a bloody heap of meat. She knew Simone was right, and hated that she was.

The seething rage slowly subsided. She slumped in the seat. "All right. All right. I was just so close." She laid her head back, eyes closed. "Why are we parked here?"

"We are waiting for them to leave so we can follow them."

"They would have taken us there."

"But they would be in control."

Justine sighed. Reluctant to give up control, she resolved to follow Simone's lead, while learning what she needed to know. But she could be patient only so long.

After a few minutes the two SUVs came out from behind the bar and headed south.

# Chapter Twenty

Harry sat in his usual spot in the Sundowner. Bayley set another beer down. Over the noise of a busy Friday night she said, "She'll be back."

"But will it still be her?" Harry said, knowing Bayley wouldn't understand.

"I'm jealous." Then he told her Justine had to leave town and he didn't know when or if she would return. Once again Bayley said, "She likes you. She'll be back." For the hundredth time he thought, *Will it still be her?*

Harry had been on paid administrative leave since the shootings at Teresa's house. Policy. There'd been several witnesses. No doubt it was a good shoot. Killing people can mess with your head. Policy. They didn't want him out on the street getting all Dirty Harry on them. They also didn't want him so upset he inadvertently—or purposely—put himself on the other end of the same scenario. Policy.

He hadn't mentioned vampires to anyone. With Gurvitz's surreptitious help he worked his cases. He kept a separate file for anything related to Brittany Kroft's murder. The file thickened quickly, although it contained few facts of any use. Sinakov the vampire remained elusive.

Though not for lack of trying. He checked out all the Sinakovs in San Diego and Orange County. There weren't many, and none gave any indication they were vampires. He checked out real estate owners, taxpayers, voters, criminals with aliases similar to "Sinakov."

Then they released Latch Standard.

Standard's girlfriend, Sharon, drove him to her home in Escondido. The only activity outside the house until full dark was pizza delivery about six o'clock. At seven, a large Mercedes sedan, accompanied by a Cadillac SUV, both out of place among the neighborhood's pickups, old SUVs, and cheap cars, took him silently into the night.

Harry followed.

He followed to I-15 south. The Mercedes took the first exit and got right back on heading north. At Gopher Canyon Road, Harry followed east, on two-lane Old Castle Road, toward Valley Center.

Some miles later Harry rounded a sharp corner and had a view of the road for almost half a mile ahead. The road was empty.

Harry's first instinct was to go fast and catch up. But the other car had only been out of site for ten or fifteen seconds.

He slowed and searched for small roads. At the far end of the half-mile stretch he pulled over to let two cars pass, then U-turned and drove slowly back. The dirt road he found angled sharply back into uphill woods. Hidden by brush, it was invisible from east-bound traffic. Harry stopped ten feet in. A faint dust cloud lingered in the headlights. A NO TRESPASSING sign hung from a length of chain, one end attached to a weathered wood post, the other laying in the dirt.

Continue, or return during daylight? Logic, procedure, and caution said to return with backup. But Harry was curious, and after all, off duty. Cautious, he drove up the road guided only by parking lights.

The way wound up the hillside, sometimes pressed close by Eucalyptus and oak, sometimes open to the valley where a few specks of light broke the black. In one of the tightly treed areas the moon illuminated a man standing in the middle of the road about two hundred feet ahead.

Harry stopped. He was unofficially on official business—he had no warrant and no cause to be there. Technically, he was trespassing. He settled his gun beside him and moved ahead slowly. This was the road to his cousin Jim Curry's house, wasn't it?

Then he noticed the pipe in the man's hand. And the two other men coming toward him. Maybe this wasn't the way to his cousin's house. With no place to turn around, Harry started backing down the road.

The men ran after him, their mouths open unnaturally wide. In the dim light from his car they looked like the jaws of the dogs that came after him one night when he was seven—jaws that engulfed his head, foul breath suffocating him, huge fangs crushing his skull, teeth piercing his leg.

Suddenly the most important thing in the world was to get away, get away, *get away!* The trees gave way to open road with a steep rise on one side and a sharp drop off on the other. Harry searched for a place to turn around while simultaneously trying to track the vampires closing in. How could they move so fast? The car ran down the dark road much too rapidly to be under control. Heart hammering in his chest, Harry didn't care. *Get away!* The car lurched across the road. The rear fender scraped rocks. Harry overcorrected. The car shot to the other side. The rear tire slipped over the edge, hit a rock and bumped back. The front tires caught and threw the car back on track.

Harry scarcely noticed. All he thought of was to get away. When Teresa killed the vampire in her house he had to believe they were real. In the back of his mind he'd really thought that one had been an anomaly, a one-time mutant, a freak of nature, now mercifully gone. Justine was a woman, powerless to help her daughter, caught up in the fantasy of being an invincible creature. They weren't really real. How could a logical man believe otherwise?

Yet three of them were chasing him and Harry had no doubt they meant him harm. He needed time alone to come to terms with what shouldn't be, but was.

Trees surrounded him, level ground on his left. The vampires were fifty feet away. He approached an opening in the trees. Harry regained some control of his fear. He spun the wheel, skidded into the opening, bumped a tree, jammed the gearshift in first and stalled the engine.

*"Ahhhhhhh! Goddamnit!"*

He fumbled for the key. The motor caught. Gas pedal to the floor, he popped the clutch. The car leaped forward, ricocheted off the opposite bank and sprayed his pursuers with dust and gravel as it raced down the road.

Harry turned on the headlights and cried out as elation swept through him and allowed him to breathe again. He sucked in deep gulps of cool air. His chest expanded with relief. *Safe.* Still, he looked in the rearview mirror more than at the road ahead until he fishtailed onto the paved road and sped away.

Some minutes later, as heavy drops of rain spattered his windshield, Harry parked along the roadside with other anonymous cars in an area of modest residences. He white-knuckled the steering wheel to keep his hands from shaking and forced himself to breath slow and evenly. The gun lay cocked and ready in his lap.

Fucking vampires. They shouldn't be real. But they were. The dead should stay dead. But they didn't. Then the logical portion of his brain kicked back in.

The whole deal was a set up. They knew he was going to follow Standard. What was their plan? To kill him or scare him? Safe, parked anonymously among other cars, able to think rationally, he figured that if they wanted him dead, he would be. They wanted to scare him, which they did, and let him know they were not scared of him and were watching. In other words, don't mess with them, don't be searching for Sinakov.

Well, Harry now believed. He also had lost his cinematically imposed preconception that vampires were mindless killing beasts. They were smart, clever, and ruthless. Fucking vampires.

Harry slugged down some water, eyes on the rearview mirror. A few minutes later the Mercedes and Cadillac swished past on the wet road. Harry followed.

They led him west on the 78 freeway, then south. Somewhere in the Rancho Santa Fe area Harry lost them. That was okay. Harry was clever, too.

Back in his condo, cleansed of the acrid stink of nervous sweat, beer in hand, Harry sat in his favorite chair, a blue leather La-Z-Boy recliner, and thought about his next move.

Somebody knocked on the door.

# Chapter Twenty-One

Through a light rain, Justine and Simone followed the two vehicles. One made a stoplight and turned left. The other didn't make the light and stopped, heading straight. Traffic prevented Simone from following the first vehicle.

When the light changed, they followed into southeast Escondido to an old neighborhood of small houses on large lots. The SUV pulled over and let off two men, mortals from the La Hacienda who walked up a short dirt drive and entered the one-story stucco house.

Stopped across the street, Simone turned to Justine. "Are you hungry?"

Justine was. Excitement over, her body reverted to its natural state. It needed blood to suppress the growing shakiness of her hands. She could drink blood now, the queasiness mostly in her mind. But as yet, the blood she drank had been supplied by Simone—small amounts, only enough to quell the nausea and ease the shaking. That was not enough. Her body craved more. The free ride was over. Justine would have to hunt her own food now.

She knew the signs—a slight tremor of her hands, a hunger growing in her gut. Dread and desire cracked her voice. "Yes."

Simone nodded. "Are you prepared to do what you must?"

Justine pressed hands against thighs to still them. "Yes. But I'm not sure how..."

"Your body will know, *ma cherie*." Simone took Justine's hand. "It is hard, the first kill. Many of my first were like feeding on my own people. *Tres horrible*. This is the life you chose. As mortals do, you must also do what is necessary to survive."

"I want to kill only three," Justine said. Her body vibrated with the hunger. The fangs pulsed in her mouth.

"You must have your strength to achieve that goal. These two would murder you, or Teresa, without hesitation. Come, we will be quick."

Simone pressed Justine's hands to her lips, then exited the car. Justine's hunger compelled her to follow. They crossed the street and went to the front door.

Simone said before she knocked, "Free your senses. Allow yourself to feel what being a dominant creature is like. Embrace the power you now have in you." She rapped on the door.

A stocky guy around thirty, with numerous tattoos, opened the door

# David Burton

on the chain.

"What do you want?" he asked, annoyed.

Simone smacked the door with her palms. It slammed open. "You, of course." She pushed in, grabbed his neck and threw him onto a leather couch far too expensive to go with the beer cans, magazines and clothes cluttering the house.

Justine entered, taking in the odors of stale beer, dirty laundry, and long-congealed food. She heard music in the back of the house, a slamming door, the *thump*-thump of the stocky man's heart.

"Dude, who was at the door?"

The other guy, wearing only jeans, entered from the hall. He stopped when he saw Justine. Then he saw Simone holding his friend down. He understood immediately what was happening. He did the only thing he could. He ran.

In a flash Justine's newly acquired hunting instinct took over. She raced down the hall. The next room reeked of the prey's scent. Through a window, she quickly spotted his form moving along the tall hedges. She dove through, then, dodging several pungent orange trees, she ran toward him at full speed, amazed how quickly she reached him.

He surprised her with a machete swinging at her neck. Her quickness saved her head, but cost her a slash on the arm as she spun away. Immediately, he came after her, hoping to slice and dice her before she recovered. She was on the defensive, unsure how to dodge his attack. Then she remembered her training.

He swung the machete.

She leaped at him and slammed him against a tree. Using both hands to bend his machete arm over a branch, she couldn't defend her midriff from a hard punch. It didn't hurt, and didn't knock the breath out of her as she had no breath. It did get her attention and pushed her back.

He tried to twist away, but the bloodlust was on her. She snapped his arm against the tree and cut short his scream by bending his head back over a low branch. Her mouth stretched wide, at once uncomfortable and natural. Her fangs extended fully for the first time, creating a heavy pressure on the adjacent teeth.

Justine knew how to twist the head back and to the side to expose and stretch the neck skin. She knew how to locate the carotid artery with a thumb. The tight skin resisted her fangs, then gave way. But she was inexperienced. There was no rush of hot blood, only a tantalizing trickle. Wild with need, she bit again and again until blood surged into her mouth. Her extended lips sealed the blood in. The vampire in Justine moaned and shuddered as each spurt over her tongue created a warm wave that traveled down her body like an orgasm.

The man ceased struggling after ten seconds. Thirty seconds later he sighed and went limp. When the last trickle of blood came from his ravaged neck, Justine released him. He slipped off the branch and crumpled to the ground. Weak from the ecstasy of the feeding, she fell to her knees. From pure habit her body breathed hard though there was no physical need for it.

"It will be easier and neater with experience," Simone said.

Justine did not look at the body. "It was horrible...and incredible." Her hands fluttered about her mouth. "When the blood..." Her body quivered. "Is it always like that? How could one stand it?"

"Alas, it is not always so fantastic." Simone picked up the machete.

"He almost cut my head off."

"But he did not. I am grateful for that."

"What about the...them?"

"They must vanish. If Sinakov knows how they died he will think it was you and be very angry and come after us...you...very hard. I know you do not wish this, but we should be low profile for a little time. A plan is necessary. Do you agree?"

Surprising herself, she did. A glance at the machete reminded her that she had almost ceased to exist, thus wasting her life and breaking her promise to Brittany. The time to be reckless was after she did what she had to do, not before. "Yes, I agree."

Simone grabbed the body by the arm and lifted it as if it weighed twenty pounds instead of two hundred. *"Bon.* Help me."

Driving back from disappearing the two men into an overgrown ravine, Justine realized it was not quite midnight. She was wide awake, rejuvenated. The blood energy tingled through her body, pushing what she'd done to the back of her mind where, dead or alive, guilt lingered.

Justine knew what Simone wanted when they returned to her house. Desire to share Simone's bed did not hide in the back of her mind. She owed Simone for the chance to avenge her daughter. Justine, however reluctantly, depended on her for guidance, for which she was grateful. Too, with its heightened senses, this new reality begged for new sensual experiences. She had felt the older vampire's touch and had every wish to explore the new possibilities that it offered.

But not that night. Justine felt too restless, too alive, to just go to bed, no matter what sensual delights she might find there. After being with Simone constantly for days she needed to experience her new world on her own.

Justine had no idea where she was going. She just had to go.

# Chapter Twenty-two

*Justine!* Harry's first thought brought a surge of elation that quickly vanished. Why would she come to see him? Did he want to see her if she really was changed? What would she be like? Would she still be her? He'd wanted her for ten years, but now that she was in his life, what? If that was her at the door, what did he do?

Harry rubbed his face to wipe away his confusion. Who was he kidding? He wanted to see her, whatever she was. He opened the door.

"Hey boss," Gurvitz said. "I know it's late, but the light was on, so..."

Harry was disappointed, and glad, that the young detective stood uncertainly in the door. "Come in," Harry said, stepping aside. "You want a beer? You're not getting paid overtime so it's authorized. Sit."

Gurvitz clutched a file folder in both hands. His eyes sparkled and he couldn't keep the grin from his heavy lips. He sat for a few seconds while Harry opened two beers, then he jumped up and paced. He called into the kitchen, "You know Standard was released today, don't you?

"Didn't you mention it yesterday?"

"Yeah, I guess I did. Do you still think he's connected with this Sinakov?"

Harry returned and handed Gurvitz a bottle of Bud Lite. He was not a connoisseur of beer or food. Plain and simple was all right for him. "I do," Harry said, amused at the younger man's obvious excitement to tell him something. He sat in his chair and put his feet up. "Why?"

Gurvitz couldn't hold it in anymore. "I might have found Sinakov. Sort of."

"Sort of?" Harry kept his excitement in check.

"Well, I found a Sinakov who isn't any of the other ones we've found."

"That's a good start. Tell me."

Gurvitz sat on the edge of the couch and opened the file on the coffee table. "I thought that if he wasn't on any list maybe he isn't a resident. Maybe he's a guest or a temporary employee from a foreign company. Quite a few of them have residences here for their executives."

"Or he's an illegal."

"I considered that. But if he is...?" He threw his hands up. "Anyway, I started checking foreign companies with offices or residences in the area. There's only about twenty in North county. So I called them. None had a Sinakov working for them. Then I checked their websites. One, Transport Francaise, mentioned a Sinakov as a co-founder." His hands flew out. "At last, a Sinakov. Between The Deuxieme Bureau and Interpol, with some prodding from my cousin, a captain in Israeli Security, I found out that this Sinakov is a shady character and is nowhere to be found and has to be about ninety years old. Transporte Francaise owns a large and very private estate in Rancho Santa Fe."

Harry had to admit Gurvitz earned the pleased grin he wore. "I'm impressed. Whether this is the Sinakov I'm looking for or not, that was some good work. Address?"

Beaming, Gurvitz handed him a paper. Harry knew the area—he'd been there earlier. "Why 'shady?'"

The younger detective flipped the file closed and sat back, holding the beer with both hands while thoughtfully studying it.

"Apparently, Transporte Francaise moves anything anywhere, including arms, drugs, and people. The people being both willing and unwilling, slavery is still alive and well in many places. There have never been any convictions. Witnesses tend to change their minds, or disappear."

"You said he was a co-founder of the company?"

"In nineteen thirty-two. Assuming he was at least twenty at the time that makes him about ninety-five."

"I find it hard to believe a ninety-five-year-old man raped and murdered Brittany Kroft. A son?"

"No record of any kids. Or relations of any kind."

*Vampire,* Harry thought. *He's the one.* "Have a photo?"

"Oh, yeah." Gurvitz pulled one from the file. "It's a surveillance photo taken at night. It's grainy, but not bad."

Harry studied the photo of a man in his mid-twenties leaving a door held by a liveried doorman and headed to a waiting limousine. Two obvious bodyguards flanked him and he had the arm of an elegant woman wearing a dark hooded cape, making her unidentifiable.

Sinakov was roughly handsome, thin, almost emaciated, with wide shoulders. He sported a short, blond ponytail. Harry scrutinized the face. Even with the poor quality, he'd bet he wasn't the only one whose first impression of the man was *arrogant son of a bitch.*

"When was this taken?"

"Nineteen ninety-two."

"What? This guy can't even be thirty."

Gurvitz took a long swallow of beer. "Tranporte Francaise has been under investigation for years, by three different governments, and an unknown number of local law enforcement. If there is a Sinakov, that's him."

"An imposter, a stand in?"

Gurvitz spread his hands and shrugged.

# David Burton

Harry made a show of checking the time. "It's late. Why don't you leave the file and go get some sleep. I'll see you in the morning. I'm told I'll be reinstated tomorrow."

"That's what I hear, too. It's about time."

At the door, Harry said, "This was great work, Paul. Good thinking, good follow up. I like to think I'd have thought of it eventually. But I probably wouldn't have."

In daylight he would have seen Gurvitz blush with pride. "Thank you, sir. That means a lot coming from you."

"I'm glad you think so. However, for the moment, we need to keep this between us. This guy doesn't need to know we're looking at him."

Not at all tired, Harry sat down and began to study the file.

A few minutes later a knock on the door interrupted him.

# Chapter Twenty-three

Justine didn't know where she wanted to go. She was antsy, full of energy with no place to use it. She headed east on the 78 freeway, pushing through traffic at eighty miles per hour. Without thinking about it she exited at Sycamore and found herself driving past her house.

Simone had warned that Sinakov and his people would be watching. They knew where she lived. They'd be after her.

"Let 'em come," Justine had said, the full meal of fresh blood making her bold.

A quick U-turn brought her back to her driveway. The night sounds entered the car's open windows. Traffic noises mostly, the susurrus of normal people going about their normal pursuits. Not like her, a dead person whose only business was to track down and kill three more men.

She'd killed and fed on a man earlier. That's who she was now. A killer with no mercy. So what if she didn't know his name, if he had a girlfriend or a kid, or if a few weeks ago they might have met and had a pleasant conversation about the traffic or the weather, or that damn war.

She swiped at phantom tears annoying her cheeks.

From now on, no mercy for mortal or vampire. She was dead and the dead gave no quarter in their quest to avenge the death of a beautiful live being who had made life worth living.

Again she wiped at tears that would never be real again, a habit of the body, like breathing.

A sound caught her attention: The whisper of cloth against cloth, the swish of footstep on grass. Then the awareness of motion. Justine knew what it meant: vampires.

She yanked the door handle and pushed the door open six inches before it was slammed shut from outside. A figure of a man propped a two by four against the door. Another figure did the same on the other side.

She smelled it then. If she had been paying attention it might have given her an early warning. Gasoline. The figure outside held a gas can. He sloshed gas through the window.

Primed with fresh blood, Justine moved faster than the gas the man threw, but not as fast as the gas a woman vampire tossed through the opposite window. The liquid soaked her legs.

With senses on full alert, the gasoline odor burned her nose, the scratch of a match grated on her ears, the shallow arc of flame into the car terrified her even as it spurred her on. She dove into the backseat then tumbled into the rear cargo area.

With a *whump*, the gasoline burst into flame, instantly filling the front and back seats with fire. Heat forced her to curl on the floor. Flames darted over the rear seats, searching for the gas on her legs. Smoke blinded her.

Fire found her legs as she shattered the rear window with one kick and rolled through. Pants blazing, she rolled to her feet. Moving so fast she left flutters of fire behind, she slammed into the big vampire and knocked him to the ground. He grabbed her on the way down, spun and landed on her legs, smothering the flames. He was stronger, but she was faster. Before he could gain control, her knife blade flashed, slicing halfway through his neck.

Out from under, Justine grabbed the man and shoved his head through the driver's window into the inferno. He briefly screamed, spasmed, then went limp.

Pants smoking, clicking the knife open and closed, she watched the bottom half of the man crumple to the ground—a distraction of a few seconds, but too long. A can flew over the burning car, spraying gas. Justine swatted it away. Gas splattered her.

A flaming rag arced over the car. She jumped sideways. Then another rag, and another and another followed by the female vampire leaping over the burning car. The vamp grasped Justine's knife arm as they sprawled on the ground. The knife spun onto the lawn.

The two women vampires fought. The female was slender, shorter, but unbelievably fast. Justine was tough when she was alive and tough as a vampire. Though not as quick, she could take punishment and wait for an opening.

Her time came when the vamp thought Justine was done and lunged for the knife. Justine grabbed the woman's foot and, surging to her feet, flung the attacker at the car. The impact shook the car, sending a flurry of sparks into the night. Immediately, the vamp's hair and jacket flamed up. The vamp screamed and attacked Justine again. On contact, the gas on Justine's clothes ignited.

Justine tried to damp down the pain, but, alive or dead, fire burned. She needed water. A hose lay coiled at the corner of the house. The vamp slipped past her and headed right for it. Justine raced after her.

The vamp had turned on the faucet, but the water hadn't gotten through the hose yet. Just as it hiccupped out, Justine reached her. Without thinking, because she was burning, she snatched up the vamp and threw her through a window.

Justine hissed as cold water washed away the fire. Though her hair, clothes, and skin were singed, she hung her head with relief—until she noticed that her house was on fire.

# Blood Justice

Flames from the vamp quickly climbed the drapes, then jumped to a paperback filled bookcase, newspapers, the rug and furniture. The vamp struggled to regain the window. In the end, the fire caught her.

The water hose failed to quell the flames. After a minute, Justine dropped the hose. Without a backward glance, she turned and walked away from the burning house.

The house was dead, anyway, and had been since Brittany's murder. She had removed anything of importance before her change. Brittany was dead, Justine was dead, the house they were happy in might as well die, too. Let it burn.

Justine retrieved her knife, searched what was left of the male vampire's body for car keys and slipped into the night to the sound of approaching sirens.

# Chapter Twenty-four

Teresa gazed from the deck at an idyllic postcard setting and for a full twenty seconds considered staying in hiding at the cabin for months, or years—for as long as it was deemed safe. Which, considering that vampires were basically immortal, could be forever. The log cabin was actually a faux rustic, three thousand square foot home, with four bedrooms and three baths, nestled in trees overlooking a small river that wound down the western slope of the Sierra Nevada Mountains below Lake Tahoe; a totally gorgeous setting. It belonged to a friend of Detective Frazer. Nobody was planning to use it for at least six months and they were happy to have somebody look after it. It was untraceable to Teresa and her family.

The third morning she woke up there, the charm had faded. She was bored and missed the hustle and bustle of suburban life. She didn't really hate nature, but a day at the beach or a two hour hike on a level trail fulfilled her nature requirement for at least a month.

And she was worried about Justine. Would her best friend really be turned into a vampire? Was that really possible? Would she still be Justine? Teresa wanted to know, or at least talk about it with someone.

Her husband, Miguel, was a religious man. A Catholic, he was raised on a ranch in the central mountains of Mexico. An outdoors man from boyhood, he rarely attended formal church services. Nature was his church. God was in nature, he said. He believed in the natural order of things as he saw it, life and death—not life and death and undead.

The first night at the cabin, after the kids were in bed, Teresa and Miguel sat on the deck under a brilliant half moon. Teresa explained why the police officer, Detective Frazer, had helped them leave so quickly and secretly. The official story involved organized crime. That night, Teresa told him what really happened.

He didn't believe her. No matter what she thought she saw, God would not allow vampires to exist. Only Christ died and was resurrected. "You work too hard," he said to her, implying that she allowed her boss to overwork her, allowed herself to be over-stressed, ate in an unnatural way and was therefore hallucinating. "Come and hike with us tomorrow. Relax, enjoy this beautiful area. Your friend Justine can take care of herself."

A hike with Miguel and the kids was never relaxing. It was a race to see who got to the top of the mountain first. She went anyway. Miguel and the kids had, of course, loved it. Teresa still believed in what she had seen and what it meant, regardless of what God or the trees allowed.

Teresa knew what she was going to do. She just didn't know how to tell Miguel and her kids—no, just Miguel, so that he would understand. She felt a huge guilt for leaving them, though the guilt was tempered by the hurt Miguel did to her. They had always been honest with each other and able to at least consider the other person's point of view. They'd had their arguments, and there'd been a few white lies, always, at least on her part, to avoid hurt feelings, never to get away with something.

She felt Miguel had let her down by dismissing her so thoroughly and assuredly. But what had she expected? She barely believed it herself even after what she had seen and done. How could she expect Miguel, religious beliefs aside, to accept it?

Teresa's feelings for her husband—hurt, anger, love, respect—swirled in a confused jumble inside her head with her feelings for Justine—love, respect, shared grief, and, yes, anger. She was going to help Justine, she just wasn't quite sure why.

The screen door slammed and Miguel appeared beside her. He leaned his arms on the rail and said in Spanish, "You're going to go back and to help Justine, aren't you?"

Teresa nodded, not trusting herself to speak.

"To help kill her vampires?"

"No. No vampires. I don't know where that came from. Of course there is no such thing."

"But she thinks there is?"

"I don't know what she believes anymore. She's changed since Brittany's death. I know..." Her voice broke. "I know the pain she feels. We were not even friends when she helped me. Now I have to be with her when she needs me." She wiped tears from her cheeks with a quick swipe as if they were annoying raindrops to be flicked away and forgotten.

Miguel looked out into the darkness. "That's the first time you have spoken of it in more than two months."

"She's been gone almost four months, Miguel. It's the only way I can stand the pain."

"You must let her go, Teresa. It is the natural order of things, and it is hurting us."

"Would you say that if it had been Maria or Carlos taken? Would you be so quick to let them go?"

Miguel stared into the dark. He said nothing because his answer was no. Carlos and Maria were his kids. He was Antonia's father, too, but had not wanted a child when Teresa became pregnant. Though they were Catholic, Teresa knew he would have been relieved, and said nothing, if she had gone to a clinic. She didn't, and raised Antonia mostly on her own. Miguel performed the minimum parental duties required, otherwise he had little to do with her. Antonia had been…was…Teresa's child. When she went missing, Teresa, too, had died a little. But unlike Justine, she had other kids, and a husband. They had long since accepted their differing parental roles.

"I did not think so." Teresa wanted to take the words back the instant she said them. "I'm sorry. I know you meant her no harm." She wiped more tears and said, "Justine helped me then. Now I can help her do what she needs to do."

"The vampires?"

"If that's what she wants."

Miguel snorted a quick laugh. "She always did seem a little loco to me."

"Focused. She was determined to be successful and independent." Teresa squeezed her eyes shut to keep in the tears. Why couldn't she stop crying? "She wanted Brittany to have all she needed to be a happy child. Not like Justine."

"Things."

"Sure, things. Also, love, respect, support, education, safety. When Brit died, Justine thought she had failed. She had nowhere to direct her energy so she's directing it to revenge."

"What happens to her after she gets her revenge?"

"I don't think Justine knows, or cares. If there is a God, only He knows. Though at this moment, I don't think He cares."

# Chapter Twenty-five

Justine stood in front of Harry's front door with her hands in her jacket pockets, unsure whether to push the doorbell or not, unsure of her reception if she did. Would he reject her, accept her? She didn't know how she felt, either. The surprising thing was that she felt anything. She sensed something in the man, a goodness that she had rarely encountered in her life. Besides Justine's mother, Brittany was the only member of her family to ever possess the quality.

Too, he had an open mind, which he would need if...? If what? She was a vampire with every intention of murdering two men and another vampire. He was a cop. Open-mindedness would only go so far.

She shouldn't be there. But she needed to connect, however briefly, with the mortal life she'd so recently left behind. Her hand paused an inch from the door. She remembered the smell of him, the touch of his hands, the taste of his sweat, the feel of his skin against hers. If she had a heart that beat, it would be racing. With a sudden eagerness, she knocked, then backed up against the railing as if afraid of the door.

Harry appeared in the doorway, his expression unreadable through the screen. After a long mutual inspection Justine stepped forward. "Hello, Harry."

Harry unlatched the screen door, but didn't open it. "Justine?"

"Yes." He still didn't open the door. "You have nothing to fear from me."

The door screeched as it swung open.

"Have you...? Are you...?"

"Yes, I have been changed."

Another long moment passed while Harry processed that statement. He stepped back. "Do I need to invite you in?"

"No. That's for movies and books. Not real...life."

Harry closed the door behind her, then sniffed and noticed her burnt clothes and the black smudges on her face. "You look like you've been to Hell and back."

"Not yet."

They looked each other over, neither knowing what to say. Justine felt twitchy inside, like a schoolgirl approached by the object of her first crush.

Harry said, "Are you all right? Where did you go? What happened to you? Are you sure you were...you know? Are you...okay? Can I do

# David Burton

something?"

Justine moved close and looked into his eyes. "I'd like to take a shower, with you."

They kissed. At first they were tentative, then they gave in to the loneliness and desire to connect with another being that had built up in them over years.

Justine allowed her senses free rein. His scent intoxicated her, his touch was electric on her face when he drew her to him. She let go long enough to throw off her jacket and yank off his shirt. His hands traced fiery trails on her skin as he slipped off her T-shirt.

The hair on his chest sent exquisite shocks through her nipples. She shivered each time his frenzied touch grazed her breasts as he held her to him and kissed her face and neck and shoulders. Then she was wrapped about him and he carried her to the bedroom and dropped her on the bed. He yanked off her jeans and she opened herself to him, frantic to feel his heat on and in her body.

Justine ignored Simone's warning not to leave her senses at full reception when she had sex for the first time. The intensity of feeling went beyond pleasure into pain. Yet, she came quick and hard with an orgasm that stunned her. Recovering, she thought she might have hurt Harry. He lay beside her, gasping for breath.

Justine sat up. She leaned over him and gently placed a hand on his chest. "Did I hurt you?"

"I couldn't breathe. I think you scratched my back." His respiration easier, he rolled away to expose his back for inspection.

"Oh shit." Two sets of scratches oozed blood. "Lay on your stomach." The blood excited her. She bent to lick the wounds clean, then remembered what her saliva could do.

"What are you doing?" Harry asked, a bit concerned.

With a finger she wiped up each blood trail and sucked it off. Each mini rush cranked up her craving. "Cleaning you." But the fresh blood drew her down. She licked at the smears of blood, barely able to keep her tongue from the fresh scratches.

Harry tried to turn over. Justine pushed him down on his stomach. Her licking moved toward his neck. On its own, her mouth began to open wide.

"Are you okay?" Harry twisted his head around to look at her.

His voice broke the spell of Hunger. Quickly, she turned away, pressing her forehead to the small of his back while her face returned to normal. "Do you have a first aid kit?"

After she cleaned the scratches they lay facing each other, knees touching.

"You look the same," Harry said. "But your strength is more than human." He laid his hand flat on her chest. She placed her hand on his. "No heartbeat. How is that possible?"

"I don't know the biology of it."

"Despite common sense, I know there are such things, real things, as vampires. I've seen what they can do. I guess I have to accept that you are one. Why am I not afraid?"

Justine touched her hand to his chest. "Because in here you know I'll never hurt you."

"There's hurt and there's hurt." Harry eased over onto his back. Staring at the ceiling, he said, "It's going to take me a while to completely comprehend what's happened."

"Me, too."

Harry blew out a deep breath. He looked at her then back at the ceiling. "Even before, when you were a...a...."

"Mortal."

"...a mortal, it was crazy, you and me." He turned on his side to face her across the pillows. "Why are you here? Now, tonight. You could pick up any guy if it was only sex you wanted. Why me?"

Justine gazed into his eyes, recognizing the same look she'd seen that time in his office. She stroked his hair. "I like your hair, all tousled and unkempt." Her fingertips gently explored his face. "I like your face. It's square and solid, a tough face, but I bet there's a smile in there someplace. I like your eyes, big and brown, they look at me, not through me. And you were honest with me. Told me what I wanted to know and didn't sugarcoat it for the fragile mother. And I sensed a loneliness in you that matched mine. You've lost someone, too."

Harry's eyes went vacant for a long moment. "My wife left. She's in New York."

"Do you still love your wife?"

"No. Not for a while now."

Justine caressed his face with the back of her hand then withdrew it and clutched the sheets tight to her. "When Brit died, I died with her. You made me feel something besides anger. Even though I didn't want to." She felt her face tighten as that anger resurfaced.

Harry brushed the hair from her face. "You're still angry, though."

She glared at him and looked away.

"You still want to go after Standard, Dunham, and Sinakov." Justine locked eyes with him, raising her chin in defiance. "I wish you wouldn't. We'll get them. I promise. Though, we had to let Standard go."

"He's out of jail?"

"This morning. Leave him alone. We'll get him."

"I know."

A rush of anticipation sent warm shivers through Justine. Standard's

# David Burton

life belonged to her. She would get him. She couldn't promise Harry not to. No mercy, no hiding from Sinakov. She felt she was ready. Let the old bastard come after her.

But not that night. That night was for her to feel wanted and maybe loved, illusion though that may be. Powerful as Justine was, in Harry's arms, she felt safe. No vampires, no murderers, only the tiny world of his warm body surrounding her, keeping her safe from evil vampires, and murderers, and blood.

They made love again, slowly, taking time to enjoy the touch and taste and smell of each other. Justine subdued her senses, allowing herself to experience the sensations without becoming so frenzied she hurt Harry.

Some time deep in the night, before the first hint of dawn, Justine watched Harry sleep for a while, then quietly dressed. On her way to the front door she read through the file Gurvitz had left. It contained Latch Standard's address.

From the bedroom door, Harry said, "Am I going to find Standard's gutted body someplace or is he just going to disappear?"

Justine showed him a bittersweet smile. "I'm sorry." Then she turned and left.

# Chapter Twenty-six

Harry frowned as a man winched the burned-out ruin of Justine's car onto a flat bed tow truck. He turned his attention to the house. It looked like a giant had sliced it with a flaming sword from ground level to the back roof line. Water from the firefighters still glistened on the blackened floor of the living room. The last of the cleaning crew were packing up.

Justine obviously knew about the fire, the condition of her clothes attested to that. Why hadn't she mentioned it? Why hadn't he asked? Why hadn't he told her he knew where Sinakov lived?

Something happened last night. He had connected with Justine. The first time they slept together it had been terrific in an adolescent first-time way. Last night, when he opened the door and saw her, his chest had almost exploded with relief. It was all he could do not to reach out and gather her in. They had a bond that was more than lust, but not love. It was two lonely people finding each other so they could tell themselves they weren't alone anymore. It would do.

Harry could appreciate the irony that it took a dead woman to make him feel alive once again. Sex with a beautiful vampire, and the relationship that would come with it—with a dead woman bent on murder, no matter how much her victims might deserve it—both thrilled and terrified him. He knew deep in the dark areas of his brain what she was, but, in his reality, she looked, acted and felt like a living woman. It would do.

But he was a cop, sworn to prevent such crimes, and leave his personal feelings out of it. That was a test he had easily passed, so far.

The challenge of the job was one reason he became a cop, and it had been a long time since he felt really challenged. Occasionally, he wondered what his life would have been like if he'd stuck with his first career choice: thief.

In his twenties he had no desire for the mundane trials of regular people where the only consequences of failure were being broke and having to find a job. Crime had real consequences, something worth days and weeks and months of planning to prevent. He got a degree in criminology with a minor in finance. One year out of college he committed his first major burglary.

Harry had no desire to do armed robbery—too much chance of hurting somebody—or to be a low life conman or a petty thief or a white collar criminal. He figured the safest type of crime was stealing large amounts of circulated cash without anybody realizing it was missing until he was long gone. It involved the maximum planning, the rush of the actual taking of the money, and the minimum risk.

The burglary netted Harry eleven thousand two hundred and sixty three dollars. At the time, he worked for a major security company. It had been easy enough to disable the pawn shop's alarm, enter, open the safe and take the cash. He left ten times that amount in gold and jewelry. Cash was king.

A week later he heard that a high school friend had been murdered in prison because he disrespected an inmate. That news struck a chord within Harry. His friend had been a tough guy, a state champion boxer, able to defend himself against all comers. If he couldn't survive in prison, what chance did Harry have if he was sent away?

Another week passed. His girlfriend left him and he didn't get the promotion he'd wanted. With nothing to keep him there he used his money to move to California and eventually become a boring, unchallenged cop. And now here he was, standing at the smoking remains of a beautiful vampire's house and wondering, with barely suppressed anticipation, what the hell would happen next.

"Detective Frazer, there's a woman here to see you," a deputy said.

*Justine!* Harry looked toward the yellow tape across the driveway.

The woman wore a cap, sunglasses and a hooded jacket with the hood up. It took Harry a few seconds to recognize Teresa. "Mrs. Diaz, what are you doing here?"

"I came to help Justine. I couldn't stay hiding up there while she went through whatever she's going through. What happened here? Is Justine all right?"

The fire inspector called out, "Detective, you can see the bones now."

Teresa grabbed Harry's arm." Bones? What bones? Are they Justine's?"

Harry gently removed her hand. "No." He moved toward the house. Teresa followed.

"Detective...Harry, whose bones are they?"

"I have no idea. You shouldn't be here."

"Miguel and the kids are safe in the woods, communing with nature. I'm her best friend."

They followed the inspector to the near corner of the house. They stepped over water puddles and broken glass onto scorched carpet. Harry noticed that most of the glass was on the carpet, not outside.

"Right here." The man pointed to a pile of soaked, black debris.

The skeleton sprawled face down, one arm stretched out ahead, the other bent under. Traces of dust outlined where the hands should be and the back of the skull was burned away. Tattered remnants of seared clothing hung from ribs and hips.

"It's weird," the inspector said. "I've seen bodies burned in fires like this. There's always flesh on the bones, especially underneath. There's nothing on this one."

"Yeah, weird," Harry said. "Any ideas how it started?"

"Best guess, unofficially, someone broke the window, poured gasoline in and lit it up. Probably bashed this guy's head in, figured to burn the evidence. Anyway, it's all yours now."

The inspector went away as Harry squatted beside the bones. On closer examination, the jaws were wide open, as if screaming. Harry poked an arm bone with a pen. It disintegrated into a fine dust.

Teresa looked at the sun above the trees, shining on the skeleton. "It's been in the sun."

Harry stood up. "The forensics team is going to have fun with this. I think there was another one in the car."

"Was it...?"

"No."

"How do you know that?"

"I saw her last night, after the fire."

"Oh God, did she say what happened?"

"No. Come on. This is a crime scene now. You shouldn't be here."

∾—∾

"You don't really think this Sinakov is still after me, do you?" Teresa asked as Harry joined her in her garage. "What's the point?"

"Justine backs off or you die."

"Justine is not going to back off for me. Maybe before she was changed—"

"If she was changed. I'm not totally convinced she was." *Liar.* "Here, I'll get that." He lifted a ladder hanging from hooks on the wall.

"You said she didn't have a heartbeat. I'll get the door."

"Not that I could detect. Where was, is, it? About here?"

"*Si, si,* here. I'm sure you spent plenty of time searching for it, her heartbeat."

"No comment. Hold this."

"Even before she became a vampire, you two were a very unlikely couple. Now that she is, it's more strange. Not that you aren't a nice guy, maybe even a good guy, but what do you see in each other?"

Harry paused at the top of the ladder leaning against the patio cover at the back of Teresa's house. "We see ourselves."

"You will have to explain that to me sometime. Is there anything there?"

Harry picked up some tan colored dust wind swept into a corner. "Dust, like fine sand."

"Like at the fire?"

"Yeah." He put as much of the dust as he could into a plastic baggie, then climbed down and picked up the ladder.

Teresa opened the garage door for him. "So the bones in the house were vampire bones. You said there might be another in the car. So do you think Justine killed them, if that's the word?"

Harry hung up the ladder and they returned to the house. "I do."

"Why would she do that?" Teresa filled up a small watering can and moved about the house watering flowers and plants.

Harry sat on a stool in the kitchen. "Self defense, most likely."

"Why would other vampires attack her. Isn't she one of them now?"

"Vampires are just like people, they don't like outsiders killing their own, no matter what they've done."

"So you are a vampire expert now?"

Harry shrugged. "I've been reading up. Except for being dead, they're just like people."

"They'd probably be easier to handle if they were just crazed blood-suckers."

Teresa came into the kitchen to refill the can. "You think this Sinakov knows about Justine and is sending his...whatevers after her to stop her from killing the men who murdered Brittany?" Harry nodded. "At least he defends his own," Teresa said. "Even if he is a scumbag, murdering, raping, sorry ass, son of a bitch. That's more than some do. So do you know where the asshole lives?"

"I think I do."

"What? Where?"

"Rancho Santa Fe."

Teresa stared at him.

"What I don't know is where Justine is staying."

Teresa stopped by the door. "She's probably with Simone."

Harry followed her out of the kitchen. "Who's Simone?"

Carrying the watering can upstairs, she said, "She's the one who changed her."

"Was that the woman who took Justine away at the bar?"

"Yes."

Harry followed her from room to room. "Where does she live?"

"I don't know."

"What's her last name?"

"I don't remember. She's French. Begins with a G."

Harry punched a speed dial number on his cell phone. "Gurvitz, I need you to find a woman for me." He listened for a moment. "Very funny." They spoke for a minute and Harry rang off. To Teresa he said, "You should go back to your family."

"No," Teresa said. "I'm staying here to help Justine any way I can. They won't miss me. They have trees."

"Someday you'll have to explain to me what that means. Where are you going to stay?"

"Here. I'm not in danger any more, am I?"

"I haven't a clue, so you're not staying here."

# Chapter Twenty-seven

Y ou're making a hell of a mistake," Latch Standard said through the
cloth bag over his head.

"Not as big as the mistake you already made," Simone said, pushing
him through the back door of the house where Brittany was murdered.
The finish of the house was almost done—some paint and fixtures were
all it needed. Part of the decor was an open beam spanning the space.
Simone helped Justine tie Standard's wrists to the beam with heavy
rope. Standard fought for release. He was strong, but no match for the
two vampires.

Simone removed the bag covering his head. Justine regarded him
with anticipation and dread. She had looked forward to this time. Now
that it had arrived she wasn't sure she could do what needed to be done.
She flipped open her knife. Barely thinking about what she did, not
looking in his eyes, she cut his clothes off.

Standard hissed as he endured the lacerations left by Justine's knife.
He glared at the two women, fear behind bravado.

"You're new blood, aren't you?" he said to Justine, making "new
blood" an insult. "Your mind hasn't changed all the way yet. You'll find
it ain't so easy to murder a mortal who can't fight back, can't run."

Standard said exactly what Justine was thinking. In many ways she
still thought like a mortal. It was one thing to kill attacking vampires,
or attacking mortals. Quite another to murder a helpless man, no matter
what his crime.

Simone stepped into the growing silence. She tapped his knees with
a length of pipe. "She may or may not kill you, mortal, but I am old
blood. I will kill you, fast or slow, whichever way you prefer." She stood
square in front of him. He wouldn't connect with her eyes. "Look at
me."

Standard glanced at her.

"Look at me." When he would not she forced his head up with the
end of the pipe. Once their eyes locked he could not turn away. "Now,
what are you afraid of?"

Neither moved, then Standard's face twisted with fear. He moaned
and tried to back away. Terror distorted his face. Acrid fear sweat rolled
off him. He let out a strangled scream and begged for mercy. His back
arched, his body stiffened, and he shook as if shocked.

Then, as if the current was shut off, he went limp, supported only by the ropes. Simone walked away. He sucked in deep gulps of air and finally found his feet.

Simone faced him again. "Tell us what we want to know or I will put you in that place forever. Do you comprehend?" She grabbed his face and held it inches from her own. He gasped and uttered a low pleading moan.

Simone let go, gave him half a minute to gather himself, and asked, "What is Sinakov's name?" She poked him with the pipe.

"Stephan."

Simone shook her head. "That is not possible."

"Stephan," he repeated.

Glad to have a distraction from her embarrassing hesitation earlier, Justine said, "It must be another Stephan Sinakov."

Simone said, "No. Vampires never take a name already used in the Family. Especially the Master. Especially the name Stephan Sinakov."

"Why?"

"The other Families hated him." Simone stared into Justine's eyes, seeing the past. "They also feared him."

"So maybe this one wants to be feared, also?"

Simone nodded, then asked Standard, "What does he look like?"

He dared to glare at her. "Like you, only starving."

"What the hell does that mean?" Justin asked.

"Same face. Beautiful." He looked away as if embarrassed.

Simone frowned, thinking hard.

Justine asked, "Does it really matter now?"

"At this moment, no," Simone said, distracted.

"Good." Justine strode up to Standard and punched him in the stomach. The air whooshed out of him. He wheezed, trying to suck it back.

While Simone put fear in him, Justine stood back and looked him over. He was a big man, not tall, but broad and muscled, with curly, black hair on his arms and chest. Even though he hung naked and scared from the ceiling, she saw that he was well endowed.

This put her imagination into vampire overdrive. She imagined his hands on Brittany, squeezing and rubbing and probing her soft flesh. She imagined Brittany's fear, her powerlessness...imagined that coarse black hair against young breasts...imagined her pain and humiliation as he forced himself into her...imagined him watching her be gutted like a dead animal.

The cold anger she had lost earlier returned. It flooded through her body. Her chest tightened around it, nurtured it, contained it, prevented Justine from slicing and ripping him to shreds in uncontrolled rage.

She forced his head back, making him look at her. "I want to know what happened to my daughter the night you and Westly and Dunham and Sinakov raped and murdered her. I want to know what you did to her."

"You don't scare me, New Blood."

"But I do," Simone said from behind Justine.

He tried to look away. Justine held his head up, forcing him to look at Simone. His body jerked and trembled, then sagged against the ropes. Breathing hard, he closed his eyes and nodded once.

"Why her?" Justine asked.

He got his legs under him and shrugged. "Sinakov ordered us to take her, or a girl like her."

"Why?"

"I don't know. Not for sure." To end his silence, Simone lightly tapped his head with the pipe. "I think he sends them someplace. Sells them, I think."

Justine muttered, "Bastards." Then, struggling to control herself, she said, "You were going to sell my daughter. Why didn't you?"

"We'd been drinking, doing coke. The girl was fighting and Westly went off on her. The fucker went nuts when he did coke. He did her in the van then we went to the house."

Justine pressed the tip of her knife into Standard's belly. "Then what?"

"Then nothing."

"Was Sinakov there?"

Standard glared at her and looked away.

The hiss of the air she sucked in to calm herself echoed in the empty space. It was all she could do not to yank his heart out and rip his head off. But then she wouldn't know what happened. She needed the details to continually fuel her quest for revenge. They gave her a reason for what she had done, what she had given up and what she was going to do.

Simone grabbed his head and pushed his eyes open with her thumbs. "What are you still afraid of?"

His body began to shake, and he tried to curl into a ball even though he hung from a beam. He managed to moan, "No, don't," before his jaw locked open in a silent scream.

"Was Sinakov there?" Justine repeated.

Simone let him go. When he caught his breath, he said, "He came later. He was pissed off, said she was damaged goods."

Her knife flashed out, then stopped a fraction of an inch from puncturing his neck. *Wait,* she told herself. *Wait.* She saw in Standard's eyes that he knew how close to dying he had come. Through clenched teeth, she said, "Then?"

Standard spoke in a rush, as if hurrying past a graveyard. "He made us tie her to the wall. He said some shit about getting power from sweet blood. Then he cut her open and drank the blood from his hands. That was fucking nasty, man. I about puked at that shit."

Justine felt a deathly cold come over her. "So you're a good guy because you almost puked?"

"Fuck you. Sinakov is pissed you're fucking with his people. Let me go and I won't say anything about this."

"And what about justice for what you did?"

"Fuck justice. And fuck you, mom. And fuck your daughter, too. Again. She loved it, you know. Three guys, one after another. The little slut wanted it."

"Shut up you scumbag liar. She was a good girl."

"Ahh, the mother is always the last to know. She was a good fuck. And we fucked her good. And she loved it."

"Shut up!" The knife shook in her hand. "Shut up!" Justine rushed him.

"No!" Simone reached out to stop her. Too late.

Justine slammed her blade into Standard and in one quick motion sliced him open. He had time to utter five words: "See you again, New Blood."

"No, you won't." Simone held up a small, red gas can where he could see it.

His eyes grew wide as he realized what it meant. He would not be resurrected.

Justine felt his heart beat for the last time when she gripped it in her hand and yanked it out. The heart was hot and sticky. Blood drained from the shredded aorta. Two feelings rose within her: Hunger and revulsion. Both rolled out from the pit of her stomach in a hot wave. The tangy odor of fresh blood drew up the Hunger and put pressure on her fangs. Residual mortal guilt—she had just murdered a man—pushed away the revulsion that made even the idea of drinking blood turn her stomach. Indecision swirled the two feelings in her head.

Simone pressed against Justine's back, arms circling her waist, pulling the new vampire against her. Into Justine's ear she said, "You are Vampire now. You made the kill, you must taste the blood."

Justine resisted for a moment. Simone was right. She was a vampire now, not mortal, not human. She needed blood, and she had gained a small measure of her revenge. Why not drink his blood?

Head back, touching Simone, she raised the heart and let the still warm fluid run into her mouth. Yes, *yes,* the metallic tang flowed over her tongue, washing any guilt down her throat. He had killed first. She was Vampire. She deserved his blood.

Justine spun around in Simone's arms and held up the heart. Simone

# David Burton

tilted her head back. Justine squeezed fresh blood into Simone's mouth. When the heart was empty, she let it slip from her hand.

Simone wiped blood from Justine's cheek and sucked it from her fingers. Moving close, she licked blood from the other cheek, then the chin, then the corners of the mouth. Driven by the rush of fresh blood, revenge, and Simone's touch, and unwilling to confront the conflicting desires her new existence presented, Justine returned the favor. Kisses and hands began to wander. Clothes began to fall. For the first time Justine experienced the full pleasures of vampire sex with her senses wide open and without having to hold back in any way.

For a half hour she did not think of Harry at all.

# Chapter Twenty-eight

Simone drove while Justine reclined in the passenger seat, attempting, with little success, to keep her mind blank. Brittany's murder, Standard's murder, satisfaction that she had completed half of her vengeful quest, thoughts about what lay ahead, and sex, all vied for brain time. She didn't want to think about anything.

They had returned the Cadillac Simone had stolen—she had a way with cars—to the spot where they'd taken it. Justine felt Simone glance at her every minute or so. At a stoplight, Justine allowed her head to roll to the left. "What?"

Simone opened her mouth to speak, then thought better of whatever she intended to say. *"C'est rien."*

Justine knew it wasn't "nothing," but had no desire to push it.

She gave up trying to shut out all the thoughts she didn't want to deal with. Instead she allowed them free rein. They formed a sort of white noise she could easily ignore. With her eyes closed, she almost missed it when Simone said under her breath, *"Merde,"* and stopped abruptly.

Something in the way she said it brought Justine to full alert. They had stopped just inside the opening in the stucco wall surrounding Simone's property.

"What?" Justine asked.

Simone pointed to a car parked by the stone walk to the front door. The driver's door opened. Justine caught her breath when she recognized Harry. A woman got out the other side and walked around to stand by him.

"Oh my God." Justine jumped out of the car and ran to meet Teresa. They met halfway and embraced, hard and long, Justine mindful not to hurt her friend.

Simone drove into the garage then walked over to Harry. Justine and Teresa loosened their hug to watch them.

They stood five feet apart, neither offering a hand, taking the measure of each other.

Simone broke the silence. "You must be Detective Harry Frazer."

"You must be Simone Gireaux."

Simone raised an eyebrow at that. "How did you find this place?"

"Teresa knew your first name, that you were French, and thought you lived in Carlsbad. The rest was easy."

# David Burton

"Ah, yes, you are, after all, a detective."

"Yes, I am. A homicide detective."

"Homicide? Are you here looking for murder suspects?"

"Yes. A man named Sinakov. Do you know him?"

Simone tensed at Sinakov's name. After a long glance at Justine and Teresa, she said, "I may have heard of him."

Justine stepped forward. "Maybe we should go inside and talk about this."

∾—∾

Inside, Simone stopped and swiveled her head, sniffing the air. "You have been inside this house, Detective."

"Me?" Harry said, his expression neutral and his tone one of wounded innocence. "You have a very good security system. How could I?"

Simone regarded him with wry amusement. "I hope none of my underwear is missing."

"I'm sure your underwear is safe."

"Oh, it is, Detective. Did you find anything interesting?"

"Is there anything interesting to find?"

Simone took Harry's arm. "Ah, Monsieur Harry, do not insult me." She lead him into the house.

Justine was glad Teresa was with her, an old friend who knew her before her two new acquaintances, friends, lovers, or whatever they were. Walking into the house, Teresa had taken her arm and asked, "Are you really a...? You look the same."

"Yes, I have been changed. I'm so glad you're here, but you shouldn't be. What about Miguel and the kids?"

Teresa lowered her head. "They'll get along without me. I came here to help you with your quest, if I can. Harry did, too, I think. Justine, what have you done? I don't want to believe that you...what I've seen...I saw your house, there were some bones..."

"The bones I can explain. Otherwise it's best you don't know."

In the formal living room, they settled into plush leather furniture, Simone and Harry on opposite sides of a coffee table, openly studying each other. Justine and Teresa sat on a matching couch with their legs curled under them as they had many times before. The tension in the room was thick enough to take a bite from.

Simone, all amusement gone from her face, asked Harry, "How do you know of Sinakov?"

"A friend who seems to know a lot about vampires loaned me a book. I read all about Stephan Sinakov and his Family. Not very nice people."

Simone leaned forward in her seat, her eyes glistening with excitement. "What book is this?"

# Blood Justice

*"Blood Relations: A History of the Great Vampire Families,* by Dague Marchette. You know this book?"

After a long reflection, Simone said, "Dague Marchette was the last of a small, but respected, Vampire Family. They were scholars, not fighters, and only lasted three centuries. The book is very rare, only twenty-seven copies ever existed. Only the Master of a Family may possess one. Perhaps it was a copy you read?"

"It looked and felt old," Harry said. "Dark blue, cloth binding, held together by a gold cord."

Simone shook her head, eyes darting about the room. Her laced fingers wouldn't lie still. Her words were fast and insistent. "Your friend is a Master, then?"

"I've known him for ten years. I don't think so."

"He is mortal?"

"As far as I know."

She jumped to her feet. "That cannot be. I must see this book and meet this man. What is his name?"

"I'll ask him if he wants to meet you and—"

Simone took three strides around the coffee table, grabbed Harry's face and looked deep into his eyes. Teresa leaped up to intervene. Justine firmly held her back.

"Tell me the name of the book's owner."

Harry had no choice but to answer. "Darwin Rubinio."

Stunned by what she heard, Simone let him go and stared into the distance. "Rubinio. The lost Family. Here?"

"What are you talking about?" Justine asked.

Harry leaped to his feet, fists tight at his side. "Simone." Simone continued her vacant stare into some long past time the others couldn't conceive. "Simone!" The hard edge of Harry's fury cut through to her. She blinked. A little shiver ran over her and she turned to face Harry.

Every word Harry uttered was chipped from anger. "Don't ever do that again."

Simone was a statue.

Harry got right in her face. "Say it. You will never fuck with my mind again." Simone raised one eyebrow as if a harmless pet had threatened to rip her to shreds. "Stay out of my mind." Harry turned to Justine. "If you want my help, she'd better say it." Back to Simone. "And mean it."

"Do not threaten me, mortal."

"Simone. Please." Justine touched her shoulder.

After a long pause Simone relented. "As you say, Justine. For you."

Harry nodded his acceptance, and the tension drained from the room.

Teresa said, "You mentioned the Lost Family. What does that mean?"

Simone rubbed her eyes with her fingertips then dropped into her chair, hands hanging limp over the armrests.

"There were once twenty-seven Families. Now there are twenty-four. The Marchettes are gone, as are the Drakes. The Drakes were brutes, barely civilized. They hunted Vampire and mortal alike. The Families hunted them down and destroyed them.

"The Rubinios were similar to the Marchettes. They were mostly traders, businessmen, money men. Their crimes were more under the table, as you say. Finally, they stole too much. The Families destroyed many, but the leaders, twenty of them, vanished. With their money."

"When was this?" Harry asked, interested despite their earlier confrontation.

"Eighteen-fifty."

"Did you know any of them?"

Simone frowned and nodded. "The Master and his Family. The mother was caught. The father, son and daughter disappeared."

Justine said, "You think Darwin is the father. Is that good or bad?"

"I knew him as Darius. It might be good for you. The Rubinios had no love for the Sinakovs, except their money." She gave Harry a meaningful look. "Also, their control of mortals and vampires is stronger than mine. Another reason they were exterminated. He may be able to force Sinakov to surrender to you. Although with age we learn defenses."

Harry studied Justine. "And what would you do to Sinakov if he surrendered to you?"

Justine caught his gaze and held it. "You saw first-hand what he did to my daughter. He deserves no less."

Harry's lips pressed into a frown. "And Dunham and Standard?"

Neither Justine nor Simone moved as their eyes held a complex conversation.

Harry's cell phone broke the silence. His expression grew darker as he listened. He glared at Justine and Simone. "I guess that answered my question," he said, reaching for his coat. "They found an unidentified body in the same place your daughter was found. He was gutted and decapitated, both heart and head were burned. It's not much of a guess to say it was Latch Standard."

The two women vampires kept their expressions neutral and said nothing.

Harry shrugged into his coat and eyed the two. The tightness of his face expressed the conflicting emotions he felt. "Do you realize the untenable position you've put me in? Christ. I don't know where to start not investigating a murder when I already know who did it and why, without humiliating myself and the Sheriff's Department." He took a few steps toward the door then turned back. "Do me two favors. If you run into Dunham, at least hide the body. And don't go see Darwin without me. Teresa, do you want a ride back to my place?"

With one quizzical eyebrow raised, Teresa looked to Simone.

"She may stay here. There is much room." When concern crossed his face, she added, "Do not worry, I will not change her."

"Don't worry, Harry. I will be as safe here as anyplace."

Not happy, he spared each of them a stern warning glance. "Come and get your stuff from the car."

"I'll get it." Justine quickly took Harry's hand and led him out of the room.

Standing awkwardly by the car as Harry pulled out Teresa's suitcase and backpack, Justine said, "I'm sorry things are difficult for you at work."

Harry set the suitcase and pack on the ground. "Not just at work. You can't go around killing people, Justine. Being what you seem to be is not a license for murder."

"I've lost too much to stop now. Will I lose you, too?"

"I should arrest you both."

"Do you think that will make a difference?"

"Dunham might die on his own. You can go after this Sinakov after I retire."

"What about all the girls taken between now and then?"

Harry's eyes narrowed. "What girls?"

"Simone said the Sinakov Family has always been in the slave business. It might be that Brittany was taken to be sold, but something went wrong and she was…" Justine waved a hand in a frustrated gesture, unable to say any more.

"It might be?" Harry said, throwing his hands up. "You're saying this guy is in the white slavery business? Isn't that a little convenient? I mention arresting you and all of a sudden the guy you're after is a slave trader so I shouldn't mess with you?"

"It's not convenient. I don't know if it's true. But Brittany was not taken just for a random rape and murder. She was taken for a reason. What if I'm right? Haven't there been a lot of girls gone missing in the last few years?"

Harry's arms flopped at his side. "Justine, I'm not a missing persons expert. I don't have time to get into that right now."

"Tell Teresa that."

"Why?"

"Because her daughter went missing almost four months ago. She's still missing."

"Oh, shit. She hasn't said anything."

"She doesn't talk about it, but she hasn't forgotten. When she hears of this possibility, she'll want to get into it."

Harry jammed his hands in his pockets and walked in quick little circles. "You said you were sorry I was having trouble at work." He stopped walking. "Look, don't do anything until we talk about this. Stay here until at least tomorrow night. Okay? Please." He got in his car.

"Okay. But we need your help finding Sinakov."

"No problem," he said through his window. "I already know where he lives."

He drove off, leaving Justine to stare after him.

# Chapter Twenty-nine

Justine helped Teresa sit. "I need a drink," Teresa said. She covered her face with her hands. She forgot to breathe. *"Dios,* she could still be alive."

Teresa felt Justine kneel before her and the comforting touch of her hands. "It's a possibility," Justine said. "But she might be anywhere. You shouldn't get your hopes too high."

Teresa raised her head. Justine wiped the tears away with her thumbs. "Hope is better than the pain I've been in," Teresa said. She looked at the other women. "Help me find my daughter. I will help you in any way I can. Kill those bastards with my bare hands if I have to."

Simone said, "I suspect our searches will lead us to the same place."

"Of course we will help," Justine said.

"I need a drink," Teresa said.

❧ — ❦

It was a normal weekday night at the Sundowner, a good crowd, but with room to move. Justine checked out Harry's usual seat as soon as she stepped through the door. He wasn't there, of course, because he was at the crime scene, her crime scene, and would be for hours. At the other end of the bar, Darwin occupied his usual place. Justine hesitated. She had promised Harry they wouldn't talk to Darwin without him. However, they hadn't come to see the old man, they had come for a drink.

"That's Darwin," Justine said to Simone.

Simone studied him. *"Mon Dieu,"* she said softly, and quickly turned away.

"That's him, isn't it?" Teresa said.

To Justine, Simone said, "Speak to him, bring him to the house." She handed over her car keys and moved toward the door.

"Where are you going? How will you get back?"

"Tell him what you must, but bring him. In public is not the place for this reunion." She pushed through the crowd and out the door.

Justine attempted to sense the other vampire. No mystic feeling came that would identify Darwin as other than a scruffy old man. The lack of that ability frustrated her. Control of speed and strength and the five senses had been gained quickly, so why not the capability to know when another of her own kind was close? She could barely tell

❧— 133 —❦

when Simone entered a room in her house. "You cannot expect to have centuries of abilities when you are new blood," Simone had told her. "Patience." Screw patience.

Darwin hunched over his beer, seeming to ignore everything around him. Justine moved toward him, wondering if she was doing it because she wanted to, or because somebody was forcing her. Teresa, lost in her own hopeful misery, followed.

Justine sat on the stool beside Darwin with Teresa next to her. Bayley brought beers without being asked. Teresa drained half her mug, and frowned into the rest. Justine drank, and caught her breath.

She felt something—or not so much felt as became aware of a presence to her right. She looked left and scanned the others at the bar. The awareness continued to indicate something next to her, where Darwin sat, no matter which direction she faced. It creeped her out, and also excited her. Some of the abilities that Simone took for granted were beginning to manifest in her.

Softly she said, "You are Darius Rubinio."

She sensed something then that made her hunch her shoulders and try to inspect the bar without moving her head: a sense of lurking danger ready to strike.

"I am Darwin. Only Darwin. Always act as if someone is watching. It will keep you safer."

The sense of danger vanished. But she got the point: vigilance as well as patience. The crash of a breaking glass gave her an excuse to look behind her. Was the couple sitting in the corner paying too much attention to her? Or the two guys leaning against the wall? Or the woman down the bar checking her watch again? She got no feeling that anyone in the place was other than what they appeared to be.

Darwin said, "You have been changed since we met last."

Justine nodded.

"Simone Gireaux changed you?"

"Yes. Do you know her?"

He smiled. "It has been many years since we last met. She was a good friend to my Family."

"She said you disappeared with some others. Are they here, with you?"

"Alas, no. They are all gone. The Sinakovs are relentless hunters."

"The Sinakovs?" Her hands shook as they tightened around her glass. "They are here, in the area. Stephan Sinakov murdered my daughter."

Darwin laid a gentle hand on her arm. "Be careful. If that glass breaks you will draw attention. It is usually best to remain inconspicuous."

Justine flexed her hands on her lap while forcing herself to calm

# Blood Justice

down.

Darwin finished his beer. "Perhaps we can help one another."

"How so?"

"You want to kill Stephan Sinakov. He wants to kill me."

"I thought you could control other…others like yourself."

"It is true what you say, though the Sinakov Family least of all. And this Stephan, the least of them."

# Chapter Thirty

Harry slept in his office for a couple of hours around dawn. He had put out of his mind the fact that he knew who the killer was and proceeded as usual. The crime scene had been closed to all except those absolutely necessary. The media knew only that an unidentified body had been found.

Fortified with a large black coffee and a stale bagel, he found the missing persons file of Teresa's daughter, Antonia. Harry discovered no new insights. The girl, fifteen, had been snatched right off the street. The only witness remembered nothing. Antonia vanished, without a trace.

Gurvitz, who apparently needed no sleep, returned from the crime scene. Harry returned to his sham investigation and assigned Gurvitz to the type of assignment he reveled in, assessing missing persons data.

By five that afternoon, Harry had had it. Standard had been identified, all relevant people notified. Standard's girlfriend turned out to be more of an acquaintance. She said she wasn't surprised he was murdered. He'd been hanging out with some very secretive people, none of whom she could identify. He had told her his new boss was into some nasty, but profitable, shit. If he proved loyal, he'd have money and a long life to enjoy it—an offer hard to resist.

Others in the Sheriff's department were doing the leg work, rounding up the usual suspects, canvassing, interrogating, perusing forensic evidence. All useless endeavors, so Harry went home.

He showered, dressed in jeans and a long-sleeved T-shirt and ate a microwave meal while watching late-breaking news on TV. The latest discussions, deaths, bombings, and bickerings about the world didn't hold his interest. What to do about Justine and Simone did.

He should arrest them. Assuming they allowed themselves to be arrested, surely somebody would realize they had no heartbeat, didn't need to breathe or eat, were burned by the sun, didn't age, and had extraordinary senses and strength. What would happen if the general public found out that vampires—quite a few of them, apparently—really did exist? Panic, and a lot of innocent people staked, decapitated, burned and otherwise dispatched by fear-blinded people who would rather strike first, then determine if they had just cause.

If the government got to them, they'd disappear into a cell in some secret laboratory where they'd be subjected to endless experiments on how to keep those in power alive, and in control of their power, forever—or how to make weapons out of them.

# Blood Justice

The fact that he was attracted against all reason to Justine only complicated the matter. He'd been an honest, dedicated cop for eighteen years. Aside from his early, short-lived career choice, he'd never considered being anything else. With his integrity at risk, he considered it now. What would he be, a vampire hunter, vampire protector, vampire boy/old man toy? Maybe sit on his Lazy Boy and drink himself into oblivion?

"Fuck!" He clicked off the TV and slammed back the recliner. None of those options sounded the least bit appealing. On the other hand, if this Sinakov was involved with the missing girls, Justine and Simone were aiding law enforcement to catch a foul criminal. That was surely worth a consideration of amnesty—the greater good and all that.

A scream outside jerked him back to the reality of now.

A familiar voice shouted, "Sheriff's department. Stop there. Let her go."

Harry grabbed his gun and ran to the door.

"I said stop. I will shoot."

Two shots sounded.

Harry yanked open the door. Gun two-handed, he stepped out. To his left a man carrying a woman over his shoulder and a machete in his hand started down the stairs. He recognized the woman as Bayley's partner, Susan. Harry knew her as a fighter. Her long, dark hair swirled as she thrashed to no avail against the arm holding her.

Harry reached the top of the stairs. He had a second to assess the situation. The man carrying Susan was halfway down the stairs. A full-sized Hummer idled at the bottom. By the open back door, a woman held her side as if she'd been hurt. A man's body lay crumpled on the narrow strip of grass between the building and the sidewalk. File folders leaked papers by an outstretched hand. A streetlight illuminated the pale young face of Junior Detective Gurvitz.

"Sheriff's Department. Stop!" Harry knew damn well the man on the stairs wasn't going to stop. So he shot him three times. Two shots smacked the man's head. One went through the top of his shoulder after it creased Susan's arm.

The vampire stumbled against the railing. Susan slid out of his grip over the rail. She grabbed the rail, slipped, and fell eight feet to the ground. Even with the gunshots still in his ears, Harry heard the crack of breaking bone. The vampire sprawled twitching at the foot of the stairs.

Harry took two steps down, hoping someone had called 911. Though he held the high ground, he doubted he had control of the situation. He knew he didn't when the passenger window slid down and a hand holding a big gun pointed at him came out. The female vampire also drew a gun which she kept pointed at him while she stuffed her fellow wounded vampire into the vehicle.

*Okay, that's fine, take your wounded and get out of here,* Harry thought. They didn't shoot, so neither did he. But when she went for Susan he couldn't allow that. "No. You don't get to take her."

The woman ignored him. He shot her leg. She stumbled, but reached for Susan without looking up.

"Leave her, God damn it."

Before Harry could fire again the gun at the window fired. The slug smacked the wall behind him, stinging him with stucco chunks. He almost shot blind, but held up for fear of hitting Susan. Another shot from the window grazed his ribs. He sat down hard on the steps.

Doors thunked. Harry pushed the pain away and rushed down the steps. The Hummer sped away. Harry hesitated only a second over Gurvitz. Close up, the young detective's head was almost totally severed. "I'm sorry, Paul," he said as he snatched up the files. He then ran to the back of the building, jumped in his Mustang and raced after the Hummer.

A block up the street he turned left in time to see the Hummer turn right onto a narrow residential street. In three short blocks he fishtailed around the corner while he fumbled with his cell phone. The big vehicle was a block away. Harry floored it. He blasted through a stop light and quickly caught up with the Hummer. Too quick! Its brake lights flashed. Harry hit his brakes, jerking the wheel left, then right. The end of the Hummer's bumper creased the Mustang's fender. Harry sideswiped a parked car, crunching the left front fender, before he lurched to a stop.

As soon as he stopped, the Hummer's engine raced. It came right for him. It could easily roll over the car, crushing it and him. In an instant he was transformed from hunter to prey.

Inches from the big wheels, Harry surged away. As he steered into the first turn he realized the car didn't handle correctly. The left front tire rubbed on the mangled fender. He heard sirens, but drove away from them. He had no doubt cops would die if they attempted to take these vampires into custody.

He hit speed dial on his cell. His call was answered on the second ring. "Justine, I have a Hummer full of vampires chasing me. They've kidnapped a friend of mine. Tell me some magic way to beat them."

A minute later Harry had pulled almost a block ahead of his pursuers. Even a Hummer had to avoid hitting a bus. The tang of burnt rubber assaulted his nose as he cranked hard on the wheel to enter the alley leading to Darwin's clandestine home.

The main garage door rose just enough for his windshield to clear. He slammed on the brakes and the door rumbled shut behind him.

# Chapter Thirty-one

The Hummer came full speed through the alley into the enclosed space, bounded by bare walls, behind the garage. It screeched to a stop in front of the garage door. There was no other outlet and no Mustang.

Justine crouched behind a dumpster on the right side of the alley. She held her knife and what Darwin called *Uno Cutaso de Extem*, a blade of extermination. Justine thought of it as a fancy machete, shiny, with one eighteen inch edge and half of the other razor sharp. On the other side of the alley, Simone was armed with two of the fancy blades. Darwin told her they were originally for ceremonial use, but they also worked damn well for real.

For the first time Justine became aware of the presence of other vampires, and a mortal. The mortal's fear came to her almost as an acrid odor. Her fear was justified, Justine thought.

Nothing happened. Nothing moved. The vehicle could not be allowed to leave with Harry's friend. Justine's hands flexed on the hilts of her weapons. Why didn't they do something?

The door beside the garage rollup slammed open and Harry ran out. He stopped when he saw the Hummer, stared at it for a couple of seconds and ran back through the door.

Then things started happening.

The Hummer's two front doors swung open and two male vampires jumped out fast. Justine and Simone attacked them at full vampire speed.

One black, one white, both vampires were well muscled and mature when they were changed. Neither mortals nor young bloods, they were experienced, alert and armed with guns on their hips and machetes in their hands.

Justine swung at Black. He easily blocked her long blade, spun, and kicked the back of her knees. Her legs folded. She tried to spin back to her feet, but had to duck to avoid his horizontal strike that would have taken her head off. A kick in the ribs sent her rolling on to her back. Then he was on her, a foot on her right hand that held the *cutaso*, a knee on her chest.

Dazed, she watched him grasp his long knife at the ends and raise it up to chop down on her neck. Then he hesitated, a confused look in his eyes. That gave Justine her chance. She plunged her knife into his ribs, once, twice, three times, then straight up into his upper arm. He jerked away. Justine heaved her body up, rolled from under him and spun to her feet. With Black on his knees before her, she lifted the *cutaso* to decapitate him.

"Justine, behind you!"

She tried to look behind, but her arm was grabbed tight and bent back. A female vampire had control of her. Out of the corner of her eye Justine saw a flash of motion.

*Teresa!* With a tire iron and a bleeding cut on her cheek. She whacked the vamp on the shoulders, neck and head.

Justine twisted free, turned and jammed her knife into the woman's neck, slicing through all but the spine. She finished the job with the *cutaso.*

Teresa yelled again, "Look out," and flung the iron. Justine swiveled her head to see Black, behind her, swat away the iron, then she followed with a round house backhand strike of the *cutaso.* Black's head stayed balanced on his neck for several seconds before tumbling to the ground.

That's when a second SUV appeared.

∾—∾

The Hummer didn't move. Harry knew that if the vampires inside decided to leave, Justine and Simone might not be able to stop them. Even as he did it, he thought showing himself to lure them out was a stupid idea. Before he ran back, he glimpsed Darwin in the shadow of his doorway. Harry wondered whose idea showing himself really was.

The Hummer blocked Justine's attack from his sight. Simone's fight awed him. They moved faster than he could follow, arms, legs and blades a cartoon whirl of motion. Simone led White away from the vehicle.

Harry ran to the big SUV and yanked open the rear side door. At first glance he thought Susan was dead. She lay limp on the back seat, blood dripping from the corner of her mouth. The vampire Harry had shot lay on top of her.

The female vampire had the other side door open. She lunged at Harry, but stopped short when Teresa grabbed her leg and yanked. Faster than his eye could follow the woman slid out and punched Teresa in the face.

*Teresa can take care of herself,* he thought, and yanked on Susan's arms. She screamed when the male vampire with two slugs in his head grabbed her broken leg. Harry drew his gun and smacked the guy's hand. Off balance as Susan tumbled into his arms, they collapsed in a heap, Susan's hiss of pain raw in his ear.

Mindful of her agony he lay Susan on the asphalt. That's when he saw another one of those black, tinted window SUVs rush out of the alley and screech to a halt. The doors swung open and three tough-guy vampires emerged.

Simone also noticed, and White took advantage. He swept her feet out from under her, then punched her head against the ground. Dropping on a knee, he lifted his knife to stab her heart. Like Black, he hesitated. On the edge of Harry's vision, Darwin peered from his door, concentrating on White. *Always good to have someone watching your back.* Harry rolled to his feet and kicked White's head.

Caught off guard, White toppled over. Simone skewered his heart with her knife before he hit the ground. Two seconds later his separated head rolled to a stop against Susan.

Susan screamed.

Harry kicked the head away. The new arrivals meant trouble, so he picked up Susan in hopes of getting her out of harm's way. Then he saw a fourth man emerge from the SUV. Jay Dunham. "Oh, shit."

Justine and Simone, blood spattered and armed, came together and without hesitation advanced on the reinforcements. Justine spied Dunham.

"Shit. Shit. Shit," Harry whispered to the universe. Justine was going to kill Dunham. There was nothing Harry, a dedicated, honorable cop, could do about it. *Walk away, take Susan into Darwin's place and stay there,* Harry told himself. Maybe Dunham was a vampire now, so the woman he was falling in love with wasn't really murdering a mortal, scumbag though he may be. Stay out of sight until it was over. That was his only sane choice.

"Oh, hell." He quickly carried Susan to Darwin and put her in his arms. "Protect her," he said. Then he drew his gun and put his cop face on.

⁂

Blood lust ran hot through Justine. Her body felt like it would explode if she couldn't keep moving, fighting. She was almost happy to see new adversaries arrive. Knife and *cutaso* in hand, Justine marched past Teresa, who leaned on the Hummer, nursing a split lip.

Justine joined Simone. "We have to fight them."

"Yes."

"Then let's do it now."

The three vampires stood ready in front their vehicle. Behind them, a fourth person moved. Jay Dunham. Justin's vision narrowed. She smelled him, heard each of his rapid heartbeats. Her lust for his blood surged through her like a flash fire, and she headed for him. Three male vampires twice her size with ten times her experience were not going to stop her.

"Justine, stop."

"Stay away, Harry."

Harry strode past her toward Dunham, his gun held in both hands. The nearest vampire was too dumbfounded to stop him. He looked at Harry as if he was a stray dog walking obliviously through serious business.

"Jay Dunham, I'm arresting you for the murder of Brittany Kroft."

Dunham was more amused than intimidated. "Stay out of this, Detective. This is Vampire business. Out of your jurisdiction."

Even Harry could tell that Dunham's movements were clumsy compared to a real vampire. "You're still mortal. That makes you my business." He lowered his voice. "Besides, Justine will kill you."

"I don't think so," Dunham said.

Before Harry could move, one of the newly arrived vampires snatched the gun out of his hands, then grabbed him by the scruff of his neck like a naughty puppy.

Justine was as shocked by Harry's bold move as the rest. She knew what he was attempting to do. A wave of affection for the man briefly dulled the hunger for blood seething in her body, even as she knew he would fail. It was not only what Dunham did to Brittany. It was the arrogance of the man to show himself here, and think he would be safe, that kept the hunger barely in check while Harry made his futile, though honorable, attempt to save Dunham's life.

When Dunham laughed at Harry, as he dangled a foot off the ground, the rage for his blood exploded in her head. Justine traded quick glances with Simone. Simone nodded and went after the other new vampires.

Justine attacked the vampire holding Harry with no mercy. She struck out with the *cutaso,* and both Harry and the arm that held him fell to the oil-stained pavement. She jabbed her knife into the vampire's neck, and cut once right, then left. As he fell, a backhand sweep of the *cutaso* finished the decapitation.

A sharp blow knocked her down. Dynamite exploded inside her head. Another blow struck her back. *No.* She wasn't going to let Dunham defeat her, not now. She was so close.

She rolled away and looked up at Dunham. He loomed over her, steel bar raised, frozen. His body vibrated with the effort to move. Justine looked between the vehicles. Simone fought one of the tough guys. Against the wall, Darwin concentrated on Dunham.

"Darwin, let him go. He's mine." Darwin's eyes twitched in her direction. "Let him go."

Darwin shook his head and looked away.

Dunham struck.

# Blood Justice

Justine barely blocked with the *cutaso*. A sweep of her foot knocked him off his feet, but he executed a fancy flip and landed on one bent leg, the other stretched out behind. He struck her thigh with the bar as if playing with her.

Fear flashed through her. He was better than her. What if he beat her? Cut off her head and let it crumble to dust? Then no revenge, and, once again, no justice. She gave up life to gain the power to deliver justice. That was not going to be an empty gesture. He was good, but he was mortal.

The *cutaso* clattered on the asphalt as she grabbed the bar before it shattered her head. Simultaneously, she thrust the knife blade into his leg.

"Ahh." Dunham jumped back, knife still embedded in his calf. Justine tackled him. He went down, but he kicked the side of her knee and jumped up while yanking the blade out. He managed a slice across her ribs. But Justine was ready for him.

A punch in the stomach took the wind out of him. She broke his wrist while taking back the knife. He barely managed a groan. Hand on his neck she slammed him against the SUV then kneed him in the groin for good measure. A red stain formed on his shirt where the knife tip poked his stomach.

"Justine, don't." Harry groaned as Teresa helped him stand. "Let the courts provide the justice you're looking for."

Their eyes met and held. Justine's determination flagged briefly. But justice was her purpose and she would not waver, even for Harry's sad eyed entreaty.

"You know that won't happen," she said. "Do you really think you'd be able to hold him?"

Harry's frown was answer enough.

"Why don't you two go see Darwin?"

Teresa pushed Harry away. Then she stopped and faced Dunham. "Did you take my daughter, Antonia? About four months ago?"

Dunham tensed, his brow wrinkled in thought, then his eyebrows raised.

Teresa ran to him and beat on his chest. "Where is she? What have you done with her? Where is she, you God-damned son of a bitch?"

Justine loosened her grip on his neck.

"I don't know where she is."

"Is she alive?"

"I don't know. Maybe."

"What happened?" Teresa had to gather herself to continue. "What happened after you took her?"

Dunham shrugged. "She went to market. After that...?" Another shrug.

"What market?" Justine asked.

Dunham looked her in the eye. "Pretty young virgins fetch a good price all around the world, from vampire and mortal."

"Oh God." Teresa's hands pressed her chest. "She might be alive?"

Dunham shrugged again.

"How do I find her? Who would know? You?"

"I just find them and take them."

"And rape them." Justine tightened her grip on his throat. "Stephan must have been pissed you spoiled his goods."

"That was Westly." Dunham's voice came out rough as he fought to breathe. "After that, what did it matter?"

"What did it matter? That was my daughter, damn you."

Justine shoved the knife to the hilt in Dunham's belly. Before she could slit him open, things began to happen fast.

Dunham stabbed her between the ribs with his own knife.

To Justine, the blade penetrated her in slow motion, pushing a point of pain deep inside her. The pain vanished when one of the three new vampires slammed into her. Stunned, she landed hard on her back and saw the same vampire grab Teresa.

Harry made a futile attempt to free her. He got his face slapped hard with the gun for his trouble as the vampire dragged Teresa around the front of the vehicle.

Justine leaped to follow. Dunham grabbed her. She responded by slicing his arm, then sweeping the blade against his neck. Then she ran after Teresa.

The vampire opened the driver's door, smacked Teresa's head against the door pillar, stuffed her in ahead of him, got in, slammed the door, started the engine, and with a squeal of tires raced through the alley and onto the street.

Helpless, Justine, and the others watched it happen.

Simon ran to the Hummer and checked inside. "Where are the keys?" In a blur she searched the vampire bodies, but found no keys.

Harry punched numbers on his cell. A possible kidnapping, he told the Sheriff's dispatch. He gave out information on the vehicle and the driver. Armed and extremely dangerous, he told them.

Justine said, "You know they'll never catch him. And if they do, Teresa might die and the cops, too."

"I had to call. He took Teresa."

"But you know where Sinakov lives, do you not?" Simone asked.

"Gurvitz figured it out," Harry said, face tight.

Simone rested a hand on Justine's shoulder. "Then we will bring her back."

Harry stepped up to her. "We will bring her back. They murdered my partner and...Damn, Susan."

Dunham coughed.

Justine and Simone traded glances. Simone took Harry's arm and said to him, "Come Harry, let us see to your friend."

Justine knelt beside Dunham and said, "Blood for blood, sick bastard," then plunged her knife into his heart. Dunham shuddered and exhaled his last breath.

Susan sat by the door to Darwin's lair. Darwin knelt over her. Her eyes were closed and she seemed free of pain. "She'll survive, Harry," he said. "But she may require some explanation."

"Don't we all." Harry surveyed the dead. "Christ, more bodies." They looked down at Dunham who lay on his side in a pool of blood. "This one especially. What the hell kind of story am I going tell about him?"

Justine and Simone nodded to each other. "We can take care of him if you like," Justine said. "No story necessary."

Harry sighed a deep, weary sigh. "I must be mad."

# Chapter Thirty-two

It was well past midnight as Simone looked down from her kitchen at Darius Rubinio. He sat in a leather armchair like an old man, feet flat on the floor, arms flat on the armrests, staring straight ahead. From a generously filled glass, she sipped a superb French Burgundy. She'd resided in America for almost a hundred years, and still had only French wines in her small cellar. Maybe in fifty years the Californians would have a place. Though as she sipped, she had the feeling that this affair of blood justice had more to it than was apparent, and changes were coming in days rather than years.

*Signore* Rubinio—though she was a hundred and seventy years older than he, she couldn't bring herself to call him Darwin, or even Darius— looked old. A young woman, and she had still felt like a young woman at the time, did not call an older man by his given name, especially if he was the Master of the Family. He had attended the Rubinios as a mortal for fifty years. He knew what they were, yet served them well as retainer, daylight protector, and friend, as did his family. When he became sixty he fell ill. As reward for his faithful service he and his wife, two daughters and two sons were brought into the Rubinio Family. Fifty years later he became Master.

Though, like all in the Rubinio Family, he was of a studious bent, at the time Simone knew him he was a vital, energetic man, at the forefront of the Vampire financial universe. He loved his wife, Sophia, but was not above the occasional dalliance. "After all," he explained to Simone, "after a hundred years of marriage one deserves to be assured that he made the right choice." He was well aware that Sophia deserved the same assurance, but he never mentioned it.

Simone smiled, remembering his attempts to dally with her. They had been more for forms' sake than out of any real desire for her. Now he sat quiet like an old mortal, not speaking, not moving, lonely, waiting patiently for death. Simone wanted to know why, and she had other questions, also.

Justine entered the kitchen. She wore baggy sweat pants and a long sleeved T-shirt. Her hair was still damp from the shower and she'd only finger-combed it back so it hung loose and a bit wild, like the woman. Simone watched her pour a glass of wine, then sip it and with head laid back, eyes closed, savor it, most likely thinking about the last few hours.

After a necessarily quick debate, Simone and Justine had loaded all the bodies, Dunham included, into the Hummer, finding the keys in the process. With Simone following in her car, they'd driven East into another rugged, sparsely populated area and made the evidence disappear. They threw the vampires into the open. They'd be dust by noon.

Dunham was last. He lay in the back of the Hummer, his blond ponytail an ivory slash in the moonlight.

"Are you satisfied?" Simone asked. "He is dead, as you wished."

"Almost." Justine flicked open her knife, stuck it into the body down low and ripped it open up to the sternum. Her hand held up the bloody knife. Simone nodded, and Justine licked one side of the blade clean. The blood hit her stomach like a bomb. A blast of Hunger spread through her like an electric shock. Barely able to control the shaking, she held the blade out for Simone.

Simone grasped Justine's wrist and licked blood from her fingers with long, sensuous movements of her tongue. Last, she licked the blade. Her body shuddered and exhaled a low moan of pleasure. Blood pooled in the open cavity. Simone dipped a cupped hand into the still warm body and offered the thick, pungent liquid to Justine.

Driven by Hunger, they drank until satisfied. Afterward, they placed Dunham in the driver's seat and sent him down a steep ravine to vanish into thick brush.

Justine brought her thoughts back from wherever they'd been and joined Simone observing Signore Rubinio.

"Is he all right? He looks...old. I thought they...we, didn't age."

"Not physically."

"So what he was telling us earlier, before Harry called, about losing his wife, and three of his kids, and having to hide from the Families all those years has made him a bit crazy?"

"Being on the run for over a hundred years, not able to reveal himself to anybody, constantly having to shield himself, missing Sophia, yes, it might make one mad."

"That would be a lonely way to live." Justine shivered and touched shoulders with Simone.

Simone returned the gesture. "Yet, you say he seemed happy before, had lots of friends, Harry and that bartender among them. Look at him now."

"Something's changed," Justine said. "What?"

"Indeed."

The two women moved out of the kitchen toward the old vampire.

"Do you think Harry is okay?" Justine asked.

"Harry can take care of himself, I think."

Justine settled on the couch next to Darwin while Simone took a simple armchair from the wall and placed it in front of him.

# David Burton

"*Signore* Rubinio," Simone said gently. "Something worries you."

He raised his head and attempted to square his shoulders. "Darwin. I am Darwin now."

"Darwin, then." Simone suppressed a knot of sadness in her gut. "What troubles you?"

He sighed deeply and said, "You noticed I could not control those you fought tonight. Yes?"

"Several hesitated at crucial times." Simone said.

Justine added, "I saw that, too. You saved my ass, more than once."

Darwin almost managed a smile. He bowed his head to her. "I am happy I could save your lovely ass, Justine. But it took every bit of my concentration to affect one at a time. Not so long ago I could have had all of them dancing like puppets simultaneously. Not now. Not for three or four years."

Simone raised an eyebrow at Justine, who returned the gesture.

"What happened then?" Simone asked.

"I don't know for sure. I think that is when Stephan Sinakov arrived in the area."

Justine leaned toward him. "Do you know where he lives?"

"No."

"The Sinakovs were always ones you could not manipulate well," Simone said.

"Yes, yes, that is true. It was not easy, but I could do it. These young bloods now I can't control at all, except for what little you've seen. There was only one other vampire I could not control, no matter how hard I concentrated." He looked straight into Simone's eyes.

"Who?" Simone had a sudden tightening in the pit of her stomach that told her she would not like the answer.

"You."

"You tried to control me?"

Darwin shrugged. "An old man like me with so many young and beautiful lovers?" He shook his head with regret. "You never felt me in your head, urging you to me?"

"*Jamai.* I did not need to be told to like you."

"Ah, my dear Simone, many times I have thought of you and how you helped us escape the Families' assassins." He leaned toward her. "I believe I am happy I did not succeed with you. That would have lessened you in my eyes, which you do not deserve."

Simone reached out to take his hand, and with great affection said, "*Merci,* my old friend."

Justine gave them a few moments, then asked, "Darwin, why can't you control Simone?"

The old friends leaned back and took a second to return their thoughts to the present.

Darwin said, "I do not know why. Some anomaly in her brain prevents it."

"The same for the Sinakovs?"

"I believe so. But they are not so strong as Simone."

"So it must be hereditary. If a Sinakov changes a mortal into a vampire they also are hard to control with your mind. Simone, could these vampires be "related" to you?"

"No. I have changed few mortals. I know each one. I remember them all. Only one, besides you, is in this country."

Justine slumped in her seat. "So how does this get Teresa back?" She paged through Gurvitz's file, which Harry gave her before he rushed away with Susan.

Simone stretched her legs out on the coffee table. "Dunham could have told us."

"Harry knows where he lives," Justine said, frowning at the pages on her lap. "Gurvitz figured it out."

"This Gurvitz sounds like a most useful man."

"Too bad he's dead," said Simone. "What are those papers?"

Justine spoke while turning pages. "An analysis of missing persons for the last five years, focusing on girls fourteen to seventeen. You said your ability to control the vampires changed about three years ago, yes?"

Darwin nodded. "That's correct."

"About three years ago the number of girls between fourteen and seventeen gone missing in Southern California spiked up about twenty-five percent, and has stayed at that level since. All pretty, most blonde, rich and poor, smart or dumb. The percentage of girls in that group eventually found, dead or alive, is barely ten per cent. Before that the percentage was about eighty percent. Unhappily, Teresa's daughter is in the ninety percent that aren't recovered now."

"Are you sure you understand all that?" Simone asked.

"Have you ever read real estate analysis? This stuff is a piece of cake."

Simone stared at the ceiling. Her enthusiasm for revenge had waned over the centuries. She went along with Justine out of boredom, mostly, and to be close to her. Besides beauty, the woman had a special *je ne sais quoi* about her that could lead to a splendid long life or a spectacular quick death. Simone was determined to follow along to either conclusion. "So Sinakov arrives and starts a trade in young girls. If he was looking for virgins, I think he may have had, as you say, slim picking."

"Slavery has always been an interest in that Family," Darwin said.

Justine dropped the file on the table then jumped up and paced. "What will he do with Teresa? And how do we get her back?"

# David Burton

"Like Harry said, and I agree, Sinakov won't hurt her, at first. He will use her as leverage to get to you."

"Well, how do we get to him first?"

"You said Harry knows where he lives," Simone said.

"Then what? We march in there and free her? Well, maybe we could, but getting out might be a problem."

"What we need is somebody who knows the house and grounds, but is not in the Sinakov Family."

"If we have the address, we can go to the Building Permit office and get blueprints of the house." Justine jammed her fists into her pockets. "I wish Harry would call."

# Chapter Thirty-three

Teresa woke with a blazing headache. Without opening her eyes, she put a hand to her head to keep it from exploding. She felt a bandage there and a sharp pain. "Oh *Dios*," she groaned, not yet wondering where she was.

"She's awake," someone whispered.

Miguel? No, a girl's voice. Antonia? "Antonia? Is that you? Are you here?"

A cool cloth touched her face. "Are you okay?"

Teresa's eyes flickered open. She saw white. A white coat? Was she in the hospital? What had happened? It came back to her in a rush—the fight at Darwin's place, Dunham shot, a hazy car ride, opening the door, falling out, a blast of pain—and now...somewhere.

The cool cloth dabbed at her head and neck. "Ma'am, are you okay?"

Teresa pushed away the cloth and opened her eyes again.

Two girls knelt beside the low bed. Blondes, one long haired, one short-cropped, mid-teens, tanned, cute, scared. Like her they wore light blue pajamas.

"'Mm okay. Where. . .?"

"We don't know," said shorthair. "All we've seen is this room."

A quick survey of the windowless cement walls and ceiling of the chamber, which contained six metal cots bolted to the concrete floor, told Teresa all she needed to know. They weren't in a room, they were in a cell.

Longhair held out a paper cup and some pills. "Here, for your head. Dee left them for you."

Anything to stop the pounding. Teresa lay back after downing the pills. "Who are you?"

"I'm Crissy," said the girl with long hair.

"Beth," said the other.

"I'm Teresa. How long have you been here?"

Beth said, "Three days for me, I think. They feed us three meals. I've had three breakfasts."

"I've had six breakfasts. Like, who are these people? What do they want with us?" Tears ran down her perfect cheeks. "My parents must be freaking out."

Teresa knew what they wanted. The same thing they wanted Antonia for, to sell her as a sex slave. She didn't have the heart to tell them. "I don't know what they want. But whatever it is, know that your family loves you, stay strong, and don't give up hope."

Beth stared hard at her. She knew Teresa wasn't telling everything, but didn't push it. Teresa looked away, she had her own tears to spill.

Teresa used the toilet in an open alcove at the end of the room with a shower and sink. She thought of a shower, but the girls told her she was clean, as they had been, when she was brought in.

Dizzy and a bit disoriented by the pills, Teresa lay down and quizzed the girls. Crissy, from Santa Monica, was abducted a block from her home as she walked back from a girlfriend's house only two blocks away. "A van stopped and two men grabbed me. It was like, so fast, I didn't have time to run or scream or anything. I think they gave me a shot or something, and I woke up here."

"Were you alone?"

Crissy held tight to Teresa's hand, clearly relieved to have an adult to cling to. "No. There was another girl here, I think her name was Sally. Oh my God, she was mad. She like swore all the time, kicked at the door, yelled out the little window in the door to let her go. She even attacked Dee."

"Who's Dee?"

Beth said, "The woman who brings the meals. She's the only other person I've seen."

"What happened when Sally attacked her?" Crissy's grip tightened.

"It was so scary. Sally was like seventeen. She was tall like you and played basketball. She was really in good shape, you know. And Dee is little, like me."

"Yeah, she is," said Beth. "But I wouldn't mess with her."

"Yeah, no lie. Anyway, Sally swung at her and Dee moved so fast I couldn't even see it and all of a sudden Sally was on the floor and Dee was saying stuff like, 'You're a liar,' and, 'You think you're tough? You'll get your chance.'"

Crissy shivered, sniffed, and wiped tears away. "When the lights were out, Dee and two men came in and took Sally. For a long time I heard screaming." Beth put a comforting arm around Crissy. "I haven't seen her since."

Beth took Crissy to her cot and sat with her, talking quietly.

It took all of Teresa's self-possession to keep calm. *Cristos,* Antonia had probably been in this very cell. What had happened to her? She was a sweet, obedient girl, but she had a stubborn side which on occasion got out of hand. Had her screams echoed through this place? Or was she at this moment being raped or beaten in some filthy room in a remote village halfway around the world? Or, having been used up, was her daughter rotting in the jungle, or shriveling to dust in the desert, or had

# Blood Justice

she been cast away in a heartless city, prey to merciless predators?

The solid clank of heavy bolts shot open outside the door interrupted Teresa's out of control imagination. Crissy gasped. "It's okay," Beth whispered. Teresa's gaze locked on the door.

For a moment Teresa saw Antonia before her—smooth, dusky skin, short black hair, broad shoulders. But the eyes of the woman standing in the doorway quickly dispelled her illusion. Antonia's big eyes were full of humor and love and life. The eyes that froze Teresa were hard and uncaring, with no hint of lightness. The smile on her thin lips did nothing to change that.

Dee held two stacked wooden trays each with several covered plates. She put them on the table. The door swung closed on its own, but didn't latch.

"Crissy," Dee said. "You have your favorite tonight. Chicken parmesan, roast veggies and spaghetti bolognaise."

"Really? That is so good." Crissy wiped her eyes and went to the table. "There's only two. What about Teresa?"

"She's coming with me. Don't worry, she won't be hungry. Enjoy your meal, Crissy." Ignoring Beth, though the girl stood by the table taking in her every move, Dee turned to Teresa. "Come with me."

Teresa sat on her cot, back against the wall. Remembering what happened to Sally, she glanced at the girls. They sat at the table, eyes on her. Suddenly, Teresa thought going with Dee was the thing she wanted to do most in the world. She swung her legs off the cot and stood up. Just as suddenly, the idea vanished. Why would she want to go with this obviously dangerous woman?

Dee waited by the door, head cocked just enough to say, *I can make you come with me or you can come on your own, but you will come with me.*

Teresa went. Before she exited the room, Beth caught her eye. *Be careful,* her gaze said. *Something is going on.*

"Be strong. Remember hope," Teresa said before the door clanged shut.

Dee led her down a short, roughly finished passage, past a second door, then into a large basement with concrete support columns, wires and pipes running along the ceiling, and old furniture piled along the opposite wall. They passed a noisy room with hot water heaters and a furnace, then two storage rooms, mostly empty. Three steel doors to other concrete cells lined up on the right. At the end of the basement was an elevator door. Dee pointed to several thick white bathrobes and slippers and told Teresa to put one on. On the ride up three floors, Teresa welcomed the warmth of the robe and slippers.

The elevator opened into a large multi-purpose room at least a hundred feet long. One corner featured a huge flat screen TV surrounded by stacks of electronics and comfortable furniture. One corner contained pool and card tables. A huge fireplace dominated the center of the far wall that was otherwise mostly windows. A workout mat took up another corner. A full height dividing wall hung with martial arts weapons separated that area from a six-stool bar close to an elegant dining table

Dee pointed her toward the bar where a figure waited. Teresa tugged the robe tight about her and went to meet Stephan Sinakov.

# Chapter Thirty-four

At nine o'clock in the morning, Harry leaned his fists on his desk as Gurvitz's parents left his office. That was the second time in his career he'd had one of his men die. It was the first time he'd lied. Vampires killed your son as he tried to stop them from kidnapping a lesbian to stop me from investigating their virgins-for-sale scheme. Right.

He didn't like to lie, even for a good cause. He'd been doing a lot of it lately and couldn't remember what he'd said to whom. Nobody had said anything, but he'd been around long enough to know that prickly feeling on the back of his neck when quiet questions were being asked behind his back.

It was all going to fall apart soon, and the excuse that he was involved with, or infatuated with, or in love with—he didn't know which—a beautiful vampire would not sit well with an internal affairs investigator.

He hadn't slept. He was so tired he was afraid that if he sat down he wouldn't be able to get up, and there was so much to do. Like he'd told Justine, Teresa should be okay for a few days. Sinakov would want the investigation of the missing girls to cease. It wouldn't if she were dead. Justine and Simone would go after her if they knew where Sinakov lived. Harry knew. One of Sinakov's minions had murdered Gurvitz on his doorstep and Harry wanted to be there when he went down. Revenge consumed Justine. Harry now appreciated how she felt.

"Go home, Harry."

Harry's head jerked up. Lieutenant Mike Bullock leaned in his door. "You're asleep on your feet. Go home. Sleep. We'll let you know if anything breaks."

"Yes, sir. I'm going."

Lieutenant Bullock stood by his door to make sure he left.

But Harry didn't go home. He drove his humdrum rental sedan a circuitous route to Simone's house.

Justine opened the door. She looked a bit pale to him as she stood back, avoiding a square of sunlight on the tile floor. She wore jeans and a T-shirt, her hair unbound. He smiled with relief. He had been afraid she wouldn't be there, that she had gone after Sinakov, or something had happened to her, or she had simply gone and he'd never see her again. He knew in his heart that losing her would finish him. She was his last chance, he didn't have it in him to try again. He didn't like knowing that. The last thing in the world he wanted was to love somebody so much that they had that power over him. It scared and attracted him at the same time, confusing him. Confused was not a good thing for a detective to be.

"You look tired," she said.

He nodded and entered.

"Have you any word of Teresa?" Simone asked.

"Nothing. But the message is obvious."

"We're going after her," Justine said.

Harry leaned against the kitchen counter. Justine leaned next to him, their arms touching. He was surprised to see Darwin there as well, though he was too tired to make anything of it.

Harry drew a piece of paper from his pocket. "Gurvitz thought Sinakov was here. It belongs to a company called Transporte Francaise."

"I know of it," Simone said. "A very shady, as you say, company."

"One condition, I'm going with you. Gurvitz was a good man, a good cop, one of mine."

The three vampires traded looks. Simone took the paper.

Justine took his hand. "Agreed, but not before you get some sleep."

Harry started to protest, but Justine firmly led him from the kitchen.

Justine shut the door to her bedroom. Harry took her in his arms. They clung to each other. She held him so tight he could barely breathe, but he took strength from her. For the moment his fatigue faded, along with his fear and the past and future. There was just them, now.

He buried his face in her neck and hair. She wore the same scent as always, but now it was slightly altered, more subtle, yet more intoxicating. In the back of his mind he knew that her body chemistry was altered and so her perfume was too. He didn't care. He inhaled it as if they were the last breaths he would ever take.

She held his face and kissed his eyes, nose, chin, lips—each one a searing spot of sun heat on a chilly day.

"You stink," she breathed, pushing off his jacket.

"You don't," he said, pulling off her T-shirt.

In the shower, she knelt before him, took him in her mouth. Her lips and tongue made his eyes roll. He grasped at the glass enclosure to keep his feet. When he could take no more he raised her up and pressed her against the wall with his body. More than ready, almost frantic, she wrapped her arms and legs around him. They moved against each other, desperate for connection.

Harry came hard. Ordinarily a considerate lover, he rammed into her with unintended fury. It was her fault she had come back into his life and changed it from an ordered, somewhat tedious existence, to one of lies, revenge, and improbable vampire lovers; her fault he had been attracted to her from the second they met; her fault he had overstepped the ethical bounds of law enforcement to help her, save her, be with her.

Later, lying in her bed, in her arms, his unconscious anger spent, Harry said, "I'm sorry if I hurt you, in there."

She pressed his palm to her lips. "I don't hurt easily, physically anyway. Are you mad at me?"

"No."

"Mad at the universe?"

"The universe is just being the universe."

"Mad at yourself?"

Harry didn't let himself think. "I was afraid you'd be gone. I don't want you to have that much power."

"I know. I was afraid you wouldn't come back to me."

"You could always force me to come back."

He felt her body stiffen. Justine propped her head on an elbow and turned his face toward her. "Harry, I would never do that. I promise. I don't want you if I have to force you."

Harry touched her face. "Still..." After a long period of silence, during which he could barely keep his eyes open, he said, "When this is all over, and Sinakov is destroyed, what then for us?"

Justine rested her head on his chest. He loved the feel of her against his skin. Her still damp hair smelling of the exotic tropics brushed his face. The cool smoothness of her breasts, belly, and legs thrilled him. He held her tight, sure he knew what she would say.

"I can't allow myself to think of a future. I can't allow myself to care."

Though she had told him she couldn't cry, Harry was sure he felt tears on his chest. He touched his lips to her hair. "I know," he whispered, and floated into sleep.

# Chapter Thirty-five

A handsome woman, Sinakov thought, as Teresa strode toward him across the open room. His taste for younger girls had faded years ago, though he did enjoy the occasional young one who turned out not to be as pure or as tractable as they could have been and so were worthless on the market. Although sometimes they brought more trouble than they were worth.

He only appeared to be twenty-five, but the last centuries had brought him a more mature outlook on women. When Trake had returned with news of the evening's misfortune, he'd been angry, therefore someone had to be punished. He had locked Trake in the iron coffin and put it inside the freezer. Trake hated the cold.

The unexpected woman suffered his wrath, also. She knew things he wanted to know and he was not, at first, kind in extracting it. He had had experience on both sides of pain. He knew how to inflict it without leaving a mark and how to manipulate it to get what he wanted.

Pain has a way of distracting the mind's defenses against intrusion. Yet, she wasn't terrified of him as so many had been before. Bound to the chair, she fought with her mind as most fought with their body. He was surprised to learn that she knew who he was, and even knew a tiny bit of what he had done. That she fought him from hate, not fear, caused him to stay his hand more than once.

Of course, in the end, he got the information he wanted. Justine Kroft interested him. He had dismissed her at first, just another grieving parent. Now he admired her revenge ethic. Once, long ago, before he was changed, he had plotted revenge for crimes against him and his family. The quest for revenge had fueled him in life, allowed him permission to do what had to be done to survive. Once changed, that quest performed the same function. That revenge was sweet, was true in death as well as life. He continued to enjoy the fruits of his revenge centuries later.

A mere, mortal woman with an idea of revenge, this Justine had nevertheless proved resilient and resourceful, and was now Vampire. And so he would destroy this Justine, intriguing as she was, for he knew she would never give up her quest as long as her head remained connected to her body.

Another interesting question, who was this Simone? An unknown vampire with no Family, it seemed. Also, the old man, Darwin. They seemed familiar to him, but he hadn't been able to form a clear picture of them from Teresa. He suspected both of them had been in her mind obscuring her memory of them. Two unknown vampires in his territory warranted investigation.

But that could wait. Now that he knew Justine would be coming for him, he had given orders to let her do exactly what she wanted.

"Please, sit down, Teresa," Sinakov said graciously as the woman approached the bar.

She stared at him with the same cautious inquisitiveness as the night before when she first saw him down in the room that was forever stained with blood no matter how hard it was scrubbed. Her eyes narrowed as she tried to sort out where she had seen him before.

"You must be Stephan Sinakov?"

"I am. Sit. Please. You must be famished. Have a drink before dinner. Some wine, a beer?"

He did not want to force her to sit. The time for that was past. He did not want to risk her recognizing his voice in her head. That might shake loose memories of the night before that he did not care to have Teresa experience again.

"Some wine, I think." He poured a glass half full of white wine and set it on the wooden bar top.

She hesitated, then set herself on a high stool with a wooden back. "Where is my daughter?"

Sinakov sighed. "I do not know the whereabouts of your daughter." The truth, as far as it went.

"I don't believe you. I know what you do to girls." Her eyes glistened with her desire to strangle him.

"You know nothing of what I do. And whatever I do, I promise it has nothing to do with your daughter."

"You're lying. You kidnapped her and sold her."

"Do not believe all that someone tells you. They may have their own reasons for what they say. I do nothing to girls. There are, I am sure you are aware, many evil men, mortals, who do things to girls. If your daughter is missing, I had nothing to do with it."

Sinakov sipped his wine, then rested his arms on the bar, his well manicured fingers slowly spinning the glass. "Many think they know what I do. Which one have you been talking to? Do you know them well enough to trust what they say? What proof do they offer? Perhaps they have their own agenda?"

She thought about that, he could see it in her face.

"I believe you are a detestable creature who does despicable things and doesn't care one little bit for the welfare or feelings of mortals." Teresa hesitated, wouldn't meet his steady, neutral gaze. Finally she downed half a glass of wine and looked him straight in the eye. "But, there may be one thing you could do to change my opinion."

Of course there is. "And what would that be?" he said, as if he didn't know.

"Return my daughter to me."

Sinakov made a good show of letting out a deep sigh. "I told you, I don't know where she is."

"But you could find her. The police can't do anything. Help me bring her home."

"If I do?"

"I won't think you such a monster."

He smiled and leaned closer, still holding her eyes with his. "For me to return her to you, you must do one of two things for me. You choose."

"What things?"

"Spend one night with me."

Teresa did not seem surprised. He watched her rearrange her thoughts to make that choice acceptable. "The other?"

"Tell me where to find Justine Kroft."

Teresa leaned away from him. "I don't know where she is."

"She is your best friend, is she not? Her house burned down, where would she go? To you? Maybe to Simone's house?"

"I don't know where her house is."

But she did, even if she herself could not drag it from her memory. The night before, Sinakov was unable to obtain a clear location from her chaotic mind because she fought his attempts to probe her brain. Her mental capacity for resistance was surprisingly strong. Now though, having been asked that question, she was focused on what she did know. Sinakov reached out and touched her arm. A few seconds of concentration and he knew almost exactly where Simone lived.

"But you have been there, have you not?"

"Yes, but I don't know the address." Teresa shook her head. "I wouldn't tell you that anyway. Not for anything."

"Not even for your daughter?"

Sinakov stood back and watched Teresa struggle with her choice. How many times as a mortal had he been forced to make a choice that affected not only him, but the life or death of some other pitiful mortal. Two girls—one you can have in your cage for an hour, the other will be used for the power of her young blood. A father and son—which dies quickly, which has to watch their mother, sister, wife be ravaged by the hungry band of vampires? How many choices had he made with his eventual Master's fangs at his neck—this life or that life or his own life? The choices became easier over the years. The despair, agony, and blood meant less and less, the guilt faded, he barely heard the pitiful pleas for mercy, the curses of damnation he came to disregard because he was already in Hell.

He gulped the last of his wine to mask the bitterness in his mouth. There was a time, long ago, when he, too, would have sacrificed anything to have his family again. But by the time he realized he'd been lied to, that his family was dead and there would be no reunion, it was too late. It took over a hundred years, and a thousand choices, but he got his vengeance. So he understood how Justine Kroft felt. He also understood why Teresa would give herself to him for the return of her daughter.

Teresa's choice was easy; a night in bed with him at a future date, or betray her best friend. As he had at one time been willing to do, Teresa was willing to do anything to have her daughter back and her family whole.

Sinakov was not surprised when she said, "If you return her to me, alive, for one night you can have what you want from me."

Sinakov saw how hard, and easy, the decision was for her, so he felt sure she would honor the deal. If she didn't, he would drink the blood of both daughter and mother.

He had no idea where the daughter was, or whether she was alive or dead. She had been purchased by a Russian who, as a change from pale European girls, liked a girl on the dusky side. Especially one nobody would miss after he used her up.

"Agreed," he said. "More wine?"

As for Justine Kroft, he understood her and admired her strength and determination. He had a surprise or two for her. And if that did not stop her and her mystery vampire partner, he would destroy her, as he had so many others who had wished to destroy him. Damned murdering vampires.

He filled Teresa's glass without waiting for an answer. Then he sniffed the air. "Ah, dinner is ready." He came around the bar and held out a hand for her.

Teresa hesitated. She stared at the hand as if it were a snake ready to strike the instant she moved.

Sinakov smiled a subdued, understanding smile. "Do not be afraid, Teresa. You have nothing to fear from me. If I wanted to do you harm, I would already have done so. I have every reason to want you healthy."

Slowly, she took his hand. He led her to a rectangular dining table elegantly set for two. Sinakov sat her to the right of the head of the table. He pushed the chair in for her.

A rotund vampire, around forty when he was changed, wearing kitchen whites, entered carrying a steaming tureen.

"Potato cheese soup," Sinakov told her. "An improvement over Marie Callender's, I think you will agree." Among all the information he had taken from her mind when she first arrived, he had discovered her favorite foods.

"This is my favorite soup," Teresa said.

"Is it? What a coincidence. Well done, Santos."

Santos filled her bowl, then Sinakov's. He retreated into the kitchen.

Spoon in hand, Sinakov inhaled a long pleasurable whiff. "Ahh, exquisite. Santos is a culinary genius. He's been in the kitchen for a hundred and sixty years, so he should know how to prepare some things well."

With hands in her lap, Teresa sat motionless.

"Do you wish to say grace?"

Eyebrows raised in question, she regarded him.

"If you feel you must thank your God for this food, by all means, do so. All that crucifix and holy water nonsense is only in the movies. In real life it has no effect. Unless you use a large cross as a club. That hurts. Please proceed."

Teresa stared at her hands, then reached for a spoon. "I don't think God is listening to me, anyway." She dipped her spoon into the thick, creamy liquid. "I thought you didn't have to eat."

Sinakov savored a mouthful of soup. "True, we do not need this food for sustenance. As you may know we possess enhanced senses. Sight, hearing, touch, and smell are very useful. Taste is for pleasure. It would be a shame to waste such a sensitive palate. Don't you think?"

Teresa's blissful expression as she savored her first taste of the soup was agreement enough for him.

Dee appeared by the elevator door. Sinakov excused himself and went to her.

She said, "The recovery team is ready, but they have to wait several hours before they can begin."

"They must be as quick as possible. I will need time."

"Do you think this Justine will come tonight?"

"I do, so we must delay them. Do this." He gave her a few quick orders.

"I understand," Dee said. "Also, the girl is ready."

Sinakov looked back at Teresa finishing her soup. "Prepare her."

Soup finished, waiting for the next course, Teresa asked, "What about the two girls in the basement. Will you return them to their families?"

Sinakov sipped his wine. "Are either of them your daughter?"

Teresa opened her mouth to speak, then turned away.

Santos served them the main course, grilled mahi mahi, with roasted vegetables and Spanish rice.

"I do hope this is acceptable," Sinakov said.

"Yes. Yes, this is acceptable. It's perfect."

He knew it would be.

# Blood Justice

They ate in silence for a few minutes then Teresa asked, "How did you become...what you are?"

Sinakov sat back and pursed his lips at his meal. "Do you not yet believe?"

"After what I have seen I must believe. But it is hard."

"I always believed," he said. "We were raised to be wary of vampires, they were known as Marauders then, although little could be done to stop them.

"I was a child when my family was slaughtered. I survived somehow, and the leader kept me as a slave for almost fifteen years. Back then vampires really were blood-sucking monsters. They were mostly roving bands that raped and pillaged across eastern Europe. I saw mindless carnage you could not imagine. After they'd fed, they would continue killing for the sheer sake of killing."

Sinakov finished his wine in one gulp. He then twirled the glass by its stem and stared at it as it turned, sparkling in the light from a low chandelier.

"I was a pet, at first. I wore a collar and was led about by a leash. I grew up and they made me a slave. One of my duties was to search the dead for valuables. If I was caught trying to keep anything I found, I was given to the women vampires to use as they wanted. When I could not perform further, they beat me."

"That explains some things," Teresa said softly.

Santos removed the dinner dishes and served dessert—a decadent looking fudge brownie sundae.

Sinakov shrugged and continued. "Nevertheless, I managed to accumulate and hide a good bit of gold and gems. When I was twenty-five, I learned that the Master had lied to me about my family. So I killed one of his vampires and ran away. Of course I was caught, though it took them three days. The Master said he was proud of me. I had proved I was worthy to join his growing Family. He changed me as a reward." He stared into his past through the dark windows. "Over a hundred years passed before I was strong enough to take my revenge for what he did to me."

"You must have great patience."

"A development of being immortal. I would have acted more quickly if I had been stronger. From what I have heard your friend Justine feels the same way."

"She has never had much patience."

"And now that Time is different for her, she is still in a hurry for her revenge."

"You murdered her daughter. What do you expect?"

"Nothing less—if it was true. Perhaps she should take the time to learn what really happened."

Before Teresa could respond, Dee appeared and quickly approached Sinakov. Without any preamble, she whispered in his ear. "Jay Dunham has been found along with the remains of the others with him, as well as several mortal remains." Long pause. "Dunham is Vampire now," Dee said, both statement and inquiry. "When...?"

Sinakov waved off her question. "Where is he now?"

"A few minutes away."

His lips formed a tight line as his eyes burned a hole in the night. He forced a gracious smile and said to Teresa, "Please excuse us for a moment."

Within seconds Sinakov and Dee were on the other side of the room. Dee told him how Dunham had been trapped in the vehicle until sunset when he found his way to a road and a phone.

"So they dumped my people and my vehicle in the middle of nowhere, expecting not to be found out? What if Dunham had family who gave a damn about him? Are the watchers at the house?"

"They've just arrived."

"Send all who are available. Tell them to burn the house down. This Justine has caused too much trouble already. Destroy all of them."

Back at the table, Sinakov said, "I must apologize, Teresa. Unfortunately several matters require my immediate attention. Please enjoy your dessert, and mine also, if you like. Santos will bring coffee and anything else you desire."

"And then you will release me?"

"Not quite yet, I'm afraid. Please remain in this room. Dee will escort you back soon."

Teresa instinctively glanced outside.

"Please do not try to leave. Outside, it can be very dangerous at night."

"We have a deal, correct?"

"We do."

After Sinakov left the room, Teresa watched her dessert melt for some time before picking up her spoon.

# Chapter Thirty-six

Leaning against the deck railing, Teresa searched the glitter of lights spread out below. Were any of those lights winding through the valley Justine and Simone coming to rescue her?

She sniffed at the thought. If they knew she'd made a deal with the devil, they'd turn around and consider her dead, still breathing or not. It would be worth it to have Antonia back in her arms, though she knew her daughter might be dead. At least she'd know. But, if Antonia was alive and returned to her, Teresa would honor the deal. The fact that Sinakov was attractive made it a little easier to contemplate. The fact that things between her and Miguel had not been so good lately had nothing to do with it—or so she insisted to herself.

Again, she had the feeling she'd met Sinakov before. Moving toward him from the elevator, she'd been struck by his familiar appearance. Though emaciated, she could easily imagine his features as softer, rounder, lighter. Where had she seen him before? And since she woke in the cell she'd had the strange sensation that people she couldn't see were all about her, like ghosts going about their business. She'd known Dee was in the room before she saw her, and when Sinakov had left the chamber.

In the darkness almost four stories below, the land sloped down. She felt occasional shapes moving about. Some looked like dogs, unless werewolves were real, too. *Dios*, she wasn't sure she had accepted the reality of vampires, yet, even though she'd made a deal to sleep with the local *Jefe* vampire if he returned Antonia to her.

She closed her eyes and pictured Antonia as she had last seen her leaving for school, her fine features alive with life and curiosity. She was easily the smartest in the family, but such a delicate girl. Antonia had never been more than three hundred miles from home in her life. When Teresa let her guard down, and really thought about her daughter, she could not comprehend how the girl would survive in a situation of vile abuse where nobody loved her. That thought strengthened her resolve to do what might be necessary to bring about her homecoming.

She thought she heard voices on the roof above. Obviously, the estate was well guarded. Justine would come, for Sinakov if not for her, Teresa had no doubt. How they would get in, vampire powers or not, she had no clue.

Teresa knew when Dee silently entered the room. What had they done to her?

"Are you thinking of jumping?" Dee asked.

"Would you try to stop me if I was?"

Dee peered over the rail. "I'm not sure it would be a favor to you if I did. Come with me."

Teresa continued to lean on the rail. "I made a deal with him. Do you think he will honor it?"

"In his own way, he is an honorable man. Just be careful of all the ramifications of the choices you make. Come, now." Dee took her arm, her steel grip a warning. "Now."

Waiting for the elevator, Teresa asked Dee, "How long have you been a vampire?"

"Fifty years, next month."

"You don't look a day over thirty. I suppose Sinakov changed you? How did it happen?"

"I met him at a party. He flirted with me, I, foolishly, flirted with him. My husband was a very jealous and abusive man. He made a scene and took me home to punish me." The elevator door opened, but Dee did not move. "He said he was going to make sure nobody would want to flirt with me again. Then Stephan appeared. My husband attacked and ended up with a knife in his gut."

Dee paused. Teresa asked, "Sounds like he got what he deserved. What did you think?"

"I was terrified he would die, and terrified he would live. I was terrified of Stephan, too. He explained what he was and fed on my husband to prove it. Then he gave me three choices: He would kill me and feed on me, he would let me live and go to jail for killing my husband, or he would change me and I would be bound to him for a hundred years."

"Not much of a choice."

"No. I wasn't afraid to die. In the eight years I was married I'd wished for death more than once. But, now that I was finally free of that psychopathic bastard, I was damned if I was going to spend the rest of my life in jail."

As they descended in the elevator, Dee said. "Stephan did offer me an extra incentive. My husband wasn't quite dead yet. He allowed me to stab the son-of-a-bitch right in the heart."

Out of the elevator, in the far wall just before they turned into the rough corridor to her cell, Teresa noticed a heavy metal door with a bar across it. "Where's that door go to? Your torture chamber?"

"Sort of. Outside."

At the door to her cell, Teresa asked one more question. "Given your history before, how can you let these girls be sent away? You have to know what is going to happen to them."

"Ramifications," Dee said and opened the door.

Beth sat on her bunk, hugging her legs, chin on knees. Her eyes were red and her cheeks wet with tears.

"Where's Crissy?" Teresa asked.

"Gone," Beth sniffed.

Dee closed and bolted the door.

"I thought you were gone, too," Beth said.

Teresa sat beside her. "What happened?"

"A little while after you left Dee brought her some clothes. All she said was Crissy was going away from here. Do you know where she went?"

*To Hell.* "No."

"Maybe she got to go home?"

"Maybe."

Beth studied her face. "Yeah, right. Where did Dee take you?"

*To open the door to Hell.* "Dinner." Teresa put her arm around the girl's shoulders and held her close.

"I guess I'm next," Beth said. "It probably won't be good, huh?"

*Not for Beth.* "Let's talk about something else. Like, how to get out of here."

# Chapter Thirty-seven

Justine woke with a start. Harry, spooned behind her, stirred. The feeling of approaching danger was so strong she jumped out of bed. Naked, she checked the bathroom and closet, then peered out the windows into the night. A thin indigo band stretched across the horizon.

Somebody was concentrating on her...no, not her, the house. She concentrated back. The house was being watched, by who and from where, she couldn't tell. But she sensed vampires for sure, and they weren't there to borrow a neighborly cup of blood.

"Harry, wake up. Wake up." Justine was half dressed when Simone burst into the room. "I know. I know."

Harry struggled to wake up. "What's going on?"

"Sinakov has found us," Justine said. "Get up."

In the dark living room, Darwin sat on the edge of a chair, his body taut with concentration. Simone strapped her small sword on her back. Justine repeatedly flicked her knife open and closed.

Justine asked, "Can he sense anything?"

"Not much. They're all made by Sinakov."

The two women made the rounds, peeking out of windows.

"I didn't see any, but I can feel them," Justine said.

Harry rushed in. "What's the situation?"

"Fire," Darwin said. "They're going to burn us out. Attack when we run."

"Cowards," Simone said.

"Is there an escape route they won't see?" Harry asked.

"Of course."

"How many are there?" Justine said.

Darwin shrugged as his eyes fluttered. "More have arrived, possibly twenty."

Justine looked to Simone.

"Sorry, *ma chere*. We are good together, but these ones will be experienced and ready. We cannot win against them."

"Darwin, can you control any of them out there? Maybe put an idea in their head?"

The older vampire shook his head. "I am sorry, no." Suddenly, he jerked upright. "A new one has arrived. He is only partially blocked. I could touch him." A grin lit up his eyes. "What idea?"

"It might even the odds a bit," Justine said. She quickly explained.

"Might work," Harry said.

Justine turned to Harry. "You should leave now. If they get hold of you there won't be enough left to make a zombie from, let alone a hot vampire lover."

Harry raised an eyebrow. "Yeah, well, a hot vampire lover needs a hot vampire woman to be worth a damn. I stay with you. Hell, it's my fault this is happening."

"It's my fault if anybody's," Justine said. "If we don't make it, somebody has to rescue Teresa and destroy Sinakov."

Simone stepped up. "We don't have time for this. Harry, if you want to stay, come with me. Otherwise, you should leave now." Simone walked quickly toward a small den off the living room.

"He's leaving."

"I'm staying," Harry said, following Simone.

Justine gathered up the papers that Bayley had brought in the afternoon. Harry would be furious if he knew they had gotten his friend involved. But some things had to be done in daylight.

Justine herself was at once angry and pleased that Harry was staying—and scared. They had connected more than physically before he slept. With hardly a word between them they both knew their connection was more than lust and love and loneliness. It was trouble.

Harry came out of the den loading a 12-gauge pump shotgun and carrying a short, thin, curved sword under his arm. Simone followed. She carried a shotgun and a double-edged sword which she threw handle first to Justine. "You're going to need something bigger than that butter knife of yours."

Harry handed his sword to Darwin. "Think you can handle a few punk vamps, old man?"

Darwin swished the sword a few times and made some quick moves that looked like he knew what he was doing. He turned to Simone. "You remembered." He made a few more moves. "I think I can handle it, Harry."

Simone said, "The Rubinios were mostly about brains, not fighting in combat. But, as Master of the Family, he had to defend himself against all who would be Master."

"They are coming," Darwin said.

Justine and Simone exchanged a glance and a nod.

"Idea time, Darwin," Justine said. She took Harry's arm. "You're with me, Harry."

"Lucky me," he replied with a mischievous grin.

Simone called, "No mercy. They are here to kill us. Self-defense, right, Harry?"

Harry stopped at the top of steps leading down to the pool level. "I think you'll have to ask the Supreme Court about that."

To the left, at the bottom of the stairs, a glass door led to a flagstone patio around the pool. Inside, a corridor ran the length of the house giving access to several doors. A support column and the inner side of the steps offered spaces to lie in wait. Harry waited behind the column, Justine behind the stairs.

"So where is this emergency exit?" Harry asked as he checked his gun for the fourth time that minute. "Just in case."

"The door behind you. Simone says go right, left, second left, right."

Harry found a narrow panel in the wall. He pushed it with a shaky hand and it popped slightly open. He peered in. "It's dark."

"Not to us."

"Then by all means, ladies first."

A crash came from upstairs, then footsteps, then screams. Justine listened to Simone and Darwin reap the vampires as they surged through the front door. When she heard the clang of swords, she knew the element of surprise was over. She fought the desire to run up the stairs and help.

"They're coming," Harry said, voice tight.

Justine peeked through the stair railing. The vampires ran around the house to the patio door and lost no time shattering the glass with a basketball-sized rock. The first invader, a beefy, young male, came through.

"Now!" Justine shouted.

Harry dropped the muzzle of the shotgun and blew the vampire's head off. Two more heads were vaporized in quick succession before a short, wiry vampire darted through and slammed Harry to the floor. He bent Harry's head to expose his neck.

Justine stepped out, and with one swing severed the vampire's head. More came and Justine concentrated on them—stabbing, slashing, blocking, kicking. Over the cries of attack and pain, and the clash of blades, she heard Simone cry out. She glanced up the steps. A young woman vampire took advantage of the distraction and rammed her sword through Justine, back to front.

Justine felt a sharp pain start from her back and push right through to punch out beside her navel. Her sword clattered to the steps. Looking at the five inches of protruding blade, she felt surprise and a flash of fear. She froze for a few seconds, terrified and unsure. What would happen to her?

The shotgun blasted behind her. The woman vampire's shattered body slammed against the wall. The shotgun fired again, reducing her head to fragments of brain and bone.

Harry stood beside her. "Hold the railing."

She held tight. Harry jerked the sword out.

"Justine, look out!"

A large male rushed her. With no time to grab up her sword, she drew out her knife, flicking it open. He swung. She stepped inside the swing and jammed the knife into his throat.

A flash of light and a wave of pressure came from upstairs. Justine smelled smoke and gasoline. A headless vampire tumbled down the stairs to land, twitching, at her feet. Another flash of fire billowed smoke down the steps. Two figures appeared in the smoke; Darwin, with a helping arm around Simone.

"Time to go," he shouted.

Justine hesitated, still aware that she had been run through by a sword. Where was the pain? The blood?

"Justine, come on." Harry pulled her toward the secret door.

"Hurry," Darwin shouted. "More are coming around the back."

Harry had the door open.

Justine shook off her mortal concerns about injuries. "Darwin, broadcast that we're all dead. Maybe one of them will hear it."

"Take Simone."

Simone seemed disoriented. She had slashes on her body and red burns with streaks of gore and ash. Justine helped Simone to the door.

Darwin stood still, concentrating.

"Shit." Harry grabbed Justine. "You guys can sort of talk to each other, right? That's what Darwin is doing?"

"Some can. You know that."

Surrounded by thickening smoke, Harry pointed at the vampire with a hole in his throat who stared right at Darwin. Harry rushed to the struggling vampire, and with the sword he had removed from Justine, struck at his neck. He struck again—*he's already dead*—and a third time—*he's already dead*—before the head thumped on the floor.

"Harry!"

Harry grabbed Darwin and pushed him into the escape tunnel. As he slammed the door shut behind him, tendrils of fire reached in and grasped his hands.

# Chapter Thirty-eight

Teresa and Beth lay on their beds in the dark and discussed in whispers an escape plan that had almost zero chance of working. Teresa had explained to Beth that Dee and the others were real vampires and that their legendary strength and speed were as advertised. Of course Beth didn't believe her, but she was a smart girl with common sense and an open mind.

"Getting that door open will be the hard part," Beth said.

Before Teresa could answer a great cry of anger and frustration reached them. She felt the anger more than heard it. The power behind that cry erupted in her brain. She froze. Sinakov was coming for her.

"What was that?" Beth said.

"Nothing good. Whatever it is, you have to keep out of it."

Teresa sat up, tried to steel herself for whatever was going to happen. She felt him coming closer at great speed, down stairs, through the basement, along the corridor to her door. The door flew open, exposing a rectangle of light that illuminated the room to a pale grey.

Sinakov grabbed her and slammed her against the wall. His black eyes bored into hers. "What is this Justine? How does she escape me?"

"Leave her alone. Leave her alone." Beth stood on the bed, tugging his arm.

Sinakov flung her off the bed. She bounced off the next bed into the wall. Sinakov growled a warning, his mouth vampire wide, fangs at full extension. Beth pushed against the wall, an instant believer.

"Justine?" Teresa closed her eyes to avoid his invasive glare.

"Ahhh." Sinakov threw her onto the bed and straddled her. One hand on her forehead, he loomed over her, forcing her eyes open.

The power of his eyes forced her to answer. "I told you, she's the mother of a girl you killed."

"Pah! She is a Young Blood, yet she still defies me. What power does she have?"

Against the pressure of his hand on her chest she could barely speak. "A mother's revenge."

"Who does she serve? What Family?"

"No Family." She couldn't help but think of Simone.

"Who is this Simone?"

Defenseless against the force of his anger, barely able to breathe, Teresa pictured Simone in her mind.

Sinakov sprung up as if yanked by a hangman's noose. "That is Simone?"

"Yes."

"What do you know of her?" His mouth opened wide, his fangs long and pale in the dim light. The full strength of his will tore through her helpless mind, searching for all she knew of Simone Gireaux.

He uttered one word, "No," and then he was gone. The door slammed behind him with such force it bounced open.

"Beth, the door." Teresa coughed. Beth stared wide-eyed at the slowly closing door. "The door."

Beth shook herself and ran to catch the door inches from closing. Carefully, she inspected the corridor. "There's no one there."

Teresa pushed to her feet, staggered, and sat down, head between her legs.

Beth dragged a chair to keep the door open and went to her. "Are you okay? Was that really a...? What did he do to you?"

Teresa slowly raised her head and sat up straight. "He went into my head. Something there scared him. Which is scary itself."

Her first steps were unsteady, but the open door was an irresistible lure.

In the basement proper, the door to the outside was solid and locked. There was no handle, only a round, flush lock that needed a key to open. The area around the lock face was dented and scratched. They weren't the first ones desperate to open that door.

"There's a space between the door and the frame," Teresa said. "We need something to pry it open."

At their end of the basement they searched the miscellaneous dust-covered junk that had accumulated over the years. The junk stopped about midway down the basement against a cement block wall that came out ten or twelve feet from the back wall. At the corner it ran down far enough to have three heavy doors about ten feet apart.

By the wall, Teresa searched among old boxes and furniture. A noise came from the other side. She froze, listening. She pressed an ear to the wall. Was that a scraping sound, then a shuffling noise? Somebody was in the room. Another girl?

Teresa listened hard. If it was another prisoner, she had to try and rescue her. The shuffling came again, closer, directly opposite her. But with the noise, came a cold, bone-chilling feeling that made her hunch her shoulders and hug herself. She jerked away from the wall. That was no mortal in the room. Yet, the emotions seeping through the wall were compelling—sadness, fear, confusion.

"Teresa, I found something."

Teresa jumped again, thinking for a moment that the being on the other side of the wall had spoken to her. But it was Beth, holding up a dirt-encrusted shovel. Teresa signaled Beth to wait, while she checked the other rooms for occupants, taking advantage of her new ability to sense when a vampire was near—something Sinakov had inadvertently done to her. It certainly wouldn't be to his advantage for a mortal to be aware of his movements.

Teresa swung up the bar and Beth jammed the shovel in just above the lock. They pushed. The door groaned and sprang open, revealing steps rising to darkness. Shovel in hand, Teresa led the way up. She had to get Beth away. What she would do after that, she didn't know.

They came out in shadow at the end of the house. Open lawn spread out in front of them. A line of trees at least two hundred feet away provided the nearest cover. The lawn sloped up steeply in back, ending in a low cliff. Faint car sounds came from down slope. The grass was cool and damp. The trees seemed impossibly far.

"Someone will see us," Beth said.

"Not if we go now, and fast," Teresa said, not believing it herself. She didn't mention the dogs. Maybe they were sniffing the other end of the house. "Besides, what choice do we have?"

"None."

They made it halfway before the first dog barked.

Two pairs, fast-moving, black spots against the lighter grey of illuminated lawn, came at them from front and back, avoiding the bright circles of light close to the house. The first pair positioned itself between them and the trees. A Rottweiler and a German Shepherd, both prime examples of the breed, stood their ground. The dogs' eyes fixed on them. A low growl of warning escaped between two long fangs growing from their upper jaws.

Vampire dogs. Teresa could all too easily imagine those fangs ripping at her neck. No words came to her, but she could feel the creatures' craving for blood. For a moment, she wanted to give up and let the beasts tear into her. Her heart hammered as an almost overwhelming desire to kneel and offer herself to them squeezed her chest. It would be so easy to give up, to yield to the surrender call the dogs projected. But what of Antonia? If her daughter was still alive, Teresa was her only hope.

Beth dropped to her knees, unable to fight the compulsion to surrender herself. Beth's voice quivered, but came out strong. "Teresa, what the hell kind of dogs are they?"

"Vampire dogs. You have any vampire rabbits in your pants?"

Teresa angled to the right. The dogs moved with her to keep their position between her and the trees. She looked back. The other pair came on fast.

"Sorry, dog." Teresa ran toward the Rottweiler and swung the shovel.

# Blood Justice

The blade caught the animal flat on the shoulder. Her hands tingled as if she had hit a marble statue. The dog barely yipped as it rolled with the hit. Before she could advance a step or ready another strike, the Shepherd darted in and grabbed the shovel's handle.

It was their only weapon. If she let go, the two women would be at the dogs' mercy.

Beth kicked the Shepherd. "Let go, damn dog."

The dog didn't let go. He fixed a dark eye on her, watching her every move, while not giving an inch to Teresa. Beth rushed in to kick him again. Before her foot connected, the Shepherd released the shovel and jumped sideways. Teresa fell on her ass.

The other dogs arrived, a sleek, fast Doberman and a muscular German Shepherd. The Shepherd raced through, grabbed the shovel handle and yanked it from Teresa's grip. Teresa swore, and scrabbled after the shovel. She didn't get far. The Rottweiler had circled around. It clamped iron jaws around her leg.

Frustration overcame her pain. "Beth, get that shovel. They'll tear us apart."

Beth jumped for the shovel ten feet away. The Doberman leaped with her, grasped her arm, and brought her down, sprawling on the cool grass. She fought to free her arm and got two slashes on her cheek for the effort. When she held still, the sleek Doberman let her loose and took a station between her and the shovel. Undeterred, Beth crawled forward.

One of the Shepherds clamped its jaws hard on her ankle. Cursing, kicking, Beth again struggled to free herself, but only succeeded in tearing bloody gouges in her leg. She ceased struggling.

As one, the dogs released Beth and Teresa. Then the four of them lined up between the women and the safety of the trees. They waited, alert and confident, their throaty snarl a clear warning.

Favoring her bleeding leg, fists clenched and lips pressed tight, Teresa considered how to get around the dog guards. Tears welled and her stomach twisted when Beth offered the only realistic answer. "We're not going to make it to the trees."

"Damn it." Teresa knelt to inspect Beth's torn up leg.

"Sorry I couldn't stop them," Beth said. "Maybe you could make it on your own?"

"You think so? Come on, we need to stop that bleeding."

Beth leaned on Teresa as they retraced their steps to the door. The dogs followed, ready to attack or defend. Once inside, Beth hobbled unnoticed in the direction of the elevator while Teresa shut the door and lowered the bar. She didn't trust those dogs.

When Teresa turned around, she didn't see Beth at first. She glanced up the corridor to the cell. Not there. Then she spied Beth reaching for the slightly open door to the room with something not alive in it. "Beth, no."

Beth stared into the room, not moving a muscle.

Teresa ran up to her and froze at what she saw. "You," she said. "You're here?"

# Chapter Thirty-nine

Vampires heal quickly. Cuts, slices, slashes, and bullet wounds pucker closed within minutes, to seal in the limited amount of blood in their system. The wounds aren't fully healed, but there's little pain, and range of motion is mostly restored. Heads will reattach if held in place long enough, usually overday. But recapitated vampires are seldom exactly right, in mind or body, and it is rarely done. A stake through the heart will keep a vampire down, as long as the stake remains.

If necessary, a vampire can keep going through anything, unless permanent decapitation or fire extinguishes their existence. However, some mental down time and a nap work wonders for vampires as they do for mortals. That's what the occupants of rooms 214 and 216 of the Vista Rest Motel were doing.

Simone and Darius lay on the bed in the darkened 216. They dozed occasionally, between brief conversations about old times, the good old days. Both agreed, then was better than now. They'd had freedom to use their power, when power meant something besides money.

Justine and Harry occupied room 214. They lay gently in each others' arms. Harry's hands were red and tender from the fire, but without serious burns. His other wounds were minor—cuts and bruises. Nothing some ice and Band-Aids and a pill or two couldn't handle. Justine's wounds would have killed her, if she hadn't already been dead. She had been shaken by the realization of her vulnerability. Since she had first awakened in Simone's house, in the back of her mind she had thought of herself as an Uber-vampire, undefeatable as she pursued her revenge. Every victory had reinforced that idea. She had, after all, become a vampire in order to be powerful enough to defeat all comers, vampire and mortal. Seeing the sword tip protrude from her body had gotten Justine's attention. Yet, for a little while, in Harry's arms, it didn't matter.

The sun set, and the occupants of both rooms began to stir.

❧ — ❧

They gathered in room 214. Darwin warned them to subdue their thoughts. He felt the probing of Sinakov's minions as they scoured the area for them. "Sinakov is very angry," Darwin said. "His orders are to eliminate us on sight."

Simone pointed out to Harry specific areas of the Transporte Francaise estate on the blueprints that Bayley, coached by Justine, had obtained from the county records department. Bayley had also driven down to Rancho Santa Fe and managed to take some photographs of the area.

"God damn it!" Harry paced the length of the room. "Her partner was almost killed, and Bayley is a civilian. She should not be involved in this. You should not have contacted her."

"Harry, who else could go during daylight, when the office is open?"

"Me."

"You had not slept, you were hurt. You had need of rest. Sinakov has Teresa. Would you wait another day?"

Harry rubbed his temples, trying to think. "I could have called someone I work with."

Justine said gently, "I don't think your credibility at work is very high right now. Bayley jumped at the chance to help. Anything to help get the 'people' who hurt Susan."

"Christ. Is everybody a goddamn vigilante? Did you tell her what you are?"

"No. But she's not stupid. She knows something strange is happening."

Harry rolled his eyes. "Tell me about it." He looked down at the blueprints and shook his head. "I suppose you're going to terminate this Sinakov when you find him? If he doesn't terminate you first." He gave each of them a *you guys are nuts* look. "I'm a cop. I shouldn't be in any way involved in this." The three vampires just stared at him. "Okay, it's a little late for that, but still..."

"Harry, Sinakov is dead. He's out of your jurisdiction."

He almost smiled. "Funny. What about his part in the kidnapping/sex slavery thing? Is that real?"

"We believe so."

Harry held up clenched fists and shook them at the universe. "Ahhhh!" Calmer, he said, "Okay, this is a rescue mission for Teresa. At the moment, as a cop, if I still am a cop, I don't want to know any more than that. I assume you have a plan. What do I do?"

The three vampires uncomfortably avoided his gaze.

"You drive," said Justine.

* * *

Harry parked Simone's "getaway" SUV just beyond the entrance gate to the Transporte Francaise estate. He knew better than to ask where the other car they were using came from. A high stone fence with a ring of trees on the inside separated them from the broad lawn. Harry and Justine waited for Simone to signal that it was okay to proceed.

"Good luck," Harry said. He didn't know what to do with his hands.

"Thanks." Justine quietly clicked her fingernails.

Harry reached out for her hands, but drew back. "Nervous?"

"No. Yes. You?"

"Yes. It's not much of a plan."

"I'm going in. I want it over."

"I hope sometime in your long life you'll discover patience."

"If I have a long life."

"If?"

Justine glanced at him then stared at her clicking fingers. "This guy didn't become so powerful or live this long by being stupid. He has to know we're coming, tonight."

This time he did lay his hands over hers. "Simone has experience, too. And I think you're as good as her. If you don't get cocky."

Justine absently rubbed her belly where the sword had come through. "Don't worry about that."

"Good. Just try and get Teresa back before any taking care of other business, okay? I'll be here, waiting, for you."

She shifted around to look him in the eye. "No matter what?"

"No matter what."

"You're a fool, Harry."

"I know."

∾—∾

Simone and Darwin settled into the trees along the top of the steep slope behind the Transporte Francaise estate. They had a good view of the back of the house, the front approach and the left side as seen from the front. Her newly acquired car was parked a hundred yards across the hillside in a small grove of Eucalyptus trees.

Darwin sat cross-legged against a tree and carefully concentrated on the building below. While he attempted to discern the interior population, Simone surveyed the exterior.

She noted what looked like dog runs far to the left of her position. She looked for access points into the building and into the cover of trees. A disturbed area of lawn puzzled her. Then she caught a faint whiff of fresh mortal blood. Did it come from the lawn? Tracks in the damp grass suggested dogs racing to the spot. Did Teresa or one of the girls try to escape? Did the dogs rip them to pieces? Footprints led to a side door. From the blueprints, she knew the door accessed the basement, the best place to hold captives.

Simone sat next to Darwin and tentatively focused on the house. An undecipherable mishmash of thoughts and emotions were all she detected. Darwin sat absolutely still, eyes closed. Simone spoke quietly into a short range walkie-talkie. "Are you there?"

"About time," Justine replied. "What's happening?"

"Darius is searching. When he is finished, you must be ready."

"I've been ready. Tell him to hurry up. Can we get in that side door?"

"It looks clear."

"Okay. Don't make me start without you."

Simone, also, wished to go. She had questions to ask this Sinakov face to face.

⁊— ⁊

Teresa sipped water that Beth held to her lips. It took her a moment to remember the girl's name and where they were.

"Are you okay?" Beth asked. "What did he do to you?"

Teresa's head pounded in sync with her heartbeat as she searched the scrambled images in her memory. She remembered the dogs, retreating back to the basement, Beth opening the door. She struggled to sit up. Her dog-inflicted wounds were bandaged, as were Beth's.

When the whirling subsided, she asked, "You opened that door, what did you see?"

"A...vampire? A woman, young, I think. She looked dead. Not like Dee, if she really is..."

"She is. What did the woman look like?"

Beth let out a noisy breath. "I don't know. I only saw her for a second. She was like eighteen maybe, but her skin was so pale I couldn't tell. She seemed bewildered."

"Anybody else?"

"Sinakov."

"What happened?"

"At first he seemed really pissed, then he saw you. You were like totally shocked and said something like, 'It's you?' You obviously knew her."

Teresa leaned toward Beth, headache and dizziness forgotten. "Did she know me? Did she say anything? What did she say?"

Beth shifted back a tick, away from Teresa's intense stare. "She didn't say anything. But I think she recognized you."

"*Ay, Dios mio, Dios mio, mi Antonia,*" Teresa said from behind hands covering her mouth. "What did Sinakov say?"

"He smiled and said, 'Ah, Teresa, you have ruined my surprise.' Then Dee grabbed me and put me back in here. I heard you scream."

Teresa swung her legs off the bed, then had to lower her head to fight off a bout of dizziness. Images swept through her thoughts: Sinakov suddenly appearing in front of her, grabbing her neck, pulling her into the room, an unidentifiable figure of a girl behind him, slowly vanishing. Sinakov's black eyes merging with her own, his voice in her head,

"Forget her, forget who you see. You do as I say."

"No. I don't." Teresa squeezed her head to get the images out. "I don't do what you say."

Beth sat beside her. "Teresa, what are you talking about?"

After several deep breaths, Teresa straightened up. "That girl you saw was my daughter, Antonia. I have to get to her. She needs me." She jumped up, stood still to clear her head, then went to the door and shook it, grunting with the effort.

"Teresa, that was a dead girl I saw. She's one of them, a vampire."

"No. She's alive, sick, treated badly, but alive. She needs me to get her out of here. To keep her safe." Tears spattered on the floor as she beat on the unyielding door.

The door ignored her fists. Finally she stopped and rested her head against the cool metal. Beth gently guided her back to the bed, where she sat head bowed, hands listless in her lap.

"I miss her," Teresa said.

"I know." Unsure what to say, Beth gently rubbed Teresa's back. They were still sitting when the door opened.

Dee stepped in and held the door for Stephan Sinakov. He had changed clothes. Gone was the Fashion Wear suit and shiny shoes, replaced by black martial arts pants, a tight T-shirt and sneakers. He stood over her, gazing down on her like a frustrated parent considering an exasperating child.

"We have a deal, Teresa. If you leave here before I allow it, the deal, and the protection that comes with it, is finished. Do you understand?"

"But she's already here."

"Who?"

Teresa's mind and pulse raced. "Antonia."

"Your Antonia?"

"Yes. I saw..." Her thoughts swirled with doubt. He seemed genuinely surprised at her pronouncement. It must have been her daughter. It had to be. Please God, it had to be.

After a long hesitation, Sinakov said, "Ah, I see. Patience, Teresa. You mortals."

"When will I...we be allowed to leave?"

"Soon. Possibly tomorrow."

"I want to take Beth with me." She had to try. She'd feel terribly guilty if she didn't.

Sinakov's mouth twisted with distaste as he glared at her. Beth's movements were jerky as she moved to stand, head bowed, in front of Sinakov. Teresa saw how Beth fought every movement he forced her to make. She wanted to help the girl, but knew Sinakov would not tolerate her interference.

Sinakov grabbed Beth's chin and inspected the deep scratches on her face. Finally he let go, mentally and physically. Dazed, Beth dropped to the bed. To Teresa, he said, "We still have a deal, do we not?"

Hating herself, yet unable to give any other answer, she nodded.

He nodded, then stalked to the door, where Dee stood guard. He stopped by Dee, and did not look back. "That other one is worthless now. Feed her to the dogs, then come to me."

Wide-eyed, Beth looked at Teresa, then Dee, and back at Teresa.

Lips tight, eyes narrowed, Dee studied Beth, but did not move or speak.

A surprising outrage brought Teresa to her feet. She would have her daughter back, perhaps she could give another mother the same comfort. She gave Beth's shoulder a reassuring squeeze, then confronted Dee.

Dee's face showed no emotion. Head down, eyes up, her gaze never left Beth.

"Tell me you are not going to throw her to the dogs," Teresa said, voice flat and hard.

"I have my orders."

"You don't have to obey them."

"I have a deal. Just like you."

"You were forced into it."

Dee gave her a noncommittal shrug, though her eyes were still on Beth.

Teresa frowned. "Why don't you run away? You could be free and not have to do his...dirty work."

Staring at the floor, Dee said, "He is my Master. I am bound to him. He would find me, no matter where I ran to. But in fifty years I'll be free and rich." She studied Beth who returned her examination. "Maybe I'll start my own Family."

Teresa didn't like the implications of their mutual scrutiny, but anything would be better than being thrown to those dogs. "Let Beth go. Make her forget and let her go. You can do that, can't you?"

Dee cocked her head as if listening. She stepped away from the door and said, "I have my orders."

"No, you can't have her." Teresa stepped in front of Beth before she was aware of her words. Was she crazy? She barely knew the girl. If she caused trouble she'd blow any chance of getting Antonia back. However, she would expect nothing less of Beth's mother if their places were reversed.

"Don't do this," Dee said. "It will not help her."

"I can't let you just kill her. She's not worthless."

With no idea what she was going to do, fists clenched, Teresa moved

# Blood Justice

toward Dee. In a whirl of motion, she was grabbed by the throat and slammed against the wall.

"Stay," Dee said. The word, and the idea, bore into her thoughts. When Dee let her go, she sank to the floor, sobbing. She barely acknowledged the solid thunk of the door bolts shooting home.

# Chapter Forty

"I'm leaving my position now. Meet me across from that end door. Over."

Justine jumped at Simone's voice from the walkie-talkie. She squeezed Harry's hand too hard.

"Ow." Harry jerked his hand away.

Justine fumbled with the radio. "About time. I don't know how much longer I could have kept my clothes on, sitting alone with Harry like this. What's happening inside? Over. Out. Over and out?"

"Something. Let us go in and discover. Over."

Justine handed the walkie-talkie to Harry. Harry's hand trembled as he took it. They both looked ahead into the darkness. "Call me if you need any help. My middle name is Cavalry."

"I will." Justine forced a smile. "It's not your jurisdiction. These people are dead. We're all dead."

Harry turned to her. He reached out and gently touched her cheek. "Not to me."

Justine opened up her senses to fully take in his touch—just in case. The same as with the kiss that followed.

"I have to go," she said.

"I know. I'll walk you to the fence. You never know. There might be a killer bunny out there."

"Harry, no."

"Harry, yes." He lifted the shotgun from behind the seat and opened the door.

All senses alert, Justine led Harry through the trees to the stone fence that surrounded the compound. Harry followed quietly. It was nice to have him watching her back...like they were partners. Foolish, she knew, but nice, nevertheless. They found the fence and followed it upslope until she sensed someone ahead. Simone, she thought, and was surprised to recognize the signature of her friend, and, something she'd have to come to terms with later, her Master. Justine's ability to sense other vampires, and their identities, was developing much faster than Simone had said it would. A handy sense to have. It might save her head some night.

Simone slid silently out of the dark and knelt beside them at the base of the wall. Justine had no problem understanding the *Harry?* thought in her head.

"He's my bodyguard," Justine whispered. "Can we go?"

Simone answered by standing up and reaching for the top of the wall.

Harry gave Justine's shoulder a squeeze and she flowed over the wall after Simone.

❧ — ❧

Beth stumbled when Dee pushed her out of the cell door. The anger she'd felt when she first awoke in the cell and realized what had happened to her flared. They had no right to treat her this way.

Dee turned to shoot home the bolts. Beth slipped off the flip flops, grabbed them up and silently ran down the passageway. At the basement proper, she turned right to the outside door. If the vampire dogs were going to get her, she was going down fighting. Maybe they hadn't locked the door. Though the bar was up, the door would not open.

Beth spun around. Dee stood directly in front of her. Hands on Beth's shoulders, gently, but firmly, pressing her against the door, Dee said, "Beth, you have to come with me."

Beth, strangely, was not afraid. And she didn't think Dee was in her head. It was her eyes, the way they looked into her. Though dark, they contained more—dare she think it—desire than malice. She wondered if her own eyes revealed the same.

Beth had been drawn to Dee from the moment she saw her a few hours after waking up in the cell. Dee was the kind of woman Beth was attracted to—confident, strong, older—but had never had the courage to approach. Nobody knew Beth was gay except the visiting cousin of a friend. It had been the first time for both of them, an unfulfilling week of kissing and fondling that ended almost by accident in a satisfying— finally—orgasm.

She had thought that her abduction two months later was punishment for her transgression. Locked up with scared and vulnerable cute girls who totally missed their boyfriends, not girlfriends, was a particularly cruel Hell. Fantasies of the untouchable Dee did not lessen the pain.

And now here was Dee, so close, but so far. She was ordered to feed her to the dogs by, as Beth understood it, a Master who could compel her to obey. Yet, Dee hesitated. This confused Beth. The vampire woman she was attracted to was frozen in place, pinning Beth against the door. What was she thinking behind the dark, unmoving eyes that held her in place as surely as the hands on her shoulders?

Dee gave her head a quick shake like getting rid of a pesky bug. Without a word, she took hold of Beth's arm and firmly led her through the basement toward the elevator. Somewhere along the way her hand took Beth's.

In the elevator, Beth said, "Please don't feed me to the dogs."

"Beth, don't make me force you to keep quiet."

Beth clutched Dee's arm and held it close. Her head rested on Dee's shoulder.

Out of the elevator, they followed a short passage past the main kitchen and exited a simple door to a small utilitarian wood deck. Immediately, the four dogs barked and rushed toward them, stopped by a heavy wire fence that circled their run.

"Quiet!" Dee ordered.

Their low growls signaled their reluctance to obey. Beth didn't have to be a vampire to sense the animals' need to rip her body to shreds. The air was thick with their psychic desire, like the odor of raw meat too long without refrigeration. Beth fought panic. Dee put her arm around Beth's shoulders and guided her down wooden steps onto the open lawn, then away from a gate in the fence that barely contained the four vampire dogs.

Halfway to the trees, a hundred feet from the dogs, Dee stopped and faced Beth. "There's a wall in the trees there. On the other side, you'll be safe from the dogs."

With quick glances, Beth measured the distance to the trees, to the dogs, to the house, to Dee.

"I have to loose the dogs. You have to run. Go home, Beth."

"I don't want to go home. They don't want me there."

"Why wouldn't they want...? Live somewhere else then. You can't stay here."

"But I know about this place."

"After tonight, it may not matter. Go, Beth. Run for your life." Dee spun Beth around, facing her to the nearest trees. Hands on her shoulders, lips close, she whispered, "Please, Beth. Run. For me."

Beth tried to turn. Dee held her tight.

"Make me like you," Beth said.

Dee hesitated. "No."

Dee pushed Beth hard toward the trees so that she stumbled on her wounded leg. Dee walked quickly toward the dog gate. Beth started to call after her, then, slapping away tears, embracing the pain, she ran for the trees.

As she slipped into the shelter of the trees, Beth heard the whine of an opening gate and the howl of pursuing hounds. The wall rose four feet from the steeply rising ground. Beth had no trouble clambering over. From the other side, she looked back, expecting to see the dogs racing through the moon-shadowed trees toward her. Instead, the beasts ran across the silvery expanse of lawn toward the end of the house.

# Blood Justice

*Stupid dogs*, she thought. For a moment she contemplated running down to the lawn and screaming, *Here I am. Come get me. Make me disappear for good. Don't make me go back home.*

Instead, she began the painful climb up the slope to wherever it led.

❧ — ☙

Barefoot, Stephan Sinakov walked with the confidence of a man who knew how the night's events would transpire. He trailed long, slender fingers along the smooth wood paneling of the hall from his bedroom to the stairs that rose to the open third floor. He still wore the black martial-arts pants and a long-sleeved T-shirt. Justine Kroft would come for Teresa, and then attempt to destroy him. She would not have her revenge.

❧ — ☙

He'd spent some years in Asia, learning meditation and the martial arts. That time was supposed to have been a period of rest and recuperation from years of debauchery and business in other parts of the world. A global business, human trafficking was a vastly profitable enterprise. You only needed to know what the buyers who could afford to indulge their individual, sometimes bloody, predilections, desired, and where to find it. A simple business, really, but with its temptations.

The Sinakov Family, having been in the business for centuries, had the connections for both customer and product. Unfortunately, many of the customers wanted their merchandise intact and unused. Stephan's arrogance and power as the Master of one of the oldest Families had led him to think he could do as he pleased with the merchandise before delivery and not have anyone notice or complain. They did, and business suffered. As did he.

Vampires could theoretically live forever, but they couldn't "go" forever. Like mortals, too much sex, booze, stress, and not enough sleep or "down time" had an unhealthy effect on the body. Hence, his twenty-year visit to the exotic Orient in quest of head-clearing meditation and the discipline of martial arts training. However, his head-clearing consisted mostly of forgetting all the women he'd been with, and the promises made to them. A black belt in Kung Fu had come easily to him, though distractions of the flesh prevented him from taking the art seriously. He still remembered his forms and often thought about practicing them, but he had been busy and after all, it had only been fifty years since that time.

Stephan silently entered through an inconspicuous door by the kitchen and automatically scanned the area. The large stone fireplace burned comfortably. The big-screen TV was tuned to a Jazz music station. He liked the big room. It gave him space. When first taken, before he was changed, he spent much of his time in a cage, or on a leash. If he had to be restricted during certain hours of the day, the big room gave him space to move about and entertain himself and associates of various kinds. Sometimes he watched reruns of *Buffy the Vampire Slayer* and *Angel* for hours. He anticipated that night's entertainment to be in a similar vein, though the Vampire Slayer was not going to win.

Another man occupied the room. In the workout corner, facing the full-length mirrors, he practiced martial arts moves, strikes, blocks and kicks. The heavy bag shuddered with each blow. Ironically, with each punch or kick, he shouted "Chi!" meaning, among other things, Life Force. Jay Dunham's moves were quicker than any mortal's, but sometimes off the mark or tentative. His balance was not what it should have been. He'd been a vampire for only twenty-four hours, and the initial euphoria still coursed through his body.

Stephan watched him for a minute before saying, "Would you like to test yourself?"

Dunham performed one last kick then, feet together, right fist covered by left hand, he faced Stephan. "Sir!"

Stephan returned the salute without the *Sir*. Then he stepped across a red line on the floor delineating the workout area, and assumed the ready position.

His first attacks drove Dunham back. As he pressed the attack, Dunham blocked more and more of the kicks and strikes and began to return the offensive. For fifteen minutes they fought full-contact Kung Fu at vampire speed. High kicks, low kicks, spinning, rolling, striking, punching, they went at each other at a pace that would tire the most ardent Kung Fu movie fan. Stephan landed more blows, and more take downs, but Dunham, a double black belt former California champion, held his own.

They saluted each other and stepped over the line.

"You have recovered quickly," Stephan said.

Dunham grinned. "I have been preparing for this day for years, Sir. I wanted to be ready." The smile faded. "I didn't think it would be so soon. My apologies for my failure."

"Yes, it is regrettable. You have served me well as my daylight man. Perhaps tonight you will have a chance to redeem yourself."

They moved to the bar. Stephan went behind it.

"How so, Sir?"

"I believe the woman who murdered you will be here tonight."

"Justine Kroft? Did you capture her?"

"No. She is coming to kill me. And you, when she learns you are not as dead as she might like."

# Blood Justice

"She has proved more formidable, and lucky, than expected."
"Qualities better working for me than against me."
"You're going to try and recruit her?"
Stephan set a beer in front of Dunham. "I have something she wants."
"And if she refuses?"
"Then you will have a chance to terminate her. If you can."

# Chapter Forty-one

The only dog Justine had loved since her mother's murder had been Brittany's yellow Lab, Dax. So when she heard the excited baying of dogs closing fast, her stomach tightened to remind her she was about to have an encounter she'd rather not.

"*Merde*," Simone said. "Perhaps we can make it to the door before they arrive."

If they had raced mortal dogs, they would easily have reached the door first. The first pair of dogs, the Rottweiler and a Shepherd, ran right at them. The women jumped aside and let the two animals pass between them. The dogs skidded to a stop and with no hesitation attacked again. The Rottweiler went for Justine. At the last fraction of a second she jumped back and struck out with her sword. The blade sliced through both its right side legs. The dog howled as it rolled on the grass and came up hard against Simone.

Distracted, Simone failed to avoid the charging Shepherd.

The beast sank its teeth into her leg as it passed, yanking her off her feet. Rear in the air, it dragged Simone toward the back of the house. Justine ran after them. With a quick stroke she severed the dog's head. The dog backed up a few more feet before toppling. The jaws remained fastened to Simone's leg.

Simone shook her leg. "Get that damn thing off me."

"I'm trying." Justine winced as she gripped the jaws and struggled to pull them open.

The running bark of two more vampire dogs sounded. The two women froze for a second.

"Justine..."

"I know. I don't want to meet any more dogs either."

With a full-strength jerk, Justine opened the jaws enough to release their victim. Justine pulled Simone to her feet, then pushed her toward the side door. "Go, go."

Justine turned to run, but was stopped by the Rottweiler's frustrated whine. Its remaining two legs scrabbled at the grass in an effort to get at the intruders. Justine made the mistake of connecting with its eyes, glistening in the moonlight. In her mind, the beast's frustration that it couldn't get to her and kill her, turned to whimpers of pain and a request for help and sympathy.

"Oh, hell," she said to herself.

# Blood Justice

The other dogs were seconds away.

"What are you doing? Come on," Simone said from the door.

In a blur of motion Justine moved to the wounded animal and quickly decapitated it. "Stupid dog."

The new dogs were on the top step when Simone kicked the door open and they darted through. Simone pulled it shut and slammed down the bar.

On full alert, they scanned for a welcoming committee.

"There are vampires in this house," Simone said. "Why are they not here?"

Justine peered into the passage on the left. "I think there's a mortal down there. Can you tell? Is it Teresa?"

Simone stepped cautiously around the corner. They came to the cell door. Simone placed her palm on it. "Teresa," she whispered. "No others."

Carefully, Justine pulled back the bolts. Their eyes met for a moment, each making sure the other was ready for whatever happened. Then she pulled the door open.

Teresa lay on her bed, fingers laced over her stomach, head turned to the door, face set with a neutral, fatalistic expression. Tears left shiny tracks on her cheeks.

Joy flashed through Justine when she saw her friend. "Teresa. Are you all right?" Still nervously casting her senses, she moved to the bed.

Teresa forced a crooked smile. Otherwise she held still. "You came for me."

"Of course I did. You knew I would."

"I did." Her smile turned bittersweet. "I wish you hadn't."

Justine gripped Teresa's still laced hands. "Why would you say that? What has he done to you?"

"Nothing."

Simone left the door to look into Teresa's eyes. "She seems to be correct. He is not coercing her...on this matter."

"They know you're coming," Teresa said.

Justine sat on the foot of the bed. "After the racket those damn dogs made the whole frickin' neighborhood knows."

"You heard the dogs?"

"We met them." Justine pointed to Simone's tattered pant leg. "I think there's only two left."

"You killed two of them?" Frowning, Justine nodded. "Did you see anybody else?"

"No."

"Justine, let's take her to Harry. Then we can return for the other."

"Right. Teresa, can you get up?"

"No, I can't leave yet. And you can't kill him yet."

Justine tensed. "Why do you say that? What's happened?" Still frowning, she studied Teresa's face. She wiped away a tear. "Teresa, what have you done?"

"It's what you have done that matters now."

Justine grabbed her sword and jumped up at the sound of the unfamiliar voice. What she saw by the door froze her in mid draw. Vampires filled the door. Two vampires, a short, wiry man and a tall, redhead woman, held sawed-off shotguns a foot from Simone's face. The sword in her hand pointed down. Her arm trembled with the effort to keep it there.

The redhead said, "I know you're fast, but you're not that fast."

Dee, who stood even with Simone, turned from studying Justine and took hold of Simone's sword. Simone refused to release her grip for a long beat. Finally she did.

Dee turned back to Justine. "Teresa, take her sword and bring it to me."

Teresa stood beside her friend. "No."

Dee slowly blinked. She kept her focus on Justine, while speaking to Teresa. "Teresa, there's no need to make this difficult. More difficult."

"There was no need to feed the dogs, either."

Dee looked into Teresa's eyes while her lips formed a small lopsided smile. "Damn. I knew I forgot to do something."

Justine wondered what the hell that was about. Teresa seemed to know.

"Take her sword, Teresa."

Teresa stared hard at Dee, then took the sword.

"Come, all of you," Dee said. She turned and walked out of the room.

Simone and Justine, shotguns held steady on them, were ushered out. Justine noticed that Teresa followed, unescorted.

As Justine passed the three solid doors a deep sadness overwhelmed her. She staggered, clutching her stomach, and felt her face bunch up as if to cry. The third door drew her. She lurched toward it, but her escort grabbed her arms and carried her to the elevator. The sadness dissipated. The vaguely familiar memory of it did not.

"Who's in that room?" she asked, while they waited for the elevator. Dee and Simone and three others had gone up first.

"Not your business," one of two large men with shotguns said.

*Yes it is*, she thought.

The elevator door slid open. The men made her and Teresa enter first. Justine inconspicuously steered Teresa to one corner then moved to the other side where she stood with hands in pockets. As the men entered, one went to each front corner, facing her. One of them pushed the 3 button.

When the box began to ascend, Justine pretended to stumble forward, while crossing her arms over her chest. The gun muzzles hovered inches away.

"Step back," the largest guy said.

"Sorry. I really want to see what's in that room down there."

"You can't—"

Justine had no time to hesitate. She dropped her left hand and grabbed the gun barrel of the guy on the right, yanking it up to her left. "Teresa. Down." She grabbed the other barrel with her right hand, then pushed them to the door so each gun pointed to the other man's head. Justine kneed one of them in the crotch. He jerked the trigger. The second man's head disintegrated into a red spray of hair and bone. The concussion from the blast blurred her vision, and the noise covered Teresa's scream. Justine ripped the guns from the men's grips. She thrust one into Teresa's surprised grasp, then jammed the other against the bent over man's head and pulled the trigger. Then she jabbed the stop button. The headless vampires crumpled to the floor.

"Justine, *mi Dios*, what are you doing?" Teresa cried out.

"Do you know who or what is in that room?"

Teresa's brow wrinkled. She looked like she knew, but couldn't quite remember. "I don't know," she said slowly, thinking hard between the words. "I thought I did. Now I'm not so sure."

The elevator stopped at the second floor. The door slid open. The girl waited by the door. Her naturally big blue eyes grew bigger as she took in the two bodies and the two women. In a light blue summer dress, she was a waif compared to statuesque Justine. Their eyes held for the few seconds it took the door to close.

"Who was that?" Justine asked Teresa.

"I don't know. Was she a vampire?"

"I couldn't tell. It seemed like there was nothing there, neither mortal nor Vampire," Justine said. "Emptiness."

The elevator door slid open again, but not on the basement floor. It was the third floor, a big open room with at least ten vampires armed with swords, standing about, all looking at her.

Sinakov—it had to be him—stood alone by Simone. He called out, "Come, Justine, join us."

❧ — ❧

Simone knew it was a trap when she and Justine first entered the building. But that was okay; Simone had been in traps before, even set a few herself. She wanted to see this Stephan Sinakov and discover if he was who she thought he might be. If she was right, she had no idea how she would feel. It had been such a long time.

Immediately the trap was sprung, Simone understood how they appeared with no warning. A very powerful Master had cloaked their minds. She could only sense him in her mind as a faint presence, not at all powerful enough to influence her. Another clue.

Simone didn't like being separated from Justine by the elevator. Justine was so close to her goal she would not necessarily stop to think before acting. She'd like nothing better than to rampage through the house until she found Sinakov, gutted and decapitated him, and watched his flesh crumble to ash in the sun.

The ride up with the woman in charge proved interesting in that it raised questions, the answers to which might be important later. With her hundreds of years of experience, Simone attempted to read the woman's mind, without the man and woman guards detecting it. Somebody named Beth was on Dee's mind, along with doubt and loyalty. No—questioned loyalty, and fear of what might happen if she betrayed loyalty forced upon her. Simone couldn't get a clear sense of Dee's thoughts because Dee herself was not clear about them. The two guards who enjoyed pointing their guns at her were mostly interested in getting over on each other.

When the elevator door opened to the big room, Simone again used her experience to suppress her surprise. Jay Dunham leaned on a bar stool, drink in hand, and watched her. It was obvious to her what had happened. Dunham had proven himself a loyal employee, and along with his other compensation he'd been given "life" insurance. At some time, probably with some ceremony, Sinakov had bitten him, and returned the blood. Then, all Dunham had to do was die, and wake up an immortal vampire. No wonder Sinakov's mortal henchmen were so brazen.

Dee led Simone to the bar, and left her there. She and the two guards retreated to a spot against the wall.

Dunham looked much better than the last time she'd seen him, a dead mortal at the bottom of a narrow ravine. He held out a wrist. "I haven't forgotten what you did to Ricky. He was a good friend. Would you like to drink my blood?"

"No thank you," Simone said. "It is probably sour by now."

A leggy blonde vampire came from the kitchen with a carafe of blood on a polished, stainless steel tray. She set it on the bar then rubbed up against Dunham.

"Not everyone thinks so," Dunham said. "She will be my reward for ending Justine Kroft's short time as Vampire."

Startled, Simone quickly replayed the last minutes. When did he have time to kill Justine? He hadn't. As the one who changed her, Simone would have felt her extinction. "You mean after you have attempted to destroy her, this woman will be your consolation prize. If you survive."

Dunham's eyes grew wide, then narrowed as he stood to his full six foot four. He clenched his fists and took a step toward Simone.

"Stop," said a man behind the bar whom Simone had barely noticed.

Dunham stopped. His reward girl pulled him back.

Simone caught the eye of the man behind the bar. She tried to read him as he tried to read her. He had no better success than she did. She felt the push into her mind, but had no problem resisting it. What she saw was a handsome man, six feet tall, his skin stretched tight over his wiry body. He was fifteen years older, two feet taller and had lost every ounce of his youthful chubbiness, but she knew immediately who he was.

"Henri."

The muffled sound of the first shotgun blast froze all in the room. Seconds later, the second blast animated them.

"Dee," the man behind the bar ordered. "Override the elevator. Bring it up."

Dee moved to the elevator door, inserted a key, punched some buttons, and stepped back.

The man known as Sinakov came around the bar and headed for the door. Simone intercepted him. Guards rushed to her. He waved them away. He did not look at her. "I am not Henri. I am Stephan Sinakov, Master of the Sinakov Family."

Simone reached out—the guards rustled—and raised his chin. The scar was there, pale, hard to see, but there. Gently her fingers touched the slightly raised line. "Henri. What has happened to you?"

Henri backhanded her fingers away from him. His head twisted to face her. His words held centuries of simmering anger. "Why do you care? You killed me."

The elevator pinged. Sinakov, with a final blast of hate, turned his attention to the door. The door slid open, revealing Justine, two shotguns leveled, standing over two tangled bodies. Simone rolled her eyes at the dramatic entrance, and silently thanked Justine for the interruption. How could she explain to her son the impossible choice she'd had? That she'd done what she'd done to prevent what had happened anyway? Guilt flooded into her as it had so many times before, compounded by new guilt now that she knew he had survived. She should have searched harder for him, but there had been so many bodies among the ashes. The bones she found, she had thought....

"Come, Justine, join us," Sinakov said.

# David Burton

↝ — ↜

The two shots happened so fast Teresa didn't jump until seconds after it was over. Her shoulders ached from the contained blasts—the noise had gone into her ears like sharp stakes. Though Justine was not the same woman she'd known and worked with for years, after the first minute Teresa could tell she was in a take-no-prisoners mode. She was making good on her *I don't care what happens to me afterwards* statement.

The answer to Justine's question about the basement room was in Teresa's head; she knew it, she just couldn't find it. Anything was better than having to answer her other question—What had happened to Teresa since she was abducted?

Teresa dreaded having to answer that. How did she tell her best friend she'd made a deal with the vampire who had brutally murdered her daughter to sleep with him if he got her own daughter back? How to ask Justine not to destroy that monster, until Antonia was returned to her? It was impossible, yet it had to be done.

Teresa stayed back when the elevator door opened.

"Come, Justine, join us," Sinakov said.

Justine stepped out of the elevator and did not seem surprised when two very alert guards put swords at her throat and took her guns.

"No guns allowed in the big room," Sinakov said, as if asking one to leave their shoes at the door.

With all eyes on Justine, Teresa slipped out of the elevator and tried to remain inconspicuous against the wall.

# Chapter Forty-two

Justine scanned the others circled around the room, all armed with swords and all focused on her. The gun she held would do little harm to Sinakov from that distance, and she could never get any closer. Or could she?

She could barge right in, shotgun blasting, hope to do some fatal damage before the guards decapitated her. No slicing him open, no explanations about why he did it, no looking him in the eye just before he dies, forever.

She looked back at Teresa, pressing herself into a corner. *Jesus, she looks deader than me,* Justine thought before asking, "You coming?"

Justine exited the elevator. Immediately she had two swords at her neck. Two massive hands grabbed the guns and waited for her to let go. She tried pulling them away. They didn't budge.

A tight knot formed in her stomach as she took the measure of the others in the room, just as they measured her. They were all vampires, all strong and fast, not afraid of what she might do. Justine closed her eyes. They were all equal in that room. She was equal to any one of them, but outnumbered and so, once again, powerless.

In the few seconds she held her eyes closed, Justine gave up hope. She'd given up her life to avenge Brittany's death. Now, she was as powerless as the night her daughter had died. She might as well give it up, walk away, go wait at the beach for sunrise.

She let go of the guns.

She silently said goodbye to Harry. It wouldn't have worked out anyway. A mortal cop and a vampire? She had to drink blood to survive. Harry could look the other way as long as she only assaulted, even killed, bad guys, but if she survived, how long could he continue the denial? How long could he love her?

Murmurs in her mind all wanted her to do something, but none were intelligible or persuasive. Simone watched Justine, a slight raising of the eyebrows questioning her; otherwise, she wore the patience of centuries like a comfortable old shirt. Teresa huddled into herself, obviously troubled. Hell, she was a big girl, she could handle it, she didn't need Justine's help. Justine had no power to help, anyway.

Justine studied Sinakov. He didn't look like so much, with his slicked back hair, wide shoulders, and oddly familiar face. On the street she'd dismiss him as a hip, pseudo-wannabe.

Then Jay Dunham stepped into her view.

Justine figuratively held her breath. Simone had explained about "life insurance," so Justine knew immediately what had happened. Dunham was now a vampire. That meant Justine had another chance to destroy him.

In a flash of epiphany, Justine got it. She hadn't really been powerless before; she just hadn't had the will to use whatever power she did have. That night in Freddy's apartment, Dunham and Standard hadn't been scared of her because they instinctively knew she wouldn't shoot them. At the time, they felt she cared about the consequences of shooting them, that she was only an angry woman making furious threats with no intention of action behind them.

Now, they thought any threat she posed was neutralized by their numbers, that she was powerless once again. But Justine no longer gave a damn about the consequences. Suddenly, she didn't feel powerless at all.

Taking a deep breath, Justine strode over to Sinakov. "I'm Justine Kroft," she said, holding out a hand. "You must be Stephan Sinakov." Sinakov shook her hand. She held his hand tight with both of hers, pulling him close. "The one who murdered my daughter."

She heard a collective intake of breath at her bold statement. He was in her head, probing thoughts, attempting to instill new ones—fear, submission. She did the same to him; neither was successful.

Dunham stepped forward. His hateful glare demanded her attention. Justine released Sinakov and returned Dunham's scowl.

Sinakov grinned. "Ahh. You are acquainted with Jay. A young one, such as yourself."

"You killed my friends," Dunham said.

"Unlike some, they deserved it."

"I'm sorry you won't suffer as a mortal would, before you die for real," Dunham said, his intense blue eyes impaling her.

"We'll see who suffers."

"That we will," Sinakov said. He swept a hand to indicate the workout area. "I promised Jay the first chance with you. That is acceptable, is it not?"

"And you?" Justine asked.

"Him first," Sinakov said and waved others to escort her to the fight floor.

Justine eyed Simone. To Sinakov she said, "Dunham is a big guy, I could use her help."

"If Jay kills you, then maybe she will have her chance."

"At you."

"She's already had her chance at me. And you can see how that turned out."

# Blood Justice

Justine raised a questioning eyebrow at Simone while probing her mind—*What the hell is going on?* Simone raised one shoulder a millimeter or two, but kept her thoughts and feelings closed off, so Justine got nothing helpful.

Two males escorted her to the taped-off area, then threw her sprawling on the floor. She was almost on her feet when Dunham kicked her ribs and sent her rolling away. The physical pain lanced through her, but faded quickly. She curled up as if badly injured. If that was the way they wanted to play it, she'd do it their way.

Dunham kicked her again. Ready for it, she grabbed his foot, heel and toe, and twisted it as she rose up, forcing him to stand on one leg, back to her. She kicked him in the balls, then knocked his leg out from under him. He went down hard, cradling his groin with his hands.

Justine circled him, occasionally giving him a poke with her toe. "Turnabout and all that, right, Dunham?"

When she was in just the right place, Dunham snapped into a fully extended position. His feet knocked her feet out and she went down on her butt. Dunham rolled and was on her in an instant. She got a foot under his body and with a full strength push, flipped him over her head. By the time she jumped up, he was up, too.

They wasted no time on ceremonial niceties or good sportsmanship. They went at each other, two super-strong, super-quick black belts, fighting for their lives. They struck, punched, kicked, blocked, leapt, and rolled faster than most mortal eyes could follow. A side kick to her chest sent her flying into the unfriendly spectators that made up the fourth wall of their combat area. They threw her back.

Justine and Dunham were evenly matched. He was bigger, stronger, and all things even, better, but very much a young one. Good as he was, like her when she was first changed, he had trouble controlling his new speed. His timing off, sometimes his punch arrived too early. She used that when she could, but she needed an advantage to win. Fair play be damned; she knew what she had to do.

Unfortunately, Dunham did it first.

Dunham punched, aiming for her jaw. Justine knew it would be ahead of her, so she held back to set him up for a strike that would allow her to literally take his head off. But Dunham had his own plan. He followed through with his strike, dropping down and sweeping Justine's feet out from under, front to back. Before she hit the mat, his elbow smashed her head, slamming her face to the floor.

Stunned, suddenly Justine was scared. In an instant, she lost all her confidence. She was at his mercy. She'd lost. She'd let Brittany down. Her immortality lasted barely a month. Any second she'd feel a sword slice through her neck, afterlife over.

When the strike didn't come, she looked up. Dunham stood over her left side. The bastard held the tip of his blade a few inches from her throat, wanting her to know what was coming.

"Bigger is not always better," Simone called to her. Stupid! Justine's confidence rushed back. "You're not getting away with hurting my daughter that easy, you sorry son-of-a-bitch."

Dunham sneered. "Fuck you, Mom."

Dunham pulled the sword tip back a few inches ready to jam it through her neck. He struck.

Justine slapped the blade with her left hand, just enough to miss her flesh. The blade stuck deep into the wood floor. Simultaneously, she reached into her pocket and withdrew her knife. Taken by surprise, Dunham paused to yank the blade free.

That was plenty of time for Justine to flip open the blade, surge up, and slice halfway through his arm. Instinctively, he jerked his hand away. Her blade flashed and cut deep into his other arm. No more equivocation for Justine. She slammed Dunham against the wall, and ripped him open crotch to chest.

Dunham sagged against the wall, attempting to hold his dead guts in with hands that didn't work.

Hate-filled eyes on Dunham, Justine picked up the sword.

"Stop her," Sinakov said.

The man and woman who had escorted Simone came at Justine, full speed, swords drawn. She met them halfway, rushing between them sword and knife like a propeller spun loose from its engine. The man crumpled to the floor minus a leg and his head. The woman lasted ten seconds more.

Justine closed the knife and returned it to her pocket, then turned her attention to Dunham. Dunham lurched away from the wall. One hand reached out, whether for attack or help was unclear. Justine stood in front of him, sword poised for the final strike. But she held back, searching his face for any sign of remorse. Finding none, she cut off his head with one clean swing.

She caught the head by its ponytail before it hit the floor. Her expression and raised sword brooked no resistance when she strode to the fireplace and laid Dunham's head on the flames. His hair sizzled as the fire consumed it.

Justine turned to the others in the room: Four vampire minions, Dee, who seemed more than a minion, Sinakov, Simone, and the only mortal, Teresa, who stood apart, her jaw set with something to say, but not able to say it.

"I don't want to have to kill him again," Justine said by way of unnecessary explanation. Then she focused on Sinakov.

Sinakov said, "Do you think you can kill me as easily as a young one? You yourself are a young one."

"I've aged a lot in the past month. And yes, I do think so," she said with full confidence.

Sinakov grinned. "You appear to be quite competent, Justine. But you cannot hope to defeat me, and my five best."

"She will have help, Henri," Simone said. She moved to stand between Sinakov and the five vampires.

"This is not your fight," Sinakov snapped.

"Nor ours," Dee said. She stepped in front of the four others, her sword held out as a barrier to them.

Sinakov glared at his defiant minion. "There are times when one should consider the consequences before one speaks."

"There are times when one should fight his own fight." Dee stiffened, fighting her Master's mental punishment. Through clenched jaws she continued, "If one wants the respect of the ones he has created."

Justine studied the reactions of the four minions, three men and a woman. All in their thirties or forties when they died, none were young ones. Justine assessed them as smart and experienced. They'd follow orders, what choice did they have? But the comment about earning respect would have meaning for them. By their glances between Sinakov and herself, they suspected a change might be coming, and they were calculating how it might affect them. The way the woman, a tall Latina, and the man next to her, a refugee from a romance novel cover, looked at each other, Justine figured they were hoping she'd win so they could get that white-picket-fenced house on the shady side of the street they'd always wanted.

Dee dropped to her knees when Sinakov released his hold on her.

Sinakov raised her chin with his sword. He spoke softly, but his voice was flint. "You are correct, Dee. I should fight my own battles. But you will not speak to me again in that manner. You are, after all, my right hand man." With his sword he lifted her right arm away from her body. "Perhaps we will make you my left hand man for a while so you will learn not to speak out of turn."

*Enough. Finish it.* Justine rushed him, sword poised to take off his head and be done with it. Suddenly, he was before her, blocking her blade. So quick she didn't see it happen, her sword flipped through the air to clatter across the floor. He had her. The blade, so sharp she felt her skin part each time it touched her neck, would take her head off before she saw it move.

Sinakov slapped her playfully on the cheek with his blade. "We are not finished yet, Justine. I have a deal to offer you. As soon as I take care of a small discipline problem."

# David Burton

He turned his back on her. The impudence of the move was a slap-in-the-face reminder of the impotence she felt when she was not taken as a serious threat, as well as the impotence she felt at that moment. She had only her knife as a weapon. After what she had just witnessed, to attack him with it was suicide. Unless...

Dee quivered with the effort to resist Sinakov's compulsion to keep her arm raised.

Sinakov looked down at Dee. "It will only be for a year, this time," he said, and raised the sword.

"Dee. No," a voice cried out from somewhere behind them all. Beth pushed past the minions and reached for Dee, just as the sword swept down. Beth's hand pushed Dee's arm away, and was severed for its trouble.

Freed, Dee slumped against Beth.

Beth slid her good arm around Dee's shoulders. "Oh my God, Dee. Are you alright?" Then she noticed the blood and where it came from. "Oh my God. Oh shit. Oh shit."

Teresa rushed up and knelt beside Beth. She grasped the girl's wrist and said, "Beth. I thought you were..."

"As did I." Sinakov dropped his piercing gaze on Dee like twin black lasers. "I am disappointed, Dee. You defy me, and now I find you disobeyed me. We have an agreement—"

"One I had no choice but to agree to. This girl needs to get to a hospital."

Sinakov tapped Beth's injured leg. "She is damaged goods. But, as you need two hands to serve me for the next fifty years, I will allow her to accept your punishment."

Beth tensed as if slapped, and slowly, fighting it, raised her intact right arm.

"Stephan, don't. It's my punishment. Leave her alone."

"Do not try me a third time," Sinakov warned with an annoyed grin. "Your mortal friend here may not survive it." To the woman vampire minion, he said, "Remove Teresa. We have our own agreement, and I do not want her damaged."

Justine had quietly retrieved her sword while Sinakov took care of his discipline problem. Sinakov's mention of an agreement with Teresa caught her attention.

Teresa finished winding the draw string from her pajama bottoms around Beth's arm as the Latina vampire took hold of her. "Let go of me," Teresa said, "She has to go to the hospital."

As she lifted Teresa, the woman said, "Come, *Querida*, you won't help by arguing."

"Sinakov, Stephan, *por favor*, don't do this," Teresa cried out as the woman vampire firmly pulled her away.

"Wait," Sinakov said.

Teresa turned a hopeful gaze to Sinakov.

"Teresa, I do know the location of what you most desire. But, I will let this mortal go, if you cancel our agreement."

Teresa couldn't speak. She stared at Beth, on her knees, pale, shivering, forced to hold her arms out by Sinakov's will. She imagined Antonia in the same position; in pain, scared and alone, maybe right that second in some desperate part of the world, surrounded by despicable characters. Teresa would expect any other mother to do what was required to prevent her girl from being hurt. How could she let this girl be mutilated? How could she give up the chance to find her Antonia?

Justine turned to Teresa. "Agreement? You made a deal with him?" Teresa's crumbling expression was answer enough. "What kind of deal?" Justine poked Teresa's chest with her sword. "Tell me." The unrelenting sword tip forced Teresa to scrabble backward. "God damn it, Teresa, tell me. What deal?"

Pressed to the floor by the sword, Teresa said, "He says Antonia may be alive, and he knows where she is, and can bring her back to me."

Justine stared open-mouthed, then turned her head to face Sinakov. "Is that true? You know where she is?"

"I do," Sinakov said.

"Liar." All attention turned to Simone. "I always knew when you were lying, Henri."

Every muscle in his body stood out as he broadcast waves of hurt throughout the room. "If you were my mother, why did you not know I didn't want to be left alone? Why didn't you know that?"

"I didn't know you would be alone. I thought I..."

"You thought you what? Protected me? Kept me safe from the vicious beasts by killing me."

"Henri, I'm sorry."

"I am not Henri! Do not say you're sorry. Only my mother can say that, and you are not my mother."

Sinakov turned his back on Simone and glared at Teresa. "Choose."

Teresa's mouth worked. No words came out. She silently pleaded with Justine.

Justine removed the sword with a disgusted jerk. "You made your deal with the devil. Choose."

Teresa remained on the floor, looking at the ceiling through her tears. She whispered. "Please, don't hurt her."

"Too late." Sinakov raised his sword over the sweating girl's arm.

"Stop!" The order was felt as well as heard. Sinakov held still, searching for who gave that order.

# Chapter Forty-three

Justine felt her chest swell with relief when Darwin suddenly appeared. She thought she had felt his presence when Beth made her dramatic entrance, but did not explore it as she focused on Dee, Beth, and Teresa. Justin hoped Darwin's calmness and experience would help her sort it all out. Then she saw that Darwin held a shotgun.

"That girl is a friend of mine, Stephan. Do not harm her anymore," Darwin said.

Sinakov's attention switched fully to Darwin. "So, Darius Rubinio. The Families still search for you. The rest of your Family is dead and it will be good to report that you, also, are finally exterminated. The end of the thieving Rubinio Family."

Beth collapsed when Sinakov focused on Darwin. With Sinakov's attention on the new arrival, Dee scooped up Beth and without a backward glance exited the big room. She made sure to take the severed hand with her.

"And do you think that will bring you favor with the Family Council, Henri Gireaux? The Master of a Family must be agreed on by the Family. You murdered Stephan Sinakov and stole his place."

"I am Stephan Sinakov. You know nothing, old man."

"Possibly, but your mother does."

"Henri," Simone said. "You have been a bad boy, *n'est pas?*"

"My mother is long dead, Rubinio. As you should be."

Sinakov raised his blade and rushed Darwin. The old vampire fired his shotgun, tearing the sword from Sinakov's hand and shattering a window behind him. Justine felt the pressure as the shot buzzed past her.

Spun by the blast, Sinakov cradled his hand with his arm. "Bring him," he ordered his minions with the full power of his voice and mind.

With only a hint of hesitation, the two male vampires separated and attacked Darwin. A shotgun blast to the chest knocked the lanky one backward. His sword clattered to the floor as he staggered back and collapsed in a heap among the bar stools.

The other man, a stout six footer with a military haircut, managed to grab Darwin's arm. Darwin clubbed him with the gun and got loose for a moment, but the man was too strong and quick—not that that helped him.

"Release him," said Simone, not giving him enough time to do so before using three precise swings of her blade to sever his arm, hand and head.

Romance-Cover guy moved to assist his fellow minion. Justine yanked him down flat on his back. She pressed her knife to his neck. "Just stay down."

Teresa had wrapped her arms around his partner's legs. The Latina vampire could easily have kicked Teresa off, but she disentangled herself without hurting her. Justine looked into the woman's eyes as they flicked between her face and her knife. "Tell him to stay down. Maybe you'll survive this."

The woman nodded once. Justine lifted the knife and backed away, turning to Sinakov.

Sinakov spoke as he retrieved the shotgunned vampire's sword. His rage permeated the room. The vampire couple expressed wide-eyed fear. Teresa curled into a terrified, shaking ball. Even Darwin shrank back. Justine felt it, but was not moved by it. Simone also seemed immune. She stood ready between Darwin and Sinakov, watching her son with dispassionate interest, as if she knew what was coming next but it meant nothing to her.

"I am the Master of the Sinakov Family. It matters not who you are. You will not interfere in Family or Vampire business, or you will be destroyed." Weapon in hand, he attacked Simone with a frenzy of pent-up rage finally released.

Simone was prepared for the attack, but not the ferocity of it. Their blades met with a continuous clanging as Simone defended against every slash and strike, but she lost ground with every block, unable, or unwilling, to do more than defend herself.

Justine watched them fight. They had issues, obviously. Simone had always seemed invincible with three hundred and fifty years of survival behind her. She understood how Simone, always calm and cool, must feel, up against her long-thought-dead son. Justine couldn't imagine having to defend herself against Brittany.

"Why did you not come for me?" Sinakov asked, his attack unrelenting.

"I did not know you were alive. I thought I had killed you." Half-heartedly she parried his attack. "I am sorry, Henri, my son. I loved you so much."

With a cry and a vicious blow he knocked the sword from her hand. He slammed her against the wall, pressing his blade against her neck. The skin stretched tight across his face like that of a desiccated corpse, his words coming out as a snarl.

"And I hated you so much. Though I thought you were dead, I dreamed for a hundred years of cutting your throat. I forgot about you for a long while, but now, I remember." He pressed his forehead hard against hers, his whole body quivering. "I remember." He tensed in preparation for slicing her throat.

In the past months, Justine had had her ups and downs, all leading to this moment. She'd died for this meeting. She'd thought about it for weeks, what she would do and say to the monster Sinakov. But now, she didn't want to hear the "monster" plead to his mother about why she did not rescue him. She didn't want her new best friend to die. She wanted it to be over. The fantasy of Sinakov's long, painful death, made more excruciating for him by her angry, biting words just seemed like too much trouble. Sinakov was incredibly fast, but his mercurial emotions and intense focus made him vulnerable.

Holding her sword in both hands Justine moved quickly to strike off Sinakov's head. Close up, she swung. Suddenly, Sinakov faced her, his blade blocking hers. For a long moment their eyes locked and they did not move. Justine felt him in her head, compelling her to surrender. As before, his compulsion had no effect on her. This surprised him and he withdrew his thoughts.

"I had hoped to persuade you to join me. But now I see I could not trust you to do as I say."

She did not have to use all her strength to hold Sinakov, which surprised her. His blade shook slightly against hers. This meant something, though she did not have time to figure out what. Sinakov pushed her away and attacked.

Justine did not back away as Simone had. They circled: attack, defend, attack, defend, neither giving way. Hardly a master swordsperson, she knew enough to recognize that Sinakov relied more on speed than technique. His attacks varied little and so were predictable. Even so, she sustained several wounds which would have crippled a mortal.

Justine was ready. Instead of circling right, she ducked and shuffled left. Both hands gripped her sword as she struck with all her strength. The force of her blow tore the sword from his hand. Like a choreographed dance they spun in opposite directions. Sinakov backed against a wood support post. Justine drove her blade through his body, deep into the wood.

His howl was more of surprise than pain. He sputtered with rage. "I am the Master of this house, this Family. You will not survive this night. You will be destroyed, and I will be in your head to enhance the pain." He focused hard on Justine. That she didn't respond to his silent orders infuriated him even more. He reached out to remove the sword holding him.

Justine slapped his hand away.

"Release me. I warn you, young one. If you destroy me you will regret it."

"Shut up." Justine scooped up his sword and rammed it through the side of his neck and deep into the wood column. Hate emanated from him like a physical force. She stepped back as if hit by an invisible fist. Hands grasped her from behind.

"Kill her." Sinakov's voice was rough and strained, but clear enough. "Kill her. You will be rewarded."

Justine flicked her knife open. To the Latina vampire and her partner, she said, "Release me, and you will be free."

Sinakov shouted, "I am your Master. Destroy them all."

The two minions shook as they tried to resist their Master's mental commands. Justine felt the force of Simone and Darwin's mental repetition of her words—*Release her, you will be free.* She added what little strength she could to the message.

With a cry, the male released her.

The woman said in Justine's ear. "Be sure you destroy him completely. If he survives, we are all finished."

They walked away without a word or a glance at Sinakov.

"I am your Master," he called after them. "I do not permit you to leave. You will be banished from all the Vampire Families. You cannot survive alone."

Their answer was a door slamming in the kitchen.

While everybody's attention was on the departing couple, Sinakov attempted to pull the sword out of his body. Justine sliced his hand off. "You are not the Master here anymore."

"Ahhh." Sinakov held his arm against his chest. His grimace turned into a grin. "Do not be so sure, Young One."

"You are alone. There is nothing left to be Master of."

"And now you will die forever." Darwin strode toward him, sword poised to take off Sinakov's head.

Justine blocked him. "He's mine."

"Yours? This...thing murdered my wife, my children, my Family, and countless others. You lost only your daughter."

Deep sadness enveloped Justine. The pain inside expelled all the air from her lungs. "Only my daughter? She was my life!"

Darwin's face bunched with his own hurt, but after a long pause, he backed off. "Just exterminate him."

"No, Justine, please." Teresa jumped up and stood beside Justine. "He can return Antonia to me."

Justine swung her sword backhand, stopping the blade when it touched Teresa's neck. Teresa let out a small yelp of surprise, but did not avert her eyes from the anger in Justine's. "In exchange for what?" Justine asked, her voice flat and hard as a sword blade.

# David Burton

"One night with me," Teresa said, her chin raised.

"You would do that?"

"To get Antonia back? Yes, and more. Wouldn't you?"

Justine had no answer to that. She faced Sinakov. "Is her daughter alive?"

"As long as I am."

"Don't believe him," Darwin said, pushing forward, sword ready to strike. "He must be ended."

Simone crossed swords with Darwin. Her hard glare said more than words.

"I know how you feel, my dear Simone," Darwin said. "But he cannot be allowed to exist. You know this."

Simone sought Justine's eyes. No words needed to be spoken.

Justine avoided looking at Teresa as she mentally prepared herself to finally avenge Brittany.

Teresa touched her arm. The contact burned like hot tears. "Justine, please." Her words were soft, but desperate.

Eyes on Sinakov, Justine said, "Even if you got Antonia back, do you think he'd really let you keep her?"

Teresa let her hand fall away. Her friend's sadness threatened Justine's hunger for revenge. The smirk on Sinakov's lips rekindled it.

Voice raspy but strong, Sinakov said, "If you will not allow Teresa to have her daughter back, perhaps you will give her yours."

"My daughter is dead and buried."

"Is she?" His eyes pointed in the direction of the elevator.

Justine had to look. The figure of a man emerging from the kitchen failed to register as the girl pushed a figure out of the closing elevator doors. A woman, a girl, bewildered, searching the room, seeing the people, focusing on one. Justine's chest constricted around her still heart. A surge of hope expelled all other thoughts from her mind.

"Brittany?"

"Mom?"

Justine found herself standing inches from Brittany. The girl's eyes were sunken, skin slack and grey. But she was Brittany, her daughter, thought gone forever, buried months ago. Sword dangling from twitching fingers, Justine reached out to touch the girl's face. She jerked her hand back. This was Brittany, she was sure of it, but what if she reached out to touch her, and there was nobody there? What if she was a cruel illusion? A dream turned nightmare when she attempted to embrace her sweet girl? But what if she was real?

Justine placed two fingers at first on Brittany's cheek. Eyes closed, she felt the cool softness of the skin. The same as the day she went to the library and never came back.

# Blood Justice

"How...why is she here?"

Sinakov's raspy voice answered, "I brought her here for you, a peace offering."

"Oh, Brittany." She embraced her daughter, squeezing her tight as if trying to meld their bodies so they could never be separated again. Then reality crept in to dissipate the shock of seeing her daughter again.

Brittany had been a strong, athletic, healthy young woman in life. To hug her meant feeling hard muscle under soft skin. There had been substance and strength to her body. Justine felt little of that now. Her daughter's body felt soft, as if it was hollow and to squeeze it too hard would crush it. Brittany's hug was tentative, as if hugging somebody she'd never met before. The girl in front of her was Brittany, but not Brittany.

"What have you done to her?"

"A little trick I learned in Africa. This is what you wanted, isn't it?"

Teresa, hands clutched to her mouth, gaped at the girl. "Brittany, do you know who I am?" Tears glistened on her cheeks.

Brittany's vacant eyes shifted slowly. Her words came with an effort, a breathy whisper. "Aunt Terry, are you dead, too? What's happened?"

Darwin stood next to Justine. His voice was somber, like Harry's when he told her that her daughter was dead. "When she was killed some of the fluid that changes mortals was in her. But not enough."

Justine caressed Brittany's cheek. "She seems so frail."

Darwin leaned in close. "She has to be...bitten again by the same one who first bit her. She has been underground for a long time. This sort of thing is frowned upon. It rarely turns out well."

"But she could be fully changed, like me, us?"

"Yes, she could," Sinakov said, in his normal arrogant voice. "I can do it, if I am alive, and stay that way."

Justine whirled about. Sinakov was free of the column. He held one of the swords she had stuck through him hard against Harry's throat. Out of the corner of her eye she saw the girl scurry along the wall like a mouse and slip into the kitchen. Justine had no sense of the girl's presence, as if she was an apparition, a figment, neither vampire nor mortal.

Justine snapped the sword in her hand to ready position. Simone and Darwin did the same.

"How the hell did he get free?" Darwin asked.

"The girl," Justine said.

"A ghost," Simone said. "A very few of us cannot be sensed."

Sinakov said, "Some servants are loyal to their masters."

"And so Justine, one other small thing. Something that should be easy for you." His eyes blazed with glee. "You must choose between your new boyfriend, Harry the detective, or the lovely Brittany. One lives, the other dies. Choose." His smile was as gracious as it was malicious. "If you need help, ask my mother. She has experience with such choices."

Simone's head jerked as if slapped.

Justine started toward Harry. Sinakov drew the blade an inch across Harry's throat. Blood tracked down his neck. She stopped. Justine did not want to choose. How could she? That was Brittany in that body, wasn't it? Brittany had been through hell, she was understandably confused. When Sinakov fully restored her she'd be the old Brittany, a good girl, smart and quick, full of life, a joy to be around. Wouldn't she? They would both be immortal, able to live together forever. As long as Sinakov survived.

"Harry," she said. "What are you doing here?"

Harry spoke in quick bursts, "Heard gunshot...thought you were in trouble...came to help. That girl brought me here. Not sure how."

How could she not choose Harry? He loved her, despite what she had become and all she had done; despite no promise of a future. She had brought nothing but trouble into his life which, though he was too stubborn to admit it, had been lonely since his wife left. Brittany's death had brought them together, could she let her rebirth pull them apart?

"She's your daughter," Harry said. "Save her."

Justine looked desperately between Harry and Brittany. Harry nodded to her—*save your daughter*. Brittany shuffled forward as she studied Harry and all the others. She seemed aware of what was happening.

Justine could not choose. How could anybody choose?

Darwin grasped Justine's face and forced her to focus on him. "If you sacrifice Harry, you then must allow, even aid, this fraud to live. Many in the Families will not be happy to learn he murdered the real Stephan Sinakov, bastard that he was, and took his place as Master of the Sinakov Family." He released her and stepped back. "He will be hunted. Your daughter's fate when he is eliminated will not be considered."

"Don't listen to that bitter old vampire," Sinakov said. "Choose now, or lose them both."

Justine looked to Simone. The firelight danced in Simone's glistening eyes. "It is an impossible choice, *ma cherie*. But know this, he is no longer my sweet boy, Henri."

Teresa, standing by Brittany, said, "She's your daughter, Justine. Your little girl. To have her back..."

Justine's stomach clenched into a tight ball. She felt her heart pound, though she knew it was still. She stood between Harry and Brittany, sword held in both hands, ready to strike in either direction.

"Mom." Brittany took a halting step toward her. Teresa reached out for her as if she was her own daughter. "Mom, I know you love me, but I don't want to live like this." With both hands she pulled apart the loose flaps of skin where Sinakov had slit her open. Revealed was a great hollow, with white ribs showing through patches of rotting skin and dried blood. "Please, Mom."

Justine stared at that vast emptiness. It mirrored her own void lined with memories that would never be added to—birthday parties and Christmases, shopping for prom dresses and baby clothes. There would never be enough to fill the hollowness in her. Never in a thousand years.

"I love you, Brit," Justine whispered for her only.

"I love you, too, Mom."

Brittany closed her eyes and raised her chin.

"Justine, no!" Teresa reached out.

Justine whipped the sword about in a long arc, cutting clean through Brittany's neck.

Teresa had reached too far. The tips of two fingers were caught by the blade, cut through clean and fast.

Justine dropped her blade and caught Brittany as she fell, holding her head in place until she lay on the floor.

"Good bye, baby. You won't be disturbed again." Her fingers gently caressed Brittany's face that in her second death seemed to regain the flush of mortal youth. For the third time, Justine felt as if she, too, had died. She had let her mother die and now she had killed her own daughter, how could anybody hope to expunge that guilt?

All the others looked upon her with varying degrees of shock. On her knees, Teresa held her severed fingers, silently sobbing.

"Teresa," Justine said. "We'll find Antonia. I promise." Then she picked up her sword and rose to her feet.

Simone, grim faced, nodded and fingered her weapon. Darwin crouched beside Teresa to help bind her fingers. "He is yours," he said to Justine.

Justine faced Sinakov, who still held Harry. Voice cold as her heart, Justine said, "I made my choice. Let Harry go."

Sinakov's eyes flicked from face to face. His full lips twitched at the corners. "Did you think there would be only one choice? There is always another and another...Who lives, who dies? Who dies easy, who dies hard. Who watches their family butchered? Always another choice. Always. Such as Rubinio's head for—"

"No." Justine said. "No more choices. Let...Harry...go."

Sinakov surveyed the three vampires. He took a half step back as if forced by the animosity they projected. His grin lost its usual arrogance. "I will release him, but not quite at this moment."

Darwin scooted forward a few inches. "Now."

Sinakov jerked back and tightened the blade against Harry's neck. "I choose not to. When I am free of your interference, I will release him."

"Unharmed," Justine warned.

"Of course. Harry will be unhurt when I release him." He began to back away toward the kitchen. "Do not follow, if you value this mortal's pathetic, short life. Some advice for you, young blood. Vampire-mortal relationships do not usually last long. Mortals are weak and slow and become old so quickly. It is really not worth the effort."

"Perhaps." Justine moved several steps toward him. "But if anything happens to Harry, I will make sure your immortality will be spent in pain."

"I look forward to that attempt. Stay. You have no choice."

Sinakov backed to the open kitchen door. There, with a flourish, he swung the sword away from Harry's throat. Harry swayed uncertainly. "You see, Justine," Sinakov said. "He is free and unharmed." Then he stabbed Harry in the back. The blade protruded several inches out of his body before Sinakov withdrew it and vanished into the kitchen.

Harry staggered and dropped to his knees.

"Harry!" Justine grabbed him before he hit the floor. She flashed back to her own impalement, felt the blade cut through her body.

"It is bad, Justine," Simone said. "But he may live if he goes to a hospital quickly."

Harry was barely conscious. He reached for Justine. "Love you," he murmured. Then, "Kill him. It's okay."

"You must finish him, here, now." Simone said. "We will care for Harry."

Justine gently touched Harry, then ran in pursuit of Sinakov.

# Chapter Forty-four

Stephan Sinakov, who had not been Henri Gireaux since he executed the original Sinakov, ran down three flights of stairs to the basement.

Power. He needed to replenish his strength. He had not fed recently. This Justine and her silly idea of revenge had been a distraction. He had planned to feed on sweet blood, but Justine and that woman Simone, who claimed to be his mother, arrived earlier than expected. So now, because they arrived early, he needed to finish the Sweet Blood ritual to regain his full powers to defeat the two women and that old fool Darius Rubinio.

Sinakov had suspected Rubinio still survived. Traces of the man could be felt whenever he mingled with lower mortals at the Oceanside beach area. He had tracked down and killed Rubinio's last son there years ago, leaving the body on the beach for the sun to burn. At first, when he returned to the area three years ago, he thought the son's ashes were still mixed with the sand. But the Rubinio sense was too strong to be ashes. So he was right, the Master of the Rubinio Family was in hiding and now he was in the house, and he would finally be destroyed for his crimes against the Families.

Sinakov quickly made his way into the hand-dug passage, past the holding cells, to the rough-hewn end. From the passage the end looked solid, but on the left, hidden by the rough surface, was an opening that slanted back to the right. A short, curved passage led to a steel door that opened into an irregular dome shaped chamber approximately twenty-five feet in diameter. Sinakov strode to a thick wooden crucifix stuck in the ground close to the far wall. Crissy hung naked from ropes binding her wrists to the cross beam. Blood trails ran down her arms. A small cloth draped table held various knives and a gold chalice.

*How appropriate,* Sinakov thought. The girl very much resembled the wife of Rubinio's son. He had made her watch her husband die, then taken her there on the beach beside him. Then he had left both their heads in their house so the Families would know they were gone.

Crissy roused from her stupor when he entered. She raised a leg in an ineffectual attempt to cover her nakedness.

"Ah, my dear, you smell of innocence and fear." He slid his hand over ribs and breasts down to her crotch. She moaned when he pressed her. "Has any man touched you like that, mortal?" His tongue raked her breast, teeth teased a nipple. "No man has ever tasted you, or felt you or smelled you, has he? You are pure, are you not?" He ripped away the tape from her mouth. Crissy sucked in a breath to scream. Sinakov gripped her face. Lips barely touching hers he whispered, "Don't scream. Nobody will hear you."

Instead of a scream, "Please don't," escaped her, a plaintive sound from deep within.

Sinakov released his grip and gently smoothed the red imprints of his fingers from the skin of her face. "You would have fetched a good price, young mortal."

"Please—"

He grasped her face again. "Shhh. It is too late for that. A pity there is no time for the full ritual, but I need your power now to defeat my enemies."

He placed his hand across her chest. Her heart beat wildly against his palm. He hissed in a breath. "You have my power." He reached for the long knife from the table and swung it back, ready to strike.

# Chapter Forty-five

Justine followed Sinakov's scent through the kitchen down the back stairs to the basement. On full alert she checked each door. At the third door on the left she hesitated only a few seconds. The sense of Brittany was strong there, but that was done. She had no time to dwell on it. In another room an intense sense of cold came from a coffin shaped metal box. The box was empty and no vampire presence could be detected. She moved on.

The scent led her past Teresa's cell to a dead end. Long scrutiny, seeming longer from the sense of urgency she felt, finally found the hidden entrance. A second after she burst into the chamber she spied Sinakov. He held the gold chalice up to collect the blood draining from the eviscerated body. Crissy's mouth formed an O, ready for a scream that would never come.

"No!" Justine shouted, knowing she was too late.

Sinakov downed the cup of blood before Justine overcame her shock and raced across the chamber. As if the blood really did enhance his power, by the time she struck at him, he easily blocked her and spun out of the way.

They fought. She attacked. He defended with a smirk on his face to let her know he was only amusing himself by not killing her right away. Justine did not let it get to her. She maneuvered so their hilts locked for a few seconds. She punched him in the face three times.

Taken by surprise, he let his guard down. She stepped back to take the final swing when a powerful sense of danger and the presence of others came to her like a hard slap on the back of the head.

"Jump left!"

Justine jumped and whirled just in time to observe Simone blast the sword wielding arm off Trake, the vampire who took Teresa from the fight at Darwin's place. Trake spun toward her. She felt the cold of him. Another blast knocked him to the ground. Simone strode to him and one-handedly severed what was left of his head.

She kept Sinakov at bay with the shotgun. "Harry needs to go to hospital immediately."

Justine nodded as their eyes met, then renewed her attack with a fury reserved for saving loved ones. Sinakov, feeling his new power, attacked as hard. With kicks, punches, bites and swordplay, their fight ranged over the chamber.

# David Burton

At one point, with a flurry of moves, Sinakov pushed her hard. In a devastatingly fast move he kicked the back of her legs. She dropped to her knees, for a second vulnerable. He did not finish it. On her feet in an instant, back against the wall, Justine wondered why. Only one direction of escape from his onslaught was available—along the rough wall toward where Simone watched intently.

Justine had no choice but to move that way. Why didn't he kill her when he had the chance? Her moves were purely defensive until his eyes gave his intentions away a few seconds before his plan would have succeeded. He paid more attention to Simone than to her. He had expected Justine to be cover for him when he thrust his blade at Simone. Instead Justine dropped to her knees, revealing his attack to Simone, and leaving him exposed.

Simone blocked his thrust, trapping his blade against the dirt wall with the shotgun. Justine drew out her knife, flicked it open with purpose and jammed it into Sinakov's belly. Then she stood up, ripping him open. The blade sliced cleanly through skin and guts up to his sternum.

"You have a choice, Stephan," Justine said. "Die or die."

Simone handed her a wooden stake. Justine inserted the stake into the gaping wound and rammed it into his heart.

"Blood for blood," she said in his face.

Sinakov stood frozen, looking down, mouth slightly open. He tried to speak, but produced only gurgles in his chest.

"You shouldn't have killed my daughter." She stepped back, looked directly in his eyes, and with one fast strike of the sword, cut off his head. She made no attempt to prevent its fall to the dirt floor.

Stephan Sinakov/Henri Gireaux crumpled at her feet.

Justine felt nothing for a long moment, then a slew of emotions jumbled up inside her—relief, sadness, anger, apprehension. Her body trembled and her legs went weak. Simone supported her. The two women stood side by side looking down at the body. "I'm sorry," Justine said.

Simone rested her arm around Justine's shoulders. "Me too," she said. "Come, Harry needs you."

Justine stood tall and shook off the months of tension. "One more thing."

Outside the basement door, Justine flung Sinakov's head out onto the lawn. The Eastern sky showed a thin strip of pale light.

Up in the big room, they laid Crissy's body next to Brittany's and covered them with a white table cloth. Justine said to Simone, "I'll catch up with you in a minute."

Kneeling beside her daughter, Justine quivered with the effort to cry, but her vampire physiology would not let her. One problem of being dead. She smoothed the cloth over Brittany's body and said, "Rest easy, baby, the ones who hurt you are in Hell."

Justine threw all the stacked logs into the smoldering fireplace. In the kitchen she turned on all the burners.

Outside at the gate, Justine caught up with Darwin, who carried Harry, and Simone, supporting Teresa. There was a loud *whump* sound from the house. Fire flared from the blown out windows of the big room.

In the back seat, Justine supported Harry's head on her lap. She wanted to think about nothing, and ended up thinking of everything. She barely noticed when Simone slowed for the shrieking fire trucks.

# Chapter Forty-six

Just because her Master was dead did not mean the girl's service was over. While the two women, Justine and Simone—she would remember their names—raced up the stairs with the dead mortal, the girl scuttled into the chamber. She wasted no time over her Master. She collected his sword and chalice, then with little effort she slung his body over her shoulder.

Barely leaving a footprint on the dew damp grass, a satchel slung from her neck, her Master's body across her thin shoulders, she retrieved the head and scurried across the lawn to the trees. Illuminated by the fire's glow, she crossed the wall, and made her way deeper into the shadows. Two hundred feet diagonally up the slope, she vanished from view among a group of large, round boulders. Without ceremony, she dragged the body through a narrow opening into a small cave known only to Sinakov and herself.

Inside, on bedding they had stocked years ago, just in case, she fitted Sinakov's head to his body and tied it in place with strong cord under his arms. She had removed the stake and now sewed his body together with heavy thread from a sewing kit she used to mend his clothes. Without his severed hand, she could do little but clean the wound. Then she lay next to him, prepared to wait as long as it took for him to wake up whole again.

# Chapter Forty-seven

Justine, Simone and Teresa slipped into Harry's hospital room at the end of evening visiting hours. Justine sat on the bed while the others stood around it. Simone smiled and nodded her greeting. Teresa did the same.

White bandages on Teresa's fingers drew his eye. This was the first time he'd seen her since he regained semi-consciousness when she brought him into the hospital. She looked different. Harder, he decided. After what she'd been through the last months, he figured she was entitled to harden up against a world that had turned out to be much more complicated than she ever contemplated. It sure as hell was for him.

"How are the fingers?" he asked her.

She held up her left hand. Even with bandages the last two digits were shorter than the index finger. "Missing." She drew a finger across her throat. "Could be worse."

Teresa was a mortal, but Harry wasn't sure he would have thought so if he hadn't already known.

Simone stood still, relaxed, hands in pockets, looking like a young woman tagging along to visit a friend of a friend in the hospital. But three and a half centuries of vampire superiority were evident in the slightly indulgent smile she wore. She probably had every right to that smile, and she had proved to be more or less one of the good guys, but nevertheless, it made him a little uncomfortable. A minuscule raising of an eyebrow made him wonder if she knew exactly what he was thinking.

Justine took his hand. Hers was cold, so he held it to his chest with both of his.

"How are you?" they both said simultaneously.

They laughed. Harry winced and sniffed against the pain.

"Harry, are you okay?"

"Only hurts when I laugh."

"Not funny."

"I'm good. I'm going home day after tomorrow." Harry did a quick survey of the three women and he knew the answer to his next question. He'd seen it before, the tolerant patience of people who were going someplace. Their bodies were here, but their minds were already on the road. "Will you...be there?"

Justine closed her eyes and shook her head. "No. We're going to find

Antonia. We have a lead. We're leaving now."

Harry broke the uncomfortable silence. "What about Miguel and the kids?"

Teresa tightened up and squared her shoulders. "Miguel and Antonia never really got along. He has put her disappearance behind him and moved on. I haven't. He is a good father. Carlos and Maria will be fine." She shrugged, looking at Harry's feet. "They will not miss me. They have the trees."

Harry knew that Miguel and the kids were coming back tomorrow. He wondered how much that influenced the decision to leave that night. "What lead?" he asked to fill another silence.

"An out of service phone number in Florida. We have a name, Rubicon, from files Darwin found in Sinakov's house. Some information on five girls. Bayley has the originals, if you want them."

"I can have the Sheriff's Department check that number."

"Ah, I...Simone has a friend who checked into it."

"Oh. Okay. If there's anything else I can help with?"

"Harry, you've already gotten in too much trouble because of me. Besides, this is likely to be—"

"Out of my jurisdiction."

There was a long pause while they each stared at something else beside the other. Simone and Teresa took the hint and quietly left the room.

"Harry, I'm sorry, I can't stay here. My house is gone. Simone's house is gone. Brittany's gone. And these girls. Maybe we can find them. I have to try."

"Against all that, what we have isn't worth a hill of beans."

"Harry, please don't make it any harder than it is. I love you. I want to be with you. But I have to do this."

Harry pressed her hand to his lips. "I know you do. Are you coming back?"

Carefully, Justine lay beside him, her head on his chest. He wrapped his arms around her and inhaled deeply of her scent, committing it to memory.

"I will be back," she said. "I..." She drew in a long breath and sighed. "I need you, Harry. I need to know that a man like you exists. That no matter what horrors I experience, I know a good man who..."

"Loves you?"

"Yes, loves me, like I love him."

Harry held her a little tighter as tears ran hot down his cheeks.

"I hear your heart," Justine murmured. "It sounds strange now, yet so familiar."

Harry sniffed and closed his eyes to squeeze out the last tears. "I hear yours, too."

"You should have them check your hearing while you're here."

"There's hearts, and there's heart."

Justine sat up. She wiped his tears away and studied him with eyes darker and deeper than a mortal's. "I'm going to live a long time. I can make it so that you will, too."

"I don't think I'm ready for that."

"But we could—"

He touched a finger to her lips. "—talk about it when you come back."

"Justine?"

Harry nodded toward the door. Simone and Teresa waited self-consciously. Simone said, "We have to go now." A nurse stuck her no-nonsense face in the room. "Now," Simone repeated.

Harry was well aware of his heart pounding in his chest and the tight lump in his throat. "Go," he said. "Come back."

Justine kissed him. A warm, moist kiss, full of promise that told him all she wanted to say, but hadn't. The taste and feel of the kiss he also memorized. He thought it might be a long time before he had another.

Fingertips scarcely touching, Justine said, "The Sinakov Family is in some confusion, so you know where to find Darwin if anything strange happens. Bye." Justine walked out the door.

Teresa said, "Take care, Harry. *Muchas gracias, por mi vie.*"

To Simone Harry said, "Take care of that Young One for me."

In his head a strong sense of *I will* calmed him and relaxed the knot in his stomach. "*Bon chance,* Harry," she said.

Then the door slowly swung shut, closing with a final thump and click, leaving Harry alone as he'd never been before.

# Chapter Forty-eight

The three women were quiet, thinking their own thoughts about the past, present, or future as Simone wheeled the Ford Expedition onto I-15 North.

Justine held up a cell phone. To Teresa, stretched out in the back, arm draped over her eyes, she said, "You're sure this is her phone?"

"Yes. Call. The not knowing is hell."

Justine slumped in her seat and dialed.

"Hello."

"Hello. Is this Mrs. Adelman?"

"Yes. Who is this? It's late."

"You're Crissy's mother?"

"Crissy? Do you know where she is? Who is this?"

"Doesn't matter who I am. I hate to tell you this, Mrs. Adelman, but Crissy is dead. I'm sorry."

Justine heard a sharp intake of breath. "Dead? How do you know? Who is this? Are you the police? Did you...?"

"No, I'm not the police, and no I didn't kill her. I almost saved her, but I was too late. I'm so sorry."

"How...how did she die? Where—?"

"Mrs. Adelman, I know exactly how you feel. You have a thousand questions. All I can tell you is that it was quick. She didn't suffer. The man who killed her is also dead. There won't be a body. We thought you should know."

"Oh my God. Oh my God. She's really dead? Oh God. Who did it? Who took my daughter away?"

"He's dead."

"Did he suffer? Did you kill him?"

"Yes and yes."

"I don't know if I believe you, but thank you for that. Will we ever know what happened?"

"I don't think so. Look, I have to go. Crissy was a very brave girl. I'm so sorry I couldn't bring her back to you. Good bye, Mrs. Adelman." She snapped the phone closed. "Shit."

"Did she believe you?" Simone asked.

"I don't know. I hope so. Not knowing is hell, but so is no hope." She rolled down the window and flung the phone away.

"Wake me up when we get to Florida," Teresa said.

# Blood Justice

Justine said, "We have to make a stop on the way."

"What?"

"Where?"

"St. Louis. The man who killed my mother lives there. It's time justice caught up with him. Blood for blood."